Eyes on the Past

Other Dr. Yoko Mysteries

Eye Sleuth

Eye Witness
(co-authored with Dennis Berry)

Eye Sleuth's Ghostly Vacations

Eyes on the Past

HAZEL DAWKINS

INTRODUCTION BY ROBERT A. WILLIAMS, *LHD*

Cataloguing Data:
Dawkins, Hazel.
Eyes on the Past: A Yoko Kamimura Mystery - Hazel Dawkins.

Although this is a work of fiction, some characters in the mystery like
Drs. E. Bertolli and H. Laukkanen truly are practitioners of optometric
vision therapy. Others, like Robert A. Williams, are associated in
some way with this optometric specialty. That being said, some of the
characters and events are inventions of the author. Real individuals
include Ansel Adams, Raymond Best, Kanjitsu Iijima, Dorothea Lange,
Madeline and Herbert Nicholson, Arnold Raber, Orville Robertson,
Floyd Schmoe, Kyo Takahashi, Barbara Takei and Tamie Tsuchiyama.
The ten camps where Japanese Americans were incarcerated were all too
real. All events that relate to the treatment of Americans of Japanese
heritage and the first Japanese immigrants who were refused citizenship
are historically accurate.

Published by MurderProse.com
Front cover art and design and Murder Prose.com logo by Mark Aller
Interior Design by JW Manus/QA Productions

Photos 1-10 are by Ansel Adams, from photos in his book, *Born Free and
Equal, The Story of Loyal Japanese-Americans.*
ISBN - 13: 978-0-9852592-4-2
1. Behavioral Optometry; 2. Optometric Vision Therapy; 3. OEP
Foundation; 4. The College of Optometry, State University of New York
(SUNY); 5. New York City—Fifteenth Street Friends Meetinghouse;
Gramercy Park, LaGuardia Place; 6. Manzanar Relocation Camp; 7.
Tule Lake Camp; 8. Minidoka Relocation Camp.

 murderprose.com

The moment is never more than Eternity.

Vincent Tripi
Greenfield, Massachusetts

Contents

Acknowledgments

Heartfelt gratitude to generous friends who helped in myriad ways, from Mark Aller, Bill Baker of Baker Office Supplies, Dennis Berry, Dr. E. Bertolli, Phyllis Brooks, Alix Carafiol, Garrett Connolly, Dennis Fairchild, Joe Giguere, Faith Kindness, Loren Kramer, Dr. Hannu Laukkanen, Peter Loiacono, Amy Meblin, Dorothy McIver, Mindy Nadolski, Dr. Mary Clare Powell, Diana Roberts to Ted Scott and Robert Williams. Last but certainly not least, gratitude to Maribeth Dawkins for her cogent comments, restorative shiatsu and delicious treats.

Thank you, one and all.

Introduction

A history student as an undergraduate in the 1960s, I recall being introduced to Executive Order 9066, signed by President Roosevelt in 1942, ordering over 100,000 people, most U.S. citizens of Japanese ancestry, to "relocation" camps. Years later, visiting family in Reno, Nevada, we drove Highway 395 many times, passing the site of the Manzanar Camp prior to its restoration, always intending to detour from a holiday trip but never slowing. Recalling one of the darkest moments in American history, I as well as most Americans simply chose to overlook this chapter. Having finished reading *Eyes on the Past*, I will not cruise past this monument again without stopping.

One of my first professors at Cal-State Hayward used the often repeated but perhaps not fully appreciated statement, "Those who choose to ignore history are condemned to repeat it." It is my hope that readers of this book will gain new understanding and appreciation for the contributions of Americans of Japanese ancestry not only to the war effort from 1941-45 but of the significance of the melting pot of humanity that has become the United States of America.

During my career in optometry I had the privilege of meeting two individuals who came to mind as I read the manuscript of *Eyes on the Past*. Dr. Henry Oster was a faculty member of the Southern California College of Optometry and I recall sitting in a group on campus when he rolled up his sleeve and showed us his numerical tattoo that was a lasting legacy of his time in a German concentration camp during World War II. Dr. Sumio Taniguchi told me of his experience as a young boy at Manzanar concurrent to Dr. Oster's time in the German camp. I have never been able to reconcile in my own mind which encounter had a more lasting impact on me. But I can say that I equate knowing these two survivors as heros. My thoughts now as it was then is the oft quoted slogan, "Never again."

Hazel Dawkins and The Writing Team have been committed to

behavioural*vision care for over thirty years. As with so many, her introduction came as a patient. A vision issue drove her to seek professional care and, perhaps serendipitously, she ended up seeing Dr. Ellis Edelman in Newton Square, Pennsylvania, a behavioural optometrist, Clinical Associate of the OEP Foundation and Fellow of COVD. Ellis began her introduction to the uniqueness that is the profession of optometry on her first visit. She soon gained understanding of the contributions that our profession can and has made to the lives of millions of individuals since Doctors E. B. Alexander and A. M. Skeffington teamed up in the 1920s to form the Optometric Extension Program.

Hazel is a gifted writer and editor. Many would be surprised how many OEP publications she touched through the years. Her book, *The Suddenly Successful Student and Friends,* a public information volume, first published in 1986 and now in its fifth printing, has sold more copies than any book published by OEP except the G. N. Getman classic, *How to Develop Your Child's Intelligence* (or *Student* had when I left OEP in 2014). I recall clinical associates buying them by the hundreds to give to parents and teachers. Before Dr. Yoko came on the scene, two other volumes followed *The Suddenly Successful Student and Friends:* a hardbound volume, *Suddenly Successful,* that expanded on the message in her first book, and *Focus Your Mind's Eye,* a series of case histories from the broad spectrum of patients. Her intent in writing the Dr. Yoko books was to bring the message of the importance of functional vision to a new audience in a new format, that of the mystery novel.

Long an ardent reader of mystery novels, Hazel very simply combined her two literary loves into the tenacious Dr. Yoko Kamimura. I am honored to be a minor character in two of the three Yoko novels. This book is the fourth in the series (the third is at this time an e-book). Alas, according to Hazel it will be the finale, though she does leave an opening for another sequel in the last chapter of *Eyes on the Past.*

Our profession owes a debt of gratitude to Mrs. Dawkins for her contributions to optometric literature. I trust that the readers of this

---

* The British spelling 'behavioural' is used here in deference to Mrs. Dawkins' English heritage.

novel will gain new insight into what optometry contributes to humanity as well as the need to guard against future injustices to groups of people just because of their race, religion or heritage.

Robert A. Williams, *LHD*
California, 2017
Project Coordinator
Career Planning and Placement
Western University College of Optometry
Former Executive Director, NORA

1 Sayonara

Yoko bumped the closet door shut with her hip, arms straining around a bulging plastic bag. Light though it was, the shove set the hinges protesting. The door creaked slowly inward but stopped short of closing. Not that it mattered. Open or shut, the closet was empty. She'd packed Auntie Ai's clothes—one armful, a second, another and another—until her arms ached. Wisps of fragrance curled around her and Yoko buried her face in the last pile for a lingering farewell sniff, breathing in lavender, her aunt's favorite. Soap, hand lotion, cologne, always lavender. Yoko's eyes were dry, tears exhausted. Auntie Ai was in her nineties and Yoko wondered if her aunt had ever thought, "How much longer will I live?"

Auntie Ai had been happy and active. No one, least of all Yoko, thought of her as a venerable senior. Her aunt's mantra was simple, "Let me wear out, not rust out."

Auntie Ai had plain worn out. Active into the last stretch of her tenth decade, joking about planning a party for her 100th, Ai Sasaki had lived alone since the death of her husband. She did her own shopping and cooking and was addicted to playing cutthroat, competitive contract bridge online.

Death stole Ai as she slept.

Halfway across the room Yoko stopped. Was the closet empty? A dim image floated onto her mind's eye. Something—what the hell could it be?—was still in the closet. Yoko shook her head in irritation and her shoulder-length black hair fanned out around her face. She hesitated then turned and walked back across the room, yanking the closet door wide. A lone wire hanger dangled on the empty rack. A dust bunny eddied on the floor where shoes, slippers and boots had been lined in rows. Clearing all trace of Auntie Ai from her home of decades hadn't taken long. A life disposed of with an ease that made Yoko's heart ache.

Her iPhone chirped. It was her cousin, Ben Sasaki, Auntie Ai's son.

"Hello, Ben," Yoko said, staring at the dust bunny on the closet floor.

"Hey, cuz, how's it going?" Ben asked. "Did the super take care of the furniture?"

"He did. It's stacked in the living room ready for the thrift store. I saw Gary on my way in and he told me the mattress is in the basement. He'll have it taken to the dump at the end of the week because thrift stores don't take mattresses."

"Gary's a gem," Ben said.

"One of a kind," Yoko agreed. "I just finished emptying the closets. I filled quite a few bags with clothes. Gary will make sure the guys from the thrift store pick up everything when they come next week."

"Great. Do you have anything else to do?"

"Empty the fridge, that's all. I looked in it when I arrived and there's broccoli and four eggs. The china and pots and pans are packed and I put them with the furniture."

"No sake?" Ben joked.

"I confess," Yoko said. "I drank it—we're talking a thimbleful."

For a moment, the cousins were silent. Ai had been the last of her generation in their family. Now she was gone. Yoko shuddered at the depth of sorrow rising in her. She'd lost someone integral to her. She'd miss the loving support more than she could ever explain to Ben or anyone else, even her sweetie, Dan. Two or three years back, over dinner at her apartment, Ai had urged Yoko and Ben, in her gentle way, to make arrangements. "Will you two share what needs to be done after I die," she said. "Will you plan now, so I have peace of mind?"

They'd scoffed at the thought that the time would ever come but agreed, with reluctance, to make plans.

"If you'll work with the super to clear out the apartment, I'll take care of the funeral and Mom's will. Deal?" Ben suggested and Yoko had agreed.

Yoko closed her eyes, feeling again her aunt's slender arms around her from that evening when Ai hugged her and whispered her thanks.

Ben cleared his throat to break the silence. Yoko knew he didn't have words to express his sorrow. Nor did she. Much easier to discuss what needed to be done. "The reason I called was to tell you about Mom's memorial service."

"All right," Yoko said.

"You remember Mom wanted green burial?" Ben said.

"Yes."

Ben told her the time and date and Yoko made notes on her iPhone. "The director at Greenwood Heights on Fourth Avenue in Brooklyn said Mom arranged for a Buddhist memorial service right at the cemetery when she's to be buried," Ben said. "He said it's often done. What do you think?"

"If that's what Auntie Ai wanted, I think that's good," Yoko said.

"Thought you'd say that." Emotion lent Ben's voice gruffness. "That's it." He ended the call.

Yoko had got quite warm when she was busy stuffing clothes into the bags but she felt chilled now. She zipped up her jacket and flapped her arms to get the blood moving and noticed the dust bunny on the closet floor swirling in lazy spirals at the slight change in the air. Why, she wondered, am I standing here? Then she remembered her doubt. Had she emptied everything from the closet?

Peering into the closet, Yoko made out a wooden box snug against the back wall. Even now it was hard to see it because the closet lacked lighting and the box was a sandy brown, the exact same shade as the walls of the closet. The box blended in. Was that deliberate? Was the box meant to go unnoticed?

"Ha!" she said, a little less annoyed. "My vision didn't play tricks."

Yoko dragged the box out of the closet, surprised it was quite heavy. It took some fiddling but she managed to pry open the lid. It fell back, hitting the ground with a dull thud that reverberated in a room empty except for the uneven row of bags crammed with clothing. Yoko stared at the small books that filled the box. What had she found?

Each of the books in the first layer was covered in red silk and had the name, "Ai Sasaki," written on the front. Underneath the name was a date. Yoko picked up one of the books and flipped through it. "It's a diary!" Excitement rose in her. She paused, smiling, over a sketch of a woman's profile that showed an elegant chignon like the one Auntie Ai often wore. Another sketch showed a woman's hair in a simple ponytail, which was Auntie Ai's "at home" style.

Yoko peered at the red silk covering the diary. "I thought so," she breathed as she recognized the zigzag stitching her aunt used to strengthen something she sewed. Yoko whistled. Auntie Ai had made slipcovers for the diaries. An expert on her venerable treadle sewing machine, Auntie Ai's feet could move at blurring speed so the whir of the treadle morphed into the contented purring of a giant cat as she transformed curtains, cushions, coats and, it appeared, books. Squatting, Yoko sorted through the diaries and piled them in stacks on the floor. The box was half empty when she uncovered a few with the name, "Ben Sasaki," on the covers.

What had her cousin Ben written? Yoko picked up one. The first pages were filled with hurried scrawling, the venting of a teen angry at being removed from his home and friends and school and incarcerated in the windy, dusty wilds of the Mohave Desert. Yoko skimmed through the entries but stopped and reread one. It was shocking—was it a youngster's exaggeration?

Ben Sasaki's Diary.
Manzanar War Relocation Center.
December 1942.

Dad wouldn't let me join in whatever was going on outside. We heard shouting and people running by our hut and I wanted to take a look for myself. I was mad at him but when we heard what happened, I know that by stopping me from going out, Dad saved my life.

Yoko leafed through the rest of that diary and Ben's other diaries but didn't find any other reference to the protest. What had happened? She found Auntie Ai's diary for December 1942 and leafed through it, hoping to find out more about what sounded like a serious situation. What she read made her blood run cold.

Ai Sasaki's Diary.
Manzanar War Relocation Center.
December 1942.

Ben was upset with his father but Saburo was adamant Ben not go outside to join the noisy crowd. The three of us stayed put. Later, we heard that a crowd gathered and a fight started. When they were ordered to go to their huts and didn't move, the army guards opened fire. One man was killed. We haven't been able to find out his name because there's a communication embargo and martial law has been declared. Word is that another man died later and nine were wounded. It doesn't sound as if any Bainbridge Islanders were involved, only city people from California.

The mess hall bells began to toll late that night and MP jeeps patrolled the streets nonstop. In the months that we've been here, messhall bells ring to call us to meals, to tell us of public meetings for everything from better food to higher wages. This time, the bells rang until noon for those killed.

"This is horrifying. Do I really want to go on reading?" Yoko muttered. She struggled with the decision. Should she abandon what she'd found or continue to explore what was in the box? How upsetting would it be to read the words her aunt had written during incarceration? Had she found a Pandora's box, something that held evil? Perhaps, yet did she want to ignore a unique opportunity? It was with reluctance that she picked up the diary again, knowing she'd regret it for the rest of her life if she didn't learn the truth about her family's time in the camps. She'd avoided reading any of the books written about the World War II incarceration. Some were factual, some were fiction, but Yoko waited, hoping for the day she'd discover the personal truth of what had happened to her parents and the Sasakis. Here was her chance and she would not resist.

Ai Sasaki's Diary.

Manzanar War Relocation Center.

December 1942.

Saburo left early this morning in search of news about last night's trouble. "It was nothing short of a riot," he told us when he returned. "Some men were beating an *inu,* a suspected traitor. They were arrested and chaos broke out. The military police started shooting into the crowd to try to stop the rioting." Saburo waited until Ben left and then told me in a low whisper, his voice close to my ear so our neighbors wouldn't be able to hear, for in the normal way, voices can be heard through the tarpaper walls, "Remember how the people in the JACL* who helped arrange orderly evacuations were branded traitors? Isn't <u>orderly</u> preferable to a riot?" My logical husband.

Within days of arriving in Manzanar, we'd heard rumors of informants, people spying on their neighbors and reporting to the government. We were incredulous at first, but there were enough instances where spying had to be the only answer. Arguments descend into fights, death threats are common. As if we don't have enough troubles.

Stunned by what she was reading—how many years had she visited Auntie Ai and never heard one single hint about diaries, let alone a box of them?—Yoko took out more of the small red-covered books. She'd longed to know about the years of World War II when Americans of Japanese heritage and their elders, the original immigrants, were forcibly removed from their homes in coastal areas along the Pacific in the name of national security. Yoko's parents had been silent about their years of incarceration. Would she at last find answers?

"This is terrible, rioting and shootings," Yoko said aloud. Did she want to read more? Her determination won. To her relief, entries recorded problems with food, rules, boredom, trouble between internees and yes, deaths, but they were from old age or illness, not guns. Relieved that

---

* JACL, Japanese American Citizens League.

it didn't look as if she'd be reading about more carnage, she was about to close the diary when an entry caught her attention.

Ai Sasaki's Diary.
Manzanar Relocation Camp.
January 1943.

Life has calmed down since the shock of the riot and shooting. We are allowed outside the barbed wire—a brief sense of freedom. Some hike, others collect driftwood or bring back stones to make rock gardens. Saburo loves finding what words mean (his name means third son) and he learned that Manzanar comes from the Spanish for apple orchard. When he told me that, I looked out at the barren, sandy landscape, trying to imagine a time when the Owens Valley had orchards and alfalfa fields. The area became a desert when water was diverted south to Los Angeles early in the 1900s.

A few rows of pear and apple trees remain from the orchards so there's fresh fruit. Not enough for everyone, but someone thought up a system so that when fruit is ripe, it is shared. I'm told the soil is alluvial and is rich. We have farmers in Manzanar so it wasn't long before vegetables were planted outside the barbed wire. Everything from lettuce and tomatoes, corn and eggplant, even horseradish. We were told—and found it hard to believe—that the gardeners would make an oasis in the desert. True to their word, before long, we had a small park with ponds and waterfalls, even curved wooden bridges.

Yoko was about to put the diary down again when she came across an entry about the family changing camps. What was that all about? She checked the time. If she lingered much longer over the reading, it would be late by the time she got back to Manhattan. She ought to tackle the last chore of emptying the fridge. She decided to ask the super if he'd like the eggs and broccoli.

"Thanks," Gary said when she tapped on his door with her offer. "I can always use food." He disappeared for a moment and came back holding a small box. "Will this be big enough?"

"Yes," Yoko said. "There's not much but you know what Auntie Ai said, mustn't waste."

"Your aunt was right," Gary said. "She was a good neighbor, helpful and friendly with everyone. Look, why don't I come up with you? I can get what's in the fridge, that'll save you a trip, and we can take a walk through the apartment. You want everything to go to the thrift store?"

"Yes," Yoko said. "I found a box of diaries in the closet. I'm taking the diaries home but I'll leave the box with the rest of the furniture."

"Diaries? That's an unusual parting gift. You must be looking forward to reading them," the super said with an easy smile.

They climbed the stairs to the third floor and Gary took the food from the fridge then they walked through the apartment. Yoko showed him the empty closets.

"Good work," Gary said, "Not everyone does a thorough job clearing out."

"Thank you for everything," Yoko said as they shook hands. "Ben and I appreciate your help."

"We'll miss your aunt," Gary said. "Despite what she went through in the war, she was always upbeat."

The super left and Yoko went back to the bedroom. She was tired and decided to take a breather and read another entry or two. She settled down on the floor, back against the wall, legs stretched out.

Ai Sasaki's Diary.
Manzanar War Relocation Camp.
March 1943.

We're leaving Manzanar and its thousands of people, we're told 10,000 or more. They're mostly city folk from California except for us Bainbridge Islanders, and there's less than 300 of us.

Our family has permission to relocate to a place called Minidoka. It's still a camp and will have a barbed wire fence and armed guards but we're going with most of the other Bainbridge Islanders here in Manzanar. Some have left already after getting work permits to help on farms in other locations. We'll be together, friends and neighbors. Minidoka is in southern Idaho, we're having quite a tour of the U.S.

Saburo discovered that Minidoka is Dakota Sioux for fountain or spring of water.

It was high time to leave and Yoko was ready to scramble to her feet but the box beckoned. It was irresistible though she was a little leery about what else she might find. She sat back on her heels and lifted out more of the diaries and was about to stack them in the bag when she spotted a school yearbook near the bottom of the box. It was the *Spartan Life* from Bainbridge High. Notebooks were tucked inside.

Puzzling over the pages, Yoko deciphered enough to learn they'd been written by students from Bainbridge Island who'd been exiled to the camps during WWII. The youngsters had sent news about their lives to Milly and Walt Woodward, publishers of *The Review,* the Bainbridge Island newspaper. Yoko skimmed lists of baseball scores and teams in softball games, notes about chicken pox, even the name of a winner of a beauty queen contest—a Bainbridge Islander no less. Yoko put the lists aside and lifted out the very last item, a small box covered in purple silk. She opened the lid and heard a faint clink. Money? Would Auntie Ai have kept money in the apartment? Surely not.

The contents in the small box had been packed neatly. The label read: *Medals awarded to our son Ben for bravery during WWII.*

"Ben's medals," Yoko breathed. She unwrapped the pack with care and found three envelopes. Peering inside one, she saw it held a medal and a slip of paper with writing on it. As she lifted out the first envelope, a feeling of awe came over Yoko, a reverence for Ben's bravery. Just as no one wanted to talk about life behind barbed wire, so no one had mentioned that Ben had received medals from the government that had incarcerated him and his family. The description in Auntie Ai's neat writing for the first award said it was a Purple Heart and awarded to U.S. military wounded or killed while serving.

Yoko knew that during one of the final battles of WWII, shrapnel had seared its way into Ben's left knee. He'd delayed surgery time and again, limping through the decades in stubborn pain until he'd been persuaded to have the knee replaced only a year ago. She returned the Purple Heart and the slip of paper to its envelope, putting it on the

floor beside her, and opened the second envelope. It held a Silver Star
with Oak Leaf Clusters. Auntie Ai had written that the Clusters were
a second award for bravery that had already merited a Silver Star. Yoko
slipped everything back. The third envelope held the Distinguished Service Cross. It, she read, was only awarded for action in combat.

Had Ben's medals been hidden in Auntie Ai's closet all these years?
Did Ben not want them? Yoko replaced the three envelopes in the small
box and closed the lid, considering what her discovery meant. Did Ben
even remember where the medals were? She put the small box to one
side, admiring how its purple silk cover complemented the red silk covering the diaries.

Yoko sorted through the diaries, trying to find some sort of sequence.
Which was the first? She was distracted from her search when she came
across a bundle of letters tied with a green ribbon. On the front was
written, *Letters from Hana and mine to her, returned by her family after
she passed.* Yoko recognized the name. Auntie Ai and Hana Oyama had
been at college and graduated together. What had Auntie Ai written to
Hana, her lifelong friend? It was impossible to resist reading the letters.
Just one, Yoko promised herself. She groaned and gave up any idea of
stopping soon, she wanted to read more—the letters brought Auntie Ai
close and helped ease the wrench of losing her.

Ai Sasaki to Hana Oyama in New Paltz, New York.
March 1942.
Hana dear,

This is written in haste to let you know we've been ordered to leave
Bainbridge Island because of the war. We've been given a notice that
says we have less than a week before we must abandon our home
and jobs and, I fear, most of our belongings. What to pack? For how
long? Will it be cold? As you know, it's temperate here on the Island.
Saburo jokes that we won't be sent to the North Pole because the
Arctic Ocean surrounds it and we are to be kept far from any ocean.
In a serious aside, away from Ben's ears, Saburo told me he'd feared
some reaction ever since Japan bombed Pearl Harbor. The 7th day

of December 1941 casts a long, dark shadow. I can only agree when Saburo shakes his head and says, "*Shikata ga nai*, it cannot be helped."

I cannot bear the thought of having to abandon our home, friends, neighbors, our entire community. How will Ben and the other students say goodbye to teachers and friends at school? I feel such pain over this. It is scant months before the end of term, so hard for our youngsters to leave. They number almost a quarter of the high school. Many are class leaders, others are promising athletes. Now they are to be dislocated from their school and friends and their dreams of the future shattered.

Several months ago, we Islanders had to deal with the freezing of the bank accounts of our elders, the Issei. This had a severe effect on families. Next, our radio sets, cameras and binoculars were impounded. Some people have burned precious photos and destroyed mementoes from Japan like kimonos or sake bottles. The awful truth is that we are "The Other." Our faces are the faces of the enemy. At first, we thought that we Nisei, second generation, born here, would not be imprisoned because we are American citizens. We were wrong.

This is a terrible time. The government is sending us to what is called an assembly center, probably in California. From there we will be transported to some sort of camp. Not, I fear, a place of comfort or joy. We pray the war will end quickly so that we may return to Bainbridge Island. When we are settled (whatever that means), I will write you. Saburo warns letters may be delayed because the mail may be censored. Let us hope we can continue sharing news, dear friend, something we began with our college days.

Where, Yoko wondered, was Hana's answer? She pulled out the next letter but to her surprise, it was another letter to Hana by Ai, written a month later.

Ai Sasaki to Hana Oyama in New Paltz, New York.
April 1942.
Dear Hana,

Our first stop after leaving Bainbridge Island was the Santa Ana racecourse. We were sleeping in the stables. Uncomfortable, smelly days passed before we heard we were to be moved. After a train trip—we Bainbridge Islanders filled all seven cars of the Southern Pacific Line's train—we were transferred to busses and had a ride of three hours before we reached our destination, the Manzanar War Internment Camp in California's Mojave Desert. Thick sandy dust fills the air, swirling in never ending clouds. We've been working nonstop for days like everyone else here to try to furnish where we are to live. The place is nothing more than a crude hut with tarpaper over raw pine walls. Each building has four such huts, 16 x 20 feet for a family. The building is one in a long row of many rows.

We were supplied with army blankets, that dreary olive color, metal cots and canvas mattresses we had to fill with straw plus a small oil heater that's supposed to keep us warm of an evening. It may be 80 degrees or more in the day but as low as 20 degrees at night. The green wood of the walls and flooring has dried and shrunk so sand silts in endlessly through rips in the tarpaper as well as through the gaps in the flooring.

Thousands of us mill around, learning the way to the bathrooms, the dining room, which is called the mess hall. The government charged us, the camp residents (I use the word "residents" with sarcasm) with creating departments and ways for the camp to function. An order of sorts is evolving from the chaos. Most of the people are from cities in California, there's such a difference between city folk and we Bainbridge Islanders. We Islanders have managed to be in huts near each other. How I miss Puget Sound. The sight of water is restorative to me, the sight of the desert is not. This is a sad time in a desolate place.

I take heart that families have not been separated. You remember my sister, Chika? She and her husband are nearby, a few huts down the row. We are in good health, despite dreadful food and sorry conditions. The changes are drastic but we're alive and together.

Saburo and Ben join me in sending you love.

Elated at the mention of her parents but curious at the lack of a reply from Hana, Yoko searched again for a letter from Hana and found it was next in the bundle. Her iPhone chirped and she was surprised then delighted to see it was Ben calling again.

"I've finished emptying the closets. You'll never guess what I found," Yoko said before her cousin could speak. "I can hardly believe it."

"Surprise me," Ben laughed. "I'm betting it's not cash."

"I discovered your medals and lots of diaries, mostly your mom's, as well as letters between your mom and her friend, Hana."

Ben was silent for a nanosecond.

"Are you serious?" His voice was incredulous.

"Want me to remind you which medals you received? Or I could read from your diary," Yoko teased.

"Hell no." His voice was vehement. "God, I had no idea Mom kept the medals or the diaries—there weren't many diaries. Back then, I wasn't into writing."

Yoko hesitated, had she struck a raw nerve and hurt Ben? "You're right, it's only a few diaries. But Ben, what about the medals?"

"I told Mom to do what she wanted, even sell them. I guess she didn't." Ben paused and when he spoke next his voice was so low Yoko strained to hear him. "We fought for freedom and to be accepted as citizens. We didn't fight for medals."

"I understand, but your parents must have been proud," Yoko said.

"Sure," Ben said, his voice less tense. "They were relieved to see me home almost in one piece."

"Ben, do you want me to stop reading the diaries and going through everything? I don't want to upset you," Yoko said. "Do you want what was in the box?"

"No," Ben said promptly. "No. Sheesh, kiddo, you surprised the heck out of me. No, you've asked me more than once about our lives when we were stuck in the camp. Go for it."

"You're sure?"

"I am." Ben's laugh was half-hearted. "Serves me right saddling you with the work of clearing out the apartment! You know, now I think about it, remember how Mom approved of the way we split the tasks? What's the betting she wanted you to find that box and read the stockpile in it?"

"I think you're right," Yoko said in relief. "I hope so."

"What will you do? Read it and dump the lot?"

"Good grief no," Yoko said. "I'll take everything home and go through it bit by bit. It'll be my personal history lesson."

"Fine by me," Ben said.

"Wait," Yoko said. "What about the medals?"

"I promise you I do not want them. I don't know what to tell you," Ben sighed. "It was an honor to receive them but that's all in the past. Behind me."

"What if I found a museum interested in having them?"

"If that works, fine," Ben said in approval.

"I'll let you know what I find."

"Okay. If you're sure you don't have any more surprises, I called again to check I gave you the right time for Mom's memorial service. Did I tell you eleven o'clock? The funeral home changed the time and I couldn't remember which time I told you."

"Yes, you said eleven," Yoko said. "I don't need to look at the note I made because I remember thinking we'd go out for lunch after."

When the call was ended, Yoko checked the time. It was getting late but the lure of the box's contents was strong, it was the opportunity to hear her family's voices again. She could squeeze in a little more reading before she left for Manhattan. She picked up the letter from Hana.

Hana Oyama to Ai Sasaki.
April 1942.
Dear Ai,

What a shock to learn that you were forced to leave your home on Bainbridge. I'd heard whispers about mass evacuations on the West Coast but hoped they were wrong. The strange thing is, your first letter arrived two days after the second. I'm relieved you are settled somewhere despite the appalling conditions you describe. Let me know what I can send. I will do my best to find anything you request.

I'm ready to stop reading the newspapers, full of hateful things about us because of our ancestry. I get dark looks from some neighbors. It doesn't matter that I've lived and worked here ever since I left college. Would it be different if Freddy were alive? His death left such a gaping hole in our lives. The consolation is that the insurance policy he paid for so many years means I can balance the budget, although we're on a financial tightrope.

My daughters are doing well in school. It is their good fortune that both take after their father in looks, rather than me. Imagine, they have red hair like Freddy's, he called it the mark of the Irish.

All our love to you. We pray that the war will end soon and you and your sister's family can return to Bainbridge Island.

Yoko folded the fragile paper with care and tucked the letters back under the green ribbon guarding the bundle. How sad, she thought. Would I be as brave and strong as Auntie Ai to write such letters? She sorted the diaries into stacks around her, glancing through those her aunt had written in recent years. As she'd expected, little was new, for she was familiar with her aunt's activities in the past decades. To her surprise, some recent entries were in kanji, the Japanese writing Yoko didn't know well enough to read.

Yoko wondered if her aunt wanted what was written in kanji to be private. Why? I won't try to have it translated, though some of auntie's friends from the New York JACL read kanji. I think Ben must be right, Auntie wanted me to read what she wrote about their lives during the war years. She never told me much about that time. This is the mother lode—or the auntie lode. Mother never talked about the incarceration and Dad was just as silent about those years. The one time I asked, when I was a teen, they shook their heads and didn't answer. I never dared ask again.

Later, Yoko would reverse the decision to leave the words in kanji unread. The translation would prove to be valuable.

Auntie Ai's first diary was dated 1942, the year the Sasaki family was evacuated from their home on Bainbridge Island. Auntie Ai had written on the first page, *March 30, a sad time.* That's when my parents were taken away, Yoko realized. They had little time to plan what to pack and what to abandon and didn't know where they were going or for how long. Horrendous. I'd have been a basket case. Yoko could not stop exploring what stories the diaries held.

Ai Sasaki's Diary.
Manzanar War Relocation Center.
March 1942.

The train ride from Seattle felt endless. I fear it is seared into my memory. The military guards (imagine, there were <u>military</u> guards) didn't want to talk to us, though only a few were outright hostile. Most of the guards were as confused as us, they didn't know where we were going—we were told no one knew. The train never ran during the day, just at night. Each day we were shunted into a siding and shades pulled down. Were we in the siding so not to interrupt regular trains or to keep us away from angry eyes? Ever since the bombing of Pearl Harbor there is resentment, even outright hatred of us.

Whatever the reason the train stopped in sidings, it was humiliating. When the train jolted to its last stop, we stared through grimy windows, wondering where we were.

"It's the Mojave Desert," someone who knew their geography called out. "That's the Sierra Nevada range."

I gazed at the Sierra Nevada mountains and saw in my mind's eye the view from Bainbridge Island, the snow-capped majesty of Mount Rainier rising above the peaks of the rugged Cascades. I wept. When I stepped down from the train, wind scoured my face dry with dust-filled gusts.

The place was barren, nothing green to soothe the spirit, just sand and sagebrush. Random tumbleweed blew in the wind. The very second our luggage was off the train, we were herded onto busses, rush, rush, rush. We rattled along for close to three hours then jerked to a stop. We gazed in shock at our destination, rows and rows of barracks flimsily covered in tarpaper. Some buildings were still being constructed. This was where we were to live? I didn't want to look at my dear husband, how hard he worked to provide a good home for us. We were reluctant to get off the bus and hardly a word was spoken as we struggled with our belongings. All around us, families hurried to get out of the wind and dust, anxious to settle in despite the surroundings.

Like every other hut, ours was bare except for wire-spring cots, army blankets and one small oil heater. Before we could go to bed, we had to stuff canvas bags with straw to make mattresses. How could the government allow this? Is this how citizens are treated? It is wrong. We filled mattresses for the three of us then Saburo and I took a short walk, something we often did of an evening at home on Bainbridge Island. Ben didn't want to come. Saburo and I wanted to talk in private but constant wind snatched words away and made it difficult to hear. As we walked, we took in our surroundings and discovered that barbed wire surrounded us and armed sentries watched from huge observation towers. Blinding lights pierced the night. We are like defenseless bugs under a dangerous, malicious microscope.

My heart feels wrenched out of my body at leaving our home. Bitter questions gnaw in my mind at night as I try to rest on the straw-filled canvas bag that rustles when I breathe. When will we be able to return to Bainbridge Island? How long will the war last? One year, two, more? What if we're here for the rest of our lives, penned up like cattle in this dusty, isolated place? I'm too exhausted to cry, too tired to think.

Dear God, Yoko thought, barbed wire and armed guards, what a brutal start.

Of course Auntie was frightened—and angry. How would I deal with losing my freedom and being incarcerated? Damn right I'd be angry and scared and anxious. Everyone, young and old, torn from their homes, their communities, their work, their belongings, living with uncertainty about the future.

Her aunt's vehemence in that first diary surprised Yoko. Normally she was a fast reader, super fast, but this time she turned the pages with slow care, absorbing the words written from her aunt's heart. When she reached the last page, Yoko sat clutching the diary in her hand, tears in her eyes as she struggled to take in the enormity of the words on page after page in clinical black, describing the outrage that capsized the lives of so many. Somehow her parents and the Sasakis endured and survived. Somehow they managed to thrive.

Yoko stood, easing cramped muscles, grateful for what she'd found in the bedroom closet. From what Ben said, she was meant to read the diaries and letters. One trash bag was left over from packing Auntie Ai's clothes. Yoko shook it open and filled it with the diaries and every single item from the box. She anticipated carrying the treasure trove home and reading its contents. Her aunt's death signaled the end of an era. Yoko's heart needed time to heal, the diaries might help bring some comfort. Outside the building, she hefted the bag and considered the walk to the subway with such a load. She didn't have to think twice when a roving cab slowed down as it approached where she stood. She hailed the cab and climbed in after piling the bulging bag on the back seat.

About to give her home address, Yoko reconsidered. "Let's go to Rutherford Place, between Second and Fifteenth. The Quaker Meeting House."

The driver repeated the address, executed a swift, illegal U turn and they were off. It was 7:15 p.m. when the cab drew up outside the Quaker Meeting. Yoko didn't mind that she'd missed the potluck the Women's Worship Sharing Group had each second Monday from 6:30-7 p.m. What she craved was the peace of Quaker worship, which on Mondays was from 7-8 p.m. When she reached the door where people were gathered, someone was speaking, giving a message, and Yoko waited until that ended then slipped in and found a seat at the end of a row. She joined the group now and then when she missed Sunday morning worship and she recognized a few faces among those present. It was hard to still the chatter of her mind. It often was, but the silence wrapped her in its generous care. The worship was drawing to an end when the phrase, *Shanti Nilaya*, the final home of peace, came to Yoko. Auntie Ai was home. She had passed to a place without pain or anguish. Yoko relaxed into that peaceful knowing.

*   *   *

By the time Yoko reached the spacious apartment at 34 Gramercy Park she'd inherited from her godmother the bag felt heavy. She dropped it in the living room with a grateful sigh. She was starving, reading would have to wait until she fixed something to eat. "What can I make that's quick?" she asked the brother cats who were circling her feet hoping for treats as well as dinner. After she fed the cats, her inventory of the fridge didn't take long—nada, zip and a lone stalk of limp celery. The meager contents changed her mind about cooking, better to go out for a meal. The lone bottle of Murphy's Irish Red beer in the fridge conjured up a tantalizing image of shepherd's pie from Molly's, Yoko's favorite pub. Molly's was at 23rd and Third Avenue, close enough so she could walk there and save the lone beer for another time.

A call came in on her iPhone. It was Ben.

"Great timing, Ben," Yoko said cheerfully. "Want to come to Molly's . . . ?"

Ben interrupted, his voice so weak it was hard to hear him. "I feel terrible," he said. "Something's wrong. I'm going to the hospital, can you meet me there?"

"Beth Israel?" Yoko asked, thankful she knew which was the nearest hospital to Ben's apartment.

"Right." Ben ended the call.

Hunger pangs ignored, Yoko stuffed the iPhone and her wallet in her pocket and headed out. Beth Israel was off First Avenue, between East 15th and 17th, a reasonable walk from Gramercy Park. Finding a cab might be tricky and who knew what traffic delays there'd be, better to trust shank's pony and walk. Yoko hurried across the long crosstown blocks and her quick strides ate up the short downtown blocks. The ER waiting room was crowded but she didn't see her cousin. After scanning the faces and not finding Ben, Yoko walked up to reception.

"Can I help you?" the nurse seated behind the desk asked.

"Is Ben Sasaki here? He called about ten minutes ago. He . . . ."

"Ben Sasaki," the nurse ran her finger down the list in front of her. "He was admitted just now." The nurse eyed Yoko with a cold, impersonal look. Did she think by staring hard she could check Yoko's credentials?

"Dr. Kamimura," a voice boomed in Yoko's ear and the optometrist jumped, nerves on edge. It was Vinnie, one of the detectives from the 13th Precinct where Yoko had been a civilian consultant for several years. "I thought I saw you come in. What's up? You okay?"

"It's Ben, my cousin," Yoko explained. "He called me to say something was wrong and he was going to the hospital. The nurse told me he was just admitted."

Vinnie nodded at the nurse. "Family's allowed in, right?"

The nurse didn't hesitate and pointed to her right, doubts quelled by the familiar sight of the NYPD detective. "Through that door, Doctor, I'll tell them you're on your way."

Vinnie patted Yoko's arm. "I gotta get back to the one-three. I'll let Dan know I saw you."

"Thank you," Yoko said to the receptionist, not taking time to explain she wasn't an M.D.

In the ER, one of the nurses directed Yoko to the end cubicle. "Dr. Branson is examining Mr. Sasaki," she said.

Yoko slipped into the cubicle and Ben managed a half smile when he saw her then tried but failed to stifle a groan.

"You made it, bless you," he said. "God, my abdomen hurts like hell."

Both his arms had lines running to them and Yoko peered at the bag on the nearest line. What was Ben being given?

"If you are troubled by anything you see or hear, wait outside." The doctor's voice was brusque and she shot a swift, impersonal glance at Yoko. "No talking. I help one person at a time."

"S'okay, doc," Ben panted. "She's a doc." He groaned again.

"I'm an optometrist," Yoko said, "An O.D., not an M.D."

The doctor shook her head but her voice wasn't as terse when she spoke. "Just as well you're not an M.D., rules prohibit outside doctors." The doctor kept her attention focused on the physical exam she was giving Ben, making quick notes on the computer on a stand by the side of the bed when Ben answered her questions.

Yoko stood watching, shocked at Ben's extreme pallor and irregular breathing. What troubled her most was that the pupils of Ben's eyes were shrunk to pinpoints. That was a serious indicator of trouble but what was the cause?

"D'you know if there's diabetes in the family?" the doctor asked Yoko. "A blood sample has gone for immediate laboratory analysis. The results ought to be back soon."

"No, there never has been diabetes in Ben's family," Yoko said. Or mine, she thought.

"That's what Ben told me," Dr. Branson agreed, nodding to Yoko and smiling in reassurance at her patient, stripping off her rubber gloves with practiced movements.

"Your notes say you're a veteran," the doctor said to Ben. "Were you in Asia with the military?"

"Europe," Ben said.

"Have you visited Asia recently?"

"No."

"Hmm, then I doubt we're looking at some exotic disease," the doctor said. "At this point, I won't call for special tests. I'll let you know as soon as the lab results are back. Press the buzzer if you need anything."

She started to leave the cubicle, indicating with a jerk of her head to Yoko to join her. Yoko followed the doctor out and they walked a short way down the hall.

"Have you ever seen any member of the patient's family in a similar condition?" the doctor asked.

"Never. What do you think is wrong?"

"At this point, my thinking is going in two distinct directions," the doctor said. "An intestinal disease like shigellosis or bacillary dysentery is one possibility. We can't count out chemical poisoning. Right now, in addition to the standard procedure of intravenous fluids to restore the loss of body fluids—you'll have noticed the patient was sweating and salivating—I ordered atropine injected intramuscularly every two hours. This works by inhibiting the parasympathetic nervous system. I gave the first injection moments before you arrived."

A nurse walked up to where the doctor stood and held out a sheet of paper. "Here's the lab report, Dr. Branson."

The doctor pursed her lips as she scanned the paper. "We can rule out intestinal disease. That leaves us with poison." The beeper on her belt sounded and the doctor excused herself, hurrying off to the next emergency.

Yoko walked back to the cubicle wondering about the doctor's comment. Really? How would Ben have been poisoned? Accidental ingestion? Surely not food poisoning. Her cousin was asleep and she sat watching him, grateful to see that his breathing was less ragged and his pallor not as extreme. Whatever the problem, it looked as if the swift treatment had helped. The hours passed and Ben woke when a nurse came in to check on him and administer another injection of atropine.

"Hey, I feel a whole lot better," Ben said. He sounded quite different from when he'd telephoned Yoko. "My God, I think I'm almost over whatever it was." His voice was calm and, to Yoko's relief, the pupils of his eyes were close to normal. "Thanks for coming, Yoko. Why don't you go on home now? Get some rest, you look wiped out."

"Are you're sure?" Yoko said. "I'm more hungry than tired, on the verge of starving." Her cousin managed a slight smile at the idea of food. "I was thinking of visiting the hospital cafeteria but it's probably closed now."

"Off you go," Ben said. "You'll find something to eat on the way home."

The nurse finished giving Ben the injection.

Yoko kissed her cousin on the cheek and left, stopping on the way out in the bathroom to splash water on her face. She stared at the face in the mirror. Alert brown eyes looked steadily back despite the tinge of fear that showed in them. She smoothed her shoulder-length black hair and took a deep breath, ready for the world. Out on the street, she walked until she came to a Famous Ray's. Slice after slice of hot pizza covered in roasted red pepper and anchovies filled the void in her stomach.

The next morning, Yoko had a quick shower and before starting breakfast called Beth Israel to find out how Ben was doing. "Mr. Sasaki was released from the hospital this morning," an officious voice told her. Yoko called her cousin at home.

"Morning, cuz," Ben greeted her. "Checking up on me?"

"True, I am that," Yoko said, relieved to hear that his voice was strong, the weakness of yesterday gone.

"I feel fine," Ben said. "Whatever the doc did, it worked."

"That's music to my ears," Yoko said.

"I have to thank you for hustling right over to the hospital when I called," Ben said. "I don't know what hit me, I've never felt so rotten."

"You looked terrible," Yoko agreed. "By the time I left, you were looking much better."

"I wouldn't have bothered you but I thought it was serious," Ben said by way of apology. "We two have to stick together, no one else left in our families but us," he added. "It's a two-way street, you'll call me if I can help with anything, right?"

"Always," Yoko said.

While she was enjoying her favorite breakfast of rice cakes slathered with almond butter and plum jam with a mug of green tea on the side, she reminded herself to call her cousin in a day or two. We'll meet for a meal. I want to ask Ben about the diaries. Damn, I'm relieved he felt certain Auntie Ai wanted me to read them.

2 Say It Ain't So

"Yoko, where've you been?"

It was Detective Dan Riley from the 13th Precinct. His voice was tense, his question more a demand than a question. By now, Yoko was inured to the detective's mood swings, grateful he veered toward cheerfulness most of the time. She knew Dan's breezy attitude covered the stress of police work and she understood. It was several years since Yoko narrowly escaped death in a bizarre twist of events that led to her becoming a civilian consultant to NYPD's 13th Precinct, the famous one-three. Murder and mayhem were the norm in police work—optometry was blessedly low key although it had been a bizarre case of deadly intrigue at New York's College of Optometry that first brought Yoko to the attention of Chief of Detectives Mark Sanders.

Ever since Yoko had agreed to work with the one-three on special cases, she was teamed with two of the top detectives, the brilliant Zoran Zeissing, who somehow triumphed over his OCD* to accumulate the highest crime solve rate in the country and Dan Riley, the Irish prankster. The chemistry between Yoko and Dan was irresistible and they soon found themselves in a relationship but it didn't take long for Dan's erratic schedule to wreak havoc on the pair.

"Don't tell me you haven't time to leave me a message when the chief calls you?"

"I meant to, I really did." Dan was contrite, as usual, though sometimes he tried to joke his way out of the argument. Worse yet, he'd try bribes. That irritated Yoko even more.

"Flowers and chocolates won't change my mind," she'd fume.

On-again, off-again lovers, they agreed on a friendly divorce that was,

* OCD, Obsessive compulsive disorder.

to everyone's surprise, even Yoko and Dan's, going well. "We'll spend time together when we aren't working," Yoko suggested. "When you are off duty and I'm not working," she added. Dan capitulated. The arrangement baffled those at the precinct whose bets, 10 to 1, predicted an end sooner rather than later.

"At work, that's where I've been. I just got home. What's up?" Yoko wondered why was Dan asking? Was he joking? He sounded serious.

"I swung by the college but security said you left almost an hour ago. I checked your place and mine but didn't find you."

"Your phone wasn't working?" Yoko asked in a voice dripping with innocence.

Dan ignored the sarcasm. That was a first. Uh oh, something's up, Yoko thought.

"I'm at the one-three, I'll be right over. Stay put."

"I took a long walk, why . . . ?" Yoko was talking to empty air.

"What now?" Yoko groaned and her two brother cats stared at her, trying to will her to fill their bowls—it was time for them to eat for heaven's sake.

Friday had been hell on wheels at the college. The two senior optometrists who staffed the clinic for infants and children except for the two mornings Yoko was in charge were both out, one with the flu, the other at a West Coast conference. Yoko had to leave her research and step in to run the clinic with the help of an intern. She worked flat out from 8:30 to 4:30, guiding young patients through their vision therapy. Around one o'clock, in the minutes between one family leaving and the next arriving, she inhaled a tuna sandwich from the deli. The coleslaw with it sat untouched. Later, updating patient files, Yoko noticed the container on her desk and scooped up the coleslaw, finishing it in a few mouthfuls, relishing the tang and crunch.

At last the work for the day was done. Looking forward to a quiet weekend, Yoko decided to walk back to 34 Gramercy Park when she left the college. She stopped now and then to window shop, savoring the fact that the hectic week was over. Dan's call came the instant she reached home.

True to his word, Dan was tapping at Yoko's apartment door minutes later.

One look at his serious face and Yoko knew her premonition was spot on, something was wrong. She searched her memory. Had Dan told her about a problem at the one-three? She felt a twinge of guilt. Had she forgotten whatever it was? Dan hugged her, a long hug.

"Why don't we sit?" he said.

"What is it?" Yoko sat down, feeling a growing dread. This must be bad news, unless . . . Dan had better not be playing one of his tricks. Dan settled his lanky frame on the couch next to her and took her hands in his.

"I'm so sorry, dear heart, but it's about your cousin. It's not good news."

Yoko flinched. "Ben?" Her question was tentative. "I talked to Ben this morning, he felt much better. Is he back at Beth Israel?"

Dan didn't answer right away. He took a deep breath and said, "You know Ben was in the hospital overnight but released early this morning, right?" Yoko nodded. "He insisted he was feeling fine and the doctor agreed Ben had improved."

"I know, I was at the hospital yesterday," Yoko said. Why was Dan going over old news? "Ben looked much better by the time I left. He told me to go home—he might have wanted to flirt with the nurses." She started to laugh but the laughter faltered when Dan shook his head, his face grave. When he spoke, his voice was so low Yoko bent her head closer to him to hear his words.

"Late this afternoon, the maintenance guy where Ben lives found Ben passed out near the street door. Ben must have been going out, perhaps back to the hospital. An ambulance was called but . . ." Dan hesitated, ". . . Ben was dead when they arrived. They weren't able to revive him."

Yoko was too shocked to speak. Ben dead? What happened? Thoughts tumbled over each other in her mind. Ben said he was fine when she'd called that morning. What happened? Was the doctor at the hospital right, was Ben poisoned?

Dan put his arm around her and Yoko sat in the warmth of his embrace. This was horrendous news. She gulped jagged breaths and tears poured down her face. Dan hugged Yoko, his arms tight around her, waiting for the flood to stop.

"I'm an orphan," Yoko said, her voice muffled because her face was pressed into Dan's chest. "All my family is gone." She sat up and mopped her face dry. "I don't have any tears left."

"Good to let it out," Dan said.

"Whoever said crying helps?" Yoko muttered. "I still feel dreadful." She shook her head. "Right now, there's work to be done. I'll have time to mourn. Will there be an autopsy?" She corrected herself. "There'll be an autopsy, right?"

"Yes," Dan said. He cleared his throat and started to speak then stopped. Yoko stared at him. Now what?

"Zoran had a long talk with the chief. He wants you to work with him on the case."

Zoran Zeissing, the brilliant detective whose crime solve rate was as legendary as his OCD was Dan's longtime partner. It was Zoran who had requested that Yoko be invited to join NYPD's 13th Precinct after the case dubbed Eye Sleuth in recognition of Yoko's work as an optometrist.

"The knowledge Dr. Kamimura has of the vision system and how it is affected by drugs and stress will be of value in our police work," Zoran told Chief Sanders when he suggested Yoko be invited to become a civilian consultant to the 13th. "She was instrumental in solving a savage crime at the College of Optometry and showed courage when captured by a criminal who had every reason to wish her dead."

"Chief Sanders agreed I ought to work on the case?" Yoko asked. Then blinked. This was happening too fast. "Wait, what case?"

"Yoko, Ben's death is suspicious. The doctor at Beth Israel was unable to determine the cause of Ben's illness. Because of your relationship with Ben, the chief questioned whether you ought to be part of the investigative team." Dan smiled. "Zoran convinced him that it was an advantage."

Puzzled, Yoko asked, "How is it an advantage?"

"Zoran thinks, and I agree, that there might be clues at Ben's place and also in what you found at his mother's place," Dan said. He looked inquiringly at Yoko then went on, "You'd be the person best able to interpret that information, right?"

"You mean what I found in the box at Auntie Ai's?"

"Right," Dan said. "Look, are you sure you're okay with this? You do want to be on the case, right?"

"Damn right I want to be involved," she told Dan, who hugged her tight. Yoko hugged him back, glad their relationship had survived and moved into a different dimension.

"Do you want to go out for a bite to eat or maybe call for takeout?" Dan asked.

Yoko shook her head. "Thanks, but I need space, time to chill. I couldn't eat just yet."

"Okay," Dan said, getting to his feet. "Call me if you change your mind and want to go out, or want to talk, doesn't matter the time." With that, Dan left.

Yoko lay down on the couch. Was it so only a few days ago that she'd been at Auntie Ai's place in Brooklyn packing up and Ben had called her?

3 Searching for Clues

Zoran Zeissing called early the next morning.

"My sincere condolences, Yoko, for the loss of your cousin, Ben Sasaki. A death in the family is always hard," the detective began in his pedantic way. It was familiar, even comforting, to Yoko. They'd worked on a number of cases together and Zoran's style was logical and clear though some at the one-three found his manner irritating.

Yoko murmured her thanks and waited.

"Dan tells me that you are willing to joining in our investigation of what is, I regret to say, a suspicious death," the detective continued. "I am glad you are receptive to the suggestion because we work well together. The reason I urged Chief Sanders to permit you to join the team is that my intuition informs me that some valuable information may be found not only where Ben lived but also in the documents you discovered at the apartment of your aunt."

"I'd been thinking the same thing," Yoko said, smiling. She never minded how Zoran spelled out things just in case it wasn't obvious.

"Good," Zoran said. "You are without a doubt the individual who would be most able to discern if any such information is of value in solving the cause of death. From my reading of the hospital report, I gather the doctor at Beth Israel questioned whether poison was the cause." Zoran stopped. Was he waiting for an answer?

"I believe that's true," Yoko said, noting as she often did that Zoran never used a contraction. Dan had once told her that no one at the one-three had ever heard Zoran say, "You'll" or "I'm."

"Do you think Zoran thinks that way, never using any contractions?" Yoko said.

Dan shrugged. "Perhaps it makes sense to him, hard to know what goes on inside his brain, he has a style all his own."

Yoko was startled when she heard Zoran clear his throat, she'd begun making a mental list of what she needed when she went grocery shopping.

"May I suggest you make it a priority to go through the diaries?" Zoran said. Before Yoko could speak, he added, "First, however, would you be free to meet me in an hour at the apartment where Mr. Sasaki lived? It is Saturday, so I hope you are not obligated to work at the College of Optometry?"

"My weekend is open," Yoko said. Playing civilian consultant to Zoran's detecting beat boring shopping. When they finished at Ben's, she'd pick up some cat food and kitty litter and vegetables and when she got home she'd explore what else the documents, as Zoran described them, had to offer. "I'll meet you in an hour."

"Excellent," Zoran said with satisfaction. "Together we can evaluate whatever we find. It is obvious that your vision will be more informed than mine."

Yoko's chuckle was rueful. Did Zoran sneak in a subtle reference to her optometric research. Could he be making a joke? Yoko reminded herself to tell Dan.

Zoran was waiting outside the building on Second Avenue where Ben had lived when Yoko arrived. It was clear the detective had dressed with his usual meticulous care, no casual Saturday slacks or open-necked shirt for him. Yoko knew he had his plastic baggy of wipes in one pocket of his tailored suit so he'd be ready to neutralize any free-floating germs. In deference to Zoran's need for order, she'd opted for respectable chinos topped with one of her favorite flower-covered T-shirts instead of the jeans she preferred on a weekend. The two chatted as they climbed the stairs to the third floor.

"Are you familiar with this apartment?" Zoran asked.

"It's a floor-through like the one I used to live in. You have a lot of space at a reasonable rent for Manhattan, even though it's laid out in the classic railway style, one room leading into the next," Yoko said. "I didn't visit very often, Ben and I mostly met at a restaurant or at family get-togethers."

"Had the Sasakis always lived in Brooklyn?"

"No. Before the war, World War II, they lived on Bainbridge Island."

"Ah," Zoran said. "In all likelihood, when the Pacific coastal area was declared a war zone, they were moved by the government to relocation camps, places more accurately described as concentration camps."

"That's true," Yoko said, remembering that once Zoran read or heard something, it was with him forever. God, how she envied him that gift. "My parents never talked about that part of their lives although Auntie Ai did tell me a little not long before she died. I'm keen to read the diaries because I've always wanted to learn about what happened in those war years."

"If I am correct, your aunt, Mrs. Ai Sasaki, would have been Nisei, the generation born in this country to immigrant parents who were denied citizenship," Zoran said.

"Correct."

"Therefore your cousin, Ben Sasaki, was Sansei, what is termed the third generation. Of course, all are Americans although their heritage happens to be Japanese."

Yoko nodded. Zoran had his information right.

"If the hospital report is correct," Zoran continued, "your cousin was in the military and before that incarcerated with his parents?"

"Yes," Yoko said. "Not that he ever talked about the years in the camp to me."

Zoran nodded his understanding. "People often find it easier to let the past stay in the past."

When they reached the third floor, it was clear from the yellow tape crisscrossing the door which of the two entrances on the landing was the one to Ben's apartment. Zoran meticulously undid the tapes that had the words, "No Entry" running across it in a continuous line. He rolled each tape in his neat, precise way and pocketed the two rolls before producing a set of master keys. Yoko knew that when they left, Zoran would be able to replace the strips of tape so that no one would realize they had ever been removed.

Zoran unlocked the door and courteously indicated to Yoko that she enter before him. She stepped over the threshold reluctantly, feeling a strong mingling of anxiety and sorrow. They stopped inside the doorway, looking over what they could see of the apartment from that vantage point. Light from the many tall windows filled the place so it didn't look forbidding, not that this helped loosen the knot in Yoko's stomach.

"It appears that this is the entry room as well as the kitchen."

Zoran didn't comment about the bathtub that sat along one wall of the room. The tub was covered with a slab of plywood and shelves above the tub held toiletries. Yoko knew—because Ben's place had the same antediluvian design as her old apartment—that a small room was off the bedroom, just a toilet, though probably Ben had added shelves to stack towels and bathroom supplies. The addition of a toilet was a nod to modernization and meant a tenant didn't have to walk down the hall to the single toilet used by all the other tenants on that floor. The rent was increased by such improvements but even so, for New York City, such places were cheap and more rare than a winning lottery ticket.

"Yes, this room doubles as a kitchen and a place to have a bath," Yoko said. "The bedroom is to the right and the living room is to the left of the kitchen." Yoko was glad the place was clean and neat. Ben had once told her that after his time in the military, he liked to keep his place orderly. "Spick and span," Ben said. "When we had a visit from top brass, that's what the sergeant demanded. We always kept the barracks in good shape." Yoko walked over to the kitchen table and looked at but didn't touch the lone mug on it. "This is half filled with something, I don't think it's tea, perhaps it's wine," she said. "I'll leave it for the forensic team."

Zoran still stood near the door, staring into the living room. Yoko followed his gaze and saw that he was focused on a desk, the top of which was covered in neat piles of papers, stacked tidily in rows.

"Do you want me to start with the desk?" Yoko asked. She waited, accustomed to the detective's long pauses, knowing they meant he was sorting through his memory banks for the most pertinent information about whatever needed his immediate attention.

"No," Zoran said, surprising her. "Let us examine the desk when we finish our search. First, I would prefer to go through the rest of the apartment together. Although I believe we will find the most rewarding items in the desk, I wish to save it for last." He took two pairs of latex gloves out of one of his pockets, offering Yoko one pair and pulling on the other pair.

Methodically, the two combed through the apartment and, as Zoran had surmised, they didn't find anything out of the ordinary. They went over the bedroom, the small room housing the toilet and shelving stacked with towels, then the kitchen and living room. They opened and removed the drawers in the bedroom bureau, feeling behind them for anything that might be hidden from sight. The kitchen cupboards were so well organized, it was simple enough to view the contents. Nothing surprising, packages of noodles and teas, jars of sauces, bottles of spices and herbs.

Zoran even lifted and searched under the small area rug that covered the space in front of the futon couch and between them they turned the futon over and felt it to check that nothing was hidden in or under it.

"Time for the desk?" Yoko asked when they'd finished.

Zoran nodded. "It is time for the desk," he said. "Please start by examining the papers on top of the desk. I will make notes of what you find." He held up his miniscule recorder, something he always carried. Yoko smiled. Once, when they'd been working on another case, she'd asked him why he of all people needed to make notes.

"It is true that I have an eidetic memory," Zoran told her. "But if I am murdered or knocked down and killed by a car of what value is my memory?" Baffled and almost amused all over again at the way Zoran's mind worked, Yoko could only nod her understanding of his strategy.

Yoko walked to the desk and sat on the bright blue office chair, thinking about the summer day when she and Ben had spotted it at a flea market on Houston Avenue and wheeled it back to his place. They'd hauled it up the long flights to Ben's apartment then headed out to celebrate with lunch. She sat down hesitantly, aware of her nervous tension and wished as she often did that she chewed gum. Who cared if it loosened the fillings in her teeth?

Zoran carried in one of the chairs from the kitchen, settling himself in it next to the desk. One by one, Yoko picked up the papers and gave Zoran a précis of each so that he could record the details. Many minutes later, she put the last aside with a sigh of relief. The neat piles on the desk had not yielded anything that looked as if it was connected to Ben's death. Mostly, the papers were Ben's brief notes from his decades of counseling veterans. From them, although he was retired, Ben had been writing an article on war-induced trauma for *The American Journal of Psychology*. He'd called Yoko several times to ask about optometric treatment of such trauma and she was glad to see he'd included details and links to the journal articles on PTSD she'd sent.

There had been one surprise when Yoko read off a name from one of Ben's notes. "Hans Reiniger?" She said, glancing at Zoran in astonishment.

"Ah, the Romani, who piloted his hot-air balloon from Union Square to Gramercy Park in defiance of the law against doing so?" Zoran asked, his voice calm.

"That was one of our most unusual cases."

"None other."

"You are certain?"

"Yes. Ben wrote the word Romani after the name Hans Reiniger," Yoko said. "What surprises me is that the two knew each other."

"Perhaps your cousin offered Mr. Reiniger pro bono counseling?" Zoran said. "That would be natural for a therapist such as Mr. Sasaki. You will recall that during and after the trial, there was an outpouring of support for Mr. Reiniger. He received myriad offers of shelter and money."

"I'm not sure Ben was acting as a therapist to Reiniger. There's even a phone number and if the man was a patient, this information would be in Ben's files, not in a note on his desk."

Yoko recalled her first sight of the Romani a few years earlier. She'd come across the wreckage of his hot-air balloon on 23rd Street and knelt beside the man lying in a tangle of ropes and fabric. He'd opened his eyes and Yoko had wondered if their striking Paul Newman blue meant the man was wearing contacts. But no, contacts tend to hide the pupils and

Yoko could see his clearly. They looked normal. The man kept his intense eyes locked on Yoko's. Between ragged breaths, he murmured, "Is . . . a dream?"

Yoko had watched as the man's pupils dilated and life began to ebb from his eyes—the man would die without prompt medical help. Luck, providence and the speedy EMT response rescued the man from death. When the police discovered the man's name and background, she and Dan had been sent by Chief Sanders on an official visit to the man in the hospital. Their unusual mission? To find out why he'd made an illegal balloon flight and why he had a Luger with him in the hot-air balloon.

The truth about Reiniger's flight lay under complicated layers that had been slowly peeled away by the detectives of the one-three. By the time all was revealed, the public's outraged reaction morphed to one of sympathy. Whether this affected the court's decision is moot. The Gypsy, which is how he was always referred to in the media, was ordered to pay a hefty fine and put on probation. If he dared to fly another hot-air balloon over the Big Apple, punishment would be swift. "One mo' time and he'll go up the river and not in a balloon," Dan joked. Not to be left out, Detective Baldoni in his official role as "Giver of names," dubbed Reiniger, "Our Roaming Romani."

After his release from hospital and rehabilitation, Yoko had attended the trial of Hans Reiniger then she'd lost sight of him. She'd read the occasional story in the Entertainment section of the *Daily News*, usually with a photo of him, always with the same picture, always the same caption, "Gypsy Reiniger strolling in Central Park." The Fashion section of *The New York Times* had praised one elite designer's "Gypsy Coat for Men," a flowing, romantic cloak. Nothing resembling anything Hans Reiniger had ever worn. The fascination of the glitterati and paparazzi with their "Gypsy" lasted much longer than the norm but at some point, the next sensation elbowed Hans Reiniger away from the headlines.

Zoran's voice brought Yoko back from her memories.

"Is there anything in this note that you deem suspicious?" Zoran asked, his voice grave.

"Not at all," Yoko said. "All the note has is the name and phone number."

"Since his retirement, did your cousin maintain an office somewhere other than this apartment?" Zoran asked. "Would there be files that we could check?"

"No," Yoko said. "Ben closed his office when he retired and his case files went to the New York State Psychological Association."

"Apart from the sheet of paper with the information about Hans Reiniger, the notes on the desk have been general and related to the article Mr. Sasaki was writing," Zoran said. "Do you think we need to pursue this?"

"I don't think it would be a waste of time," Yoko said slowly. "What do you think?"

"I am aware that there was monitoring of Hans Reiniger for a while, then it became somewhat loose. Nothing in his behavior gave any cause for alarm and the surveillance was discontinued." Zoran's look at Yoko was inquiring. "You and Dan were the first from the one-three in touch with him. Do you agree it would be appropriate if you are the person to contact him now?"

"I agree," Yoko said.

"You might wish to explain to Mr. Reiniger that you found his name and telephone number among the papers at the apartment of your cousin. I suggest this because these days, in light of his past and despite his exemplary behavior, Mr. Reiniger might find a visit from Detective Riley or myself unusual and alarming."

"True," Yoko said. "It might not mean anything but I'll follow through, just to be sure." She read out the phone number as she jotted it down in her notebook, knowing Zoran never needed to make notes. She picked up the last slip of paper on the desk.

"This is strange," Yoko said. "Here's a note that only has the letter E, then the word 'treatment?' and an address." She read it to Zoran. "3039 Avenue U, Caring Hospice. It's a Brooklyn number, 718-743-4600."

Zoran stared at her. "Is there a date on the paper?"

"No."

"So we do not know when it was written. Did your cousin ever mention hospice to you?"

"No."

"It is possible the information was for a friend of his."

"Perhaps," Yoko agreed.

"It is doubtful that telephoning the hospice will be helpful," Zoran said, reaching a decision. "It may be difficult to ascertain anything without a name. Unless . . ." he paused and a small smile crossed his face, ". . . unless one of the people staying at the hospice is known only as E."

Yoko nodded and raised her eyebrows to show her appreciation of the small joke.

"If Mr. Sasaki ever went to the Caring Hospice, he may be remembered and that may help clarify who he was visiting," Zoran concluded.

"What next?" Yoko asked and replaced the page with the cryptic note on the desk next to the paper with Hans Reiniger's name and number.

"If you will empty the cubby holes and then the desk drawers, one by one," Zoran said, "I will catalogue the contents of each as we go. We will leave the in-depth inspection of the items for the forensic team. What we seek are indications of potential answers to the death of Mr. Sasaki."

The desk had a center drawer and two deep drawers on the left. On the right were two cubbyholes filled with newspaper and magazine clippings. When Yoko looked through the clippings, she found that they were about veterans and were part of Ben's research. She opened the center drawer.

"Pens, pencils, stapler, paper clips, ah, here's Ben's checkbook." She put it on the top of the desk then took out a bunch of registers bundled together in a rubber band and placed them next to the checkbook.

"Kindly give me a simple overview of the checkbook entries," Zoran said.

Yoko read from the current check register. "Rent, utilities, telephone and TV, subscriptions to *The New York Times* and some magazines, donations to various organizations. Pretty straightforward," she remarked and Zoran nodded agreement.

"What about incoming amounts, are there many deposits?" he said.

"Only two types, monthly Social security and something noted as Vet. benefit."

"Straightforward enough," Zoran said and he sounded just a little disappointed. "I wonder what is in the second drawer. It is the last place for anything of significance."

Yoko opened the drawer. "It's empty except for a large brown envelope." She removed the envelope and hefted it in her hand. "It's not very heavy."

"I had hoped we might find some diaries written by Mr. Sasaki," Zoran said.

"I did, too," Yoko said. "It may be that all of Ben's diaries were at his mother's apartment in the box I found."

Yoko undid the clasp on the envelope and shook the contents out, sucking in a breath of surprise at what fluttered onto the desktop. Zoran stood in one quick move, coming close to where Yoko sat. Both stared at what had fallen from the envelope. Scattered across the desktop were several sheets of paper and one solitary red silk-covered diary.

"Now is the time for me to request expert aid," Zoran said. He pulled out his cell phone and called the one-three and asked for a forensics team to be sent ASAP.

Yoko stared at the patchwork of letters on the top sheet.

A wrong will be made right.
Your time will come.

Yoko could see parts of the words on the sheets underneath the top one, words like, *Reckoning* and *Guilty.* Why had Ben saved the threatening messages? Was he going to show them to the police or was he going to take matters into his own hands. She sat puzzling over the messages until Zoran spoke.

"Here is our first opening," Zoran said. His voice was serious but when Yoko glanced at him, she saw the gleam in his eyes. Zoran was ready for action.

"I gather from your surprise at seeing the sheets of paper with what can only be interpreted as threatening words that your cousin did not ever mention receiving such mailings?"

"Never," Yoko said firmly and heard the stress under the emphasis in her answer.

"It is possible forensic analysis will be of help and reveal some useful details," Zoran said. "However, my intuition is that the diary is where we may find details of substance."

"I hope so," Yoko said.

Zoran picked up the chair he'd been using and replaced it where he'd found it by the kitchen table. Even though her head buzzed with questions about what the diary might hold, Yoko had to repress a smile. Only Zoran would think of being neat at such a time. She glanced away to give him a semblance of privacy as he took out a wipe from his pocket and cleaned his hands. When she looked back, he was folding the used wipe and putting it in a baggie that went into another pocket. Germs vanquished, Zoran straightened his shoulders and stood without speaking for a few seconds.

"May I suggest that I wait for the forensics team?" he said. "When they have examined the diary, I will direct them to deliver it to your home so that you can read it. When you have done so, you will, of course, let me know if any of the contents are helpful with regard to the death of Mr. Sasaki. Is this arrangement satisfactory to you?"

"Absolutely," Yoko answered, marveling at the certainty of Zoran's words, suggestions created on the spur of the moment yet ones that made great sense.

Zoran moved to the door. It was time to leave.

"I do not think the forensics team will be long. It would be fine if you wish to wait with me for their arrival," Zoran said, opening the door and inclining his head to invite Yoko to walk out in front of him.

"Probably the best use of my time is to go home and start reading the diaries I have there," Yoko said.

"Of course," Zoran said. "I will come down with you and wait outside to greet the team."

They walked down the stairs, talking quietly.

"Do you have an autopsy report yet?" Yoko asked, curious to know if there was any news.

"In a way." The OCD detective gave one of his oblique answers for which he was notorious. "Our medical examiner, Dante Nicosian, has offered a preliminary report," Zoran coughed. "It indicates he does not have what he considers a true report. The good doctor is frustrated because he has not been able to determine the precise cause of death."

Yoko wasn't surprised to learn of the ME's chagrin. Dante was without doubt tops in his field. People in the business of analyzing the cause of death knew the pride he took in his record of prompt and accurate autopsy reports. Right then, her iPhone, which she had muted before she left home, buzzed. Caller ID showed it was the very person they'd been talking about, Dante Nicosian, the ME. The coincidence surprised Yoko and for a brief moment she felt heartened by the coincidence but she warned herself not to have expectations. Still, she couldn't help hoping that Dante had determined the cause of Ben's death.

"Hello, Dante."

"Greetings, Yoko," Dante said. It was unusual for the ME to call anyone about an autopsy, he much preferred people visit his immaculate morgue downtown, but he made no secret of his fondness for Yoko and often brushed his own rule aside for her. "I'm so very sorry for your loss," Dante said. "I am calling to explain that I cannot . . . ah . . . say I have results yet of the autopsy on Ben Sasaki." The ME hesitated, fumbling for words. He must have decided to plunge ahead and in a rush of words he confessed his lack of facts. "It's a first for me not to have made any progress ascertaining the cause of death."

His sigh was heavy and the sound hissed through the phone line and across the miles separating the ME from Yoko. "You will recall that the doctor at the hospital noted she hadn't been able to determine the cause of Mr. Sasaki's illness although the patient's improvement was swift," Dante said.

"I know," Yoko answered. "Ben's response to the treatment at Beth Israel was quick. At least, it looked that way, otherwise the doctor wouldn't have let him leave."

"So the hospital records indicate." The ME sighed again and Yoko jerked the iPhone away to avoid the noise. "The hospital report is comprehensive but doesn't begin to answer the question about what might have caused death," Dante said. "When I read over the report, it says, 'Signs of Ben Sasaki's health crisis were obvious. Extreme pallor, a rapid pulse, irregular breathing, a fast heart rate, nausea, vomiting and abdominal pain. The pupils of his eyes were shrunk to pinpoints. He was confused and almost comatose. Blood tests showed an elevation in the white blood cell count.'" Yoko's heart sank.

"How could Ben have recovered so quickly and then . . . then a few hours later died?" she asked.

"I need more time to run more tests," Dante said. "I hope it won't take too much longer. The truth is, the hospital's records and their lab reports only corroborate what was *not* the cause of death. Rest assured that I'll be as timely as possible in unraveling this mystery."

Yoko thanked the ME and ended the call, her mind mired in worry over the mystery surrounding Ben's death. Would the single diary she'd found in Ben's desk help?

Yoko had stopped walking down the stairs while she took the call from the ME. She hurried down the last flights and found Zoran standing outside the building. Zoran didn't ask and Yoko didn't volunteer what Dante had said, it was too upsetting. Besides, Dante hadn't told her anything new. She was about to say goodbye, when Zoran held up a hand.

"I have another question, although I will understand if you do not have the answer," he said.

"All right," Yoko said.

"Do you recall how many diaries written by your cousin you found?" Zoran said.

"Two or three, I think. Ben didn't write as many as his mother." Yoko added a caveat. "I skimmed over most of Auntie Ai's and one or two of Ben's, so this number may not be accurate. You see, I also found some letters, though they were between my aunt and her dearest friend, Hana Oyama."

"Perhaps you noted the years when the diaries of your cousin were written?" Zoran asked.

"Yes, I did look at the dates." Yoko's answer was tentative. "As far as I remember, only one was written when Ben was interned. I didn't find any for the time he was in the military. Ben wrote about his experiences in the war years later."

"I see."

"You've reminded me about something unusual in one of Auntie Ai's recent diaries," Yoko said.

"What was that?" Zoran's voice was unhurried but interest flared in his eyes.

"She wrote a few entries in kanji not English."

Before Yoko could decide whether she needed to explain what kanji was, Zoran spoke. "The Japanese term kanji is for the Chinese characters used in the modern Japanese writing system, together with hiragana and katakana." He smiled at the look on Yoko's face. "Yet one more interesting factoid that floats in my brain. You have something to add about the kanji?"

"It was puzzling that the kanji entries were in a diary she wrote just before her death, there was never any kanji in the early ones," Yoko said slowly. "At the time, I thought perhaps it was something she wanted to keep private but now I'm wondering whether those entries may have some bearing on Ben's death."

Yoko and Zoran stood in silence for a moment, considering the implications of the kanji.

Zoran spoke first. "Am I correct in thinking you do not read kanji?"

"I know a little, not a word of what Auntie Ai wrote," Yoko said. "I can get in touch one of my aunt's friends who reads kanji."

"May I suggest we use one of the translators who does such work for the precinct?" Zoran said. "It may be wise to keep the material in the hands of a professional so that it remains confidential."

"Understood," Yoko said.

"Do you have a printer that makes copies?" Zoran said. Yoko nodded and he added, "Why not make copies of the entries with kanji? I will send someone to your place to pick up the copies. That way, you will be able to keep the diaries you found at the home of your aunt."

Yoko left the detective standing deep in thought on the sidewalk outside Ben's building as he waited for the forensics team.

4 A Pilgrimage

Yoko walked home mulling over what she and Zoran had found at Ben's apartment. The questions surrounding Ben's death added a troubling confusion to her sorrow that he was gone. For a brief moment, Yoko found herself thinking that if death had taken Ben as simply as it had Auntie Ai, his mother, she and Dan and Zoran, not to mention Dante, wouldn't be wrestling with such a damn tricky puzzle. She banished the somber thought, aghast at where her mind had wandered. She forced herself to look on what was good. She'd found the diaries and letters and at long last was learning about her family's lives during World War II.

Her parents had been silent about those years. She wasn't sure they ever talked to each other about the days of their incarceration, they certainly didn't talk to her about the days and months and years behind barbed wire. When the war ended and they regained their freedom, neither her mother nor her father ever mentioned the devastating losses and hardships they and so many others had endured. They moved on with their lives in the land of their birth, the U.S., creating happy, fulfilling years.

Yoko was in high school when a magazine writer came to interview her parents about the days they were forced to leave their home and sent to live in places that President Roosevelt among others called concentration camps. Yoko listened outside the living room door.

"Many of us were American citizens," she heard her dad, a professor of linguistics at Hunter College, explain. His tone was calm, stating facts not complaints.

"Sixty-two percent, about two-thirds, were American citizens," added her mother, who had run science courses at St. Vincent's, a major

New York teaching hospital before it closed in 2010. "Even so, we were denied the rights of citizens, our constitutional rights."

Yoko couldn't make out what the writer said in reply but she jumped up guiltily when she heard her mother say, "I'll bring some tea." At the sound of her mother's light footsteps approaching the door, Yoko tiptoed away. She didn't dare imagine what her parents would say if she was caught eavesdropping.

It was years later that Auntie Ai, her mother's sister, begged Yoko to join her on the pilgrimage to the remains of a camp in a remote corner of California.

"Will you keep me company, Yoko? Please say you will—not that we were ever held in the Tule Lake War Relocation Center, your family and mine, but the place is symbolic of all ten camps. It was where those in the other camps named as dissidents were imprisoned. People go every other year over the July Fourth holiday. Hundreds of people are buried in that place. We summon their ghosts and mourn the losses suffered by the living as well as the dead."

Auntie Ai, her husband, Saburo, and their son, Ben, were even more important to Yoko after the death of her parents. Saburo was a quiet man, almost reticent in contrast to his outgoing wife. When Yoko visited, Saburo welcomed her and never failed to ask about her health and work. Courtesies over, he'd withdraw to his desk, retreating behind the piles of papers and legal books. Their son, Ben, although older than Yoko was someone Yoko counted as one of her closest friends, someone she could confide in, whether about her love life since her divorce—it consisted of on-again, off-again Detective Dan—or the politics at her workplace, SUNY's College of Optometry.

Yoko knew the trip to the camp was important to her aunt. Yoko also knew it was a unique opportunity for her to learn more about the incarceration. She searched the Internet and found an entry about the camp: "...Japanese Americans named as dissidents were imprisoned there." Yoko scrolled through the long entry and read that the camp director, Raymond Best, had previously had been director of the War Relocation Authority's jails, known as Citizen Isolation Centers at Moab, Utah, and Leupp, Arizona. He refused to negotiate with internees, in contrast to the policy in the other camps, ignoring their requests for meetings. The height of the barbed-wire fencing was increased as were the numbers of military police. Yoko studied the comment by Barbara Takei, whose mother had been incarcerated there, "Of all the wartime incarceration sites, Tule Lake tells the most extreme story of the government's abuse of power against people who dared to speak out against the injustice of their incarceration."

"I'll go with you, Auntie Ai," Yoko said with reluctance, almost a foreboding. Her gut instinct was prescient. Yoko's experience on the trip morphed the incarceration from history to stark reality. She and her aunt flew from New York to Los Angeles then joined the group traveling to the Tule Lake campsite in Modoc County in northeast California. "Confusion reigned," they learned, "because the spelling of the nearby town was one word and the camp was two."

Something about being at Tule Lake loosened Auntie Ai's tongue. She told Yoko a little about her experience at Manzanar while aunt and niece stood surveying flat, treeless land that was mostly grass and sagebrush. The scattering of tiny white shells from freshwater mollusks that once filled the shallow lake waters was scant evidence there had ever been a lake. It was a clear day and fifty miles away, Mount Shasta dominated the landscape. Yoko and her aunt walked around gazing at the remnants of the camp—a towering red chimney over what had been the boiler house for the hospital, a gaping root cellar, and a large excavation that once served as a swimming hole.

"At Manzanar, we organized everything we could think of to try to make life bearable, Little League, concerts, art classes. Can you believe it?"

Yoko shook her head at the query. Overwhelmed at what she saw and heard from her aunt and the others, she found little to say. Yoko tried to repress the haunting images of what she saw on that visit but over and over her subconscious brought them back to her. The nightmares started even as Yoko slept on the flight back to New York from California. They never stopped. They became less frequent but they never stopped.

Triggered by a sight, a smell, a sound, Yoko could not escape dark dreams of life in the ten places called relocation camps.

How different from the facts spouted by the history professor at Earlham College. Yoko chose to go to the Quaker college because it was where Ben had gone. He'd been at Earlham a shade shy of three months before he was eligible to enlist in the military.

"After Pearl Harbor, America entered World War II. In February 1942," the professor intoned, "Roosevelt . . . who knows which Roosevelt?" He paused. Not getting any answer from students, he shrugged and continued. "Franklin D. Roosevelt was the president who signed Executive Order 9066 for the mass evacuation and detention of people of Japanese descent. You'll find official figures are 110,000 to 120,000. Kyo Takahashi estimates more in his book, *Kaeranai Nihonjin, Japanese of No Return,* but he may have included births. In the Amache camp in Granada, Colorado, for instance, 415 babies were born."

Yoko scribbled notes as the professor talked. She shivered at the thought that she might have been born in one of the camps.

"Abandoning our lives and homes was hard but think how traumatic it was for youngsters like Ben, forced to leave school and friends, not knowing when they might return," Auntie Ai said. "For adults, jobs and homes were lost, most forever. Perhaps the exception was on Bainbridge Island. Our neighbors there saved as much as they could for the families who were taken away. Some farms were entrusted to the care of farm workers, who often were Filipinos. One of the Quakers, Orville Robertson, agreed to look after several farms so that ownership remained with the Nikkei. Arnold Raber bought the Kouras' farm for $1, promising to resell it to them for that price when they returned.

"Saburo explained that the ten camps were not internment camps. When countries are at war, internment is the lawful process for detaining enemy aliens. We were not enemy aliens yet we were detained under the law. Although we were U.S. citizens, we were not allowed to vote, you know, use absentee ballots." Auntie Ai's lawyer husband had made sure internees knew the distinction ignored by their government.

"It wasn't until 1988 that there was an apology for the internment. Ronald Reagan signed it based on legislation by President Jimmy Carter that created a study. It admitted that government actions were based on 'race prejudice, war hysteria, and a failure of political leadership,'" Auntie Ai said, voice low. "It's appalling the public figures who condemned us. Even Walter Lippmann. Newspapers like the *Los Angeles Times* had inaccurate and biased comments."

"Wasn't money paid to people who'd been interned?" Yoko asked her aunt. "I read that when they were president, Bill Clinton and George H. W. Bush sent payments to survivors."

"Reparation they called it, $1.6 billion," Aunt Ai agreed. "Too late for some." Her smile was watery. "Your parents saved the funds and later it helped with your college tuition. We used the money to help with Ben's college."

Yoko was amazed to fill in yet one more part of the mosaic her parents had left blank.

"Still, the apology and the money didn't balance with the losses," Auntie Ai said. "How to forget years living behind barbed wire or blot out memories of the bleak land? The walls of the huts were tarpaper! They blocked nothing. We heard every sound, every movement, even conversations in the huts next to us.

"We'd make noise so we wouldn't hear the families in the huts on either side of us. Imagine! If you needed to talk in private, you went outside. Always the wind was howling. It might be raining or snowing or blisteringly hot but outside you went."

Yoko hadn't thought much about privacy growing up. Although born in America, her parents still had a deep connection with their heritage, where privacy for the individual was paramount.

"Nothing was private. I'll never forget what Takato's dad, Wakamatsu-san, said when he warned his oldest son, the one with the hot temper, 'Takato, you must practice control. No more loud voice and strong words.' I nicknamed Takato 'Wasabi boy,' which got a frown from my husband, a frown that didn't reach the twinkle in his eyes." Auntie Ai's face softened at the memory. "Our Ben was influenced by Takato's example to join the military." Auntie Ai sighed.

"Your mother exchanged *sai-kei-rei*, the deep formal bow, with Mrs. Wakamatsu when they met outside at the start of the day and chatted," Auntie Ai told Yoko. "But they never talked about Takato's temper. It was late one night when we heard Wakamatsu-san speak in a grave voice and caution his son.

"'You could be moved to a detention camp,' he said.

"'What's the difference? Takato argued. We're being detained right here.'"

"'*Hai*,' his mother agreed. 'But the government says we're in an internment or relocation camp. Anyone who is disruptive will be sent to a detention camp. Mrs. Okubo told me your talk about wanting to fight is dangerous.'"

"'I'm sorry but she doesn't have it right. I want to fight for my country, for America,' Takato explained. The surprised gasps from Takato's parents were as clear as if they were sitting in our hut." Auntie Ai glanced at Yoko. "Your uncle and I were startled but we didn't speak for fear we'd offend the Wakamatsu family if they heard us.

"'Son, are you seeking a way out of this . . . this place?' Takato's dad's voice was low but not low enough for us to miss one syllable. We dared not get up and go out because that would make enough noise that our neighbors would realize we'd heard them.

"'I'm old enough to join up. I want to fight. I'm not the only one, some of us here feel we must go and fight. I'm not a No No.'

"The long silence was broken by the sound of feet shuffling," Auntie Ai said. "I could almost see Takato standing facing his parents, determined to wait them out but unable to keep his feet from moving nervously.

"'It's okay, Sam,' we heard Takato say to his brother. 'Not everyone wants to be a soldier. The Quaker *hakujiin* will help you get to a college on the East coast or the Midwest so you can study art and make us proud. Me, I'll come back with a chest filled with medals.'

"We heard his mother click her tongue, *tsk tsk*, at Takato calling Quakers *hakujiin* but I didn't see anything wrong with that, the Quakers who'd come to the camp *were* white."

The Wakamatsus had lived on Bainbridge Island, where they had a thriving apple orchard and grew acres of strawberries. They'd named Sam, Takato's brother, after Sam Weith, their closest friend on Bainbridge Island and the art teacher who encouraged Sam's talent.

"Life in the camp must have been difficult," Yoko said. "Was it sad?"

"We made ourselves happy," Auntie Ai said. "Sometimes, you managed to forget you were confined in a windblown square of desert surrounded by barbed wire. Everyone turned out for the football games and cheered on the players. There were Christian churches and Buddhist temples. The weekly newspaper was full of stories and announcements, weddings, births, everything. We even had a Boy Scout troop." Auntie Ai sighed. "When we lived on Bainbridge Island, we'd lived our lives however we chose. We went where we wanted, when we wanted. Before we knew what happened, our freedom vanished. Guards with guns up in the watchtowers night and day, searchlights always shining."

Yoko shook her head at the image. "Were you glad Quakers helped Ben leave the camp?" Yoko asked, in an effort to lighten the mood.

"I was grateful he could get out." Auntie Ai hesitated. "There was such racial prejudice, even hatred in the country against us. Before the war, he did well in school, he excelled. When people from religious organizations like the Quakers helped students leave the camp and get into college, Ben was admitted to Earlham but the age to join the military was dropped and as soon as he was 18, he joined the army." She choked back a sob. "He was a changed person when the war ended and he came home. Medals didn't help the torment he'd been through." She was silent for a moment then added, "He worked his way through the trauma. He's a good man." Auntie Ai didn't mention that Ben had earned a Ph.D. after leaving the military.

Ben had talked to Yoko about his own healing on the rare times when they met for a meal or a play. Yet in all the years Yoko had known Ben—which was her whole life—he never responded to her questions about life in the camps. "One day," he'd promise. "One day." A wave of sorrow swept over Yoko and her heart ached. Ben was gone. "God, I miss my cuz," she whispered.

5 Exploring the Past

Yoko's walk was unhurried as she considered the results of the search of Ben's apartment. One word summed up what she and Zoran had found: strange. She'd felt a jolt of surprise at seeing Hans Reiniger's name. That was unexpected. So was finding the slip of paper with the hospice number for someone identified simply as E. Strangest of all were the notes—were they threats? Was Ben murdered? If so, why and how? What, Yoko asked herself, did I anticipate we'd find? The answer was simple: a clue, maybe two. She walked, not paying attention to where her inner GPS led her.

"Hello, stranger, come on in." Yoko was startled out of her thoughts to find she'd reached Good Eats, the small coffee shop that had replaced KK, the Polish-American diner next to the apartment where she'd lived before inheriting her godmother's spacious co-op and moving to Gramercy Park. Good Eats was way off her normal path these days and she missed everything about it. The booming voice welcoming her belonged to Pete Soltys. The former owner of KK, now the head chef and bottle washer of Good Eats, which was his daughter's brainchild, was busy behind the counter making coffee.

"What's good today, Pete?" Yoko asked, sliding onto the end stool at the counter. The booths were filled but the counter seats were empty. She grinned when Pete shook his finger at her.

"You know it's all good, we have the best, that's why my daughter named the place, 'Good Eats.'" His comment was made in a stern voice. Then Pete relented and grinned. "Long time no see, glad you're here. What will you have?"

Over a bowl of borscht followed by a satisfying corned beef and sauerkraut Reuben, Yoko and Pete debated whether Uber was a smart way to get around in Manhattan and how Pete's team, the New York Yankees, was doing. Yoko didn't say one word about the deaths of her aunt and Ben. The losses were too recent, too raw to talk about, even with Pete, a friend she'd exchanged confidences with over the years. The visit and the tasty food lifted her spirits and by the time she reached her apartment she felt refreshed, even hopeful about the days to come.

Unearthing the treasure trove of diaries and letters in her aunt's closet had been serendipity. Whatever Yoko read in the diaries about the lives of the Sasaki family—Ai, Saburo and Ben—would mirror what happened to Yoko's parents as well as more than 110,000 people of Japanese heritage forced into the isolation of austere camps. Yoko knew from her optometric research that the intimate connection between our hormones and vision may drive trauma deep and more problems may develop. Yet she had witnessed the amazing resilience of her parents and the Sasakis, who were able to move past painful memories and losses to embrace life.

Before Yoko read more of the diaries, she went to her study and turned on her printer to make copies of the two diary entries written in kanji. She slipped the pages into an envelope and put it on the hall table ready to give to a courier when one came from the one-three. That chore done, she was ready. Making herself comfortable in her favorite armchair, a firm cushion at her back and a bowl filled with Ben & Jerry's Cherry Garcia on the side table next to her, Yoko took a deep breath before choosing a diary from the bag she'd carried back from Brooklyn.

As she read, Yoko sensed she was witness to the way life unfolded in the camps. The Auntie Ai who had penned the early diaries was a different woman from the person Yoko knew when she was growing up. It was only when Yoko got to the diaries written in the years after the war when the family lived in Brooklyn that she recognized the mellow woman of her youth. Here was the aunt who'd shown her how to make sushi and shabu-shabu and had teased Yoko because she loved to cook shabu-shabu but wouldn't try sushi after her first attempts were miserable failures.

"The art of sushi eludes me," Yoko remembered protesting. "Shabu-shabu is straightforward."

"Art, young lady? The few times you've made shabu-shabu, your friend Pete who ran the KK diner sliced the beef for you," Auntie Ai had replied, laughing. "All you did was chop veggies and boil water, not what I'd call haute cuisine." Yoko grinned, acknowledging the truth.

Yoko's aunt had been a study in contrasts with her sister, Chika, Yoko's mother. The name Chika means knowledge, intellect, and Yoko's mother was cool and pragmatic, a woman with a passion for science. She shared her knowledge with her daughter as well as the nursing students she taught at St. Vincent's. The name Ai means love and affection and Yoko knew she'd had the best of both in the sisters Chika and Ai. Mother shared her love for science with me and that's why I studied optometry and went on to specialize in vision therapy, Yoko thought. Working with patients at the clinic for infants and children is rewarding but the research brings me joy. Auntie Ai encouraged my work yet if it hadn't been for her, I'd never have learned my way around the kitchen, Yoko smiled at the memory. Cooking had never been high on her mother's priorities, meals were necessary but basic, "Sufficient to keep the body going." In contrast, Auntie Ai's simple philosophy spoke volumes, "Life is more than the basics, we need grace notes."

Yoko picked up the bowl of Ben & Jerry's. It was liquid now and she spooned up the soupy ice cream and munched the half cherries one by one. "Treat's over," she said. Putting the bowl aside, she selected the next of the little books, stroking the red silk covering. Her aunt had written May 1942 on the cover so the family had been at Manzanar for about two months.

Ai Sasaki's Diary.
Manzanar War Relocation Camp.
May 1942.

It doesn't matter what I do, our place (I cannot bring myself to call it home) fills with sand. It seeps in through the cracks in the tarpaper walls and gaps in the floorboards. The walls have multitudes of slits and gaps through which sandy dust invades us. Every time we open the door, sand sifts in. It's terrible.

My dear husband Saburo had great success establishing his law practice in Seattle. He took the ferry from Bainbridge Island to the city each day. He doesn't speak about the loss of his work or the way our lives have been disrupted. He is his usual calm self, practical as ever, ready to help me or others. How can he be this way? I feel such despair.

"What good comes from looking back?" he said the other night. He is an oasis of peace. I feel anything but calm. I try to put on a serene face even though inside I feel tormented.

Before we left our comfortable home, terrifying rumors ran like wildfire around Bainbridge. We knew the men who were taken away, one by one, to be questioned. By the time we had to leave, still no one knew what happened to them or where they were. We're tangled in what feels like a frustrating, dangerous dream only it's our lives and it's real. We're judged guilty yet of what? There's no court, no jury, no one to appeal to, no one to ask questions of, no answers to our fears. Here in the camp, rumors are as constant as the sandy dust. "Loose talk," Saburo says. "It fans people's fear."

Miyo, who is my neighbor here in Manzanar just as she was on Bainbridge, looked so worried when she tapped on the door just now. She beckoned to me to come outside with her. We walked over to the boundary and stood by the barbed wire.

"I heard that some farmers have been accused of adding poison to the vegetables they were sending to market," Miyo said in a shaky voice.

"That's not true," I burst out in a fury, then covered my mouth although no one was near and the wind tossed my words away, fragmenting them, covering them with sand.

"You remember the Sato family?" Miyo asked.

"They grew strawberries and such beautiful flowers," I replied and my mouth watered at the memory of those juicy berries. "They would never use poison."

"No," Miyo shook her head. "This time, the story is that people like our neighbors the Satos who grew flowers did so in a way that gave signals to enemy war planes."

I had no words, I felt helpless and stared at my neighbor, whom I'd known for all the years we'd lived on Bainbridge. It wasn't true, it couldn't be true. Dangerous lies.

At first, the talk we'd heard was that our elders, the Issei, would face internment because that's legal detention of enemy aliens in wartime. Yet our generation was born here, we are citizens, as are our children. We wouldn't be interned, that's what we thought. Problems began right after the attack on Pearl Harbor, when bank accounts were frozen. It was the beginning of harsh times, a bitter period. We were disillusioned of the belief that as citizens we had rights. My dear husband is philosophical, I cannot be. He says, "Often there are two reasons for an action. One is love, the other is fear."

Why would we be feared? We were born in the U.S. We have observed the laws, paid our taxes and been good citizens, as were our parents, for they set the example for us to follow. The story that we might be dangerous skirts the truth. Until the war started, for the most part we were spared discrimination on Bainbridge. Yes, there were some who were hostile but there were more who were friendly and good neighbors despite racial prejudice that runs deep throughout the country.

When we arrived here in Manzanar, whatever we'd brought was the sum of our belongings. We hadn't known what to pack because we didn't know where we were being sent. My choices were a hodgepodge. Besides, what could you pack in two suitcases? That's all we were allowed. Not everyone was as literal. Some people hauled much, much more. Good for them!

It's revealing what each of us chose to bring. Saburo included his well-thumbed copy of Nietzsche's *Beyond Good and Evil: Prelude to a Philosophy of the Future,* as well as what he nicknamed his "almost useful tools," for he is the first to admit his carpentering abilities are modest. Two hammers, one large, one small, a screwdriver with different size heads, nails and a tape measure. I brought needles and thread because I love to sew. I wonder if I'll ever find fabric. If nothing else, I can mend our clothes. I enjoy drawing but charcoal pencils and paper will have to satisfy my impulse to sketch if I have that desire again.

Dan, the father of the family three huts down our row, was a chef at a fine restaurant in Seattle. He brought his knives. Mary, the mother, is a nurse. Her suitcase had her stethoscope, the blood-pressure cuff (a sphyg-something, she rattles off the name and I don't like to ask how to spell it), a thermometer, a set of scissors, and the scales used to weigh infants as well as herbs and tinctures. She was loved and respected around Bainbridge as a nurse and a healer and she had great success with herbs. Some she grew, others she foraged from the land. I question whether she'll be able to forage here but she talks in optimistic terms, which is heartening.

In the hut next to them, the husband is a farmer and managed to bring spades, shears, trowels and a selection of tools, the names of which neither Saburo nor I know. When I asked how he was able to bring so much, he shrugged and said he strapped tools to the outside of his suitcases and his wife's suitcases. "No one said anything," he assured me. He looks as strong and determined as a sumo wrestler—who would want to argue with him? Most of us arrived in good health, some arrived with illness and now a nasty chest cough is circulating.

We settled in, trying to organize ourselves. Everyone was scrounging for wood scraps to build tables and chairs in between vaccinations and learning the way around the camp. It's confusing. Thousands of people milling around, most are city folk from California. We're in what is described as the residential area and cordoned off in one square mile. The desolate Mohave Desert surrounds us. We Bainbridge Islanders chose huts close to one another, familiar faces are comforting.

Barbed wire hems us in, penning us up like cattle in this dusty, isolated place. You can barely see the Sierras through the fence because the jagged barbs of wire block your view. And the swirling, endless dust. Oh God, the dust.

Strong wind greeted our arrival. None of the soft breezes that cool

Bainbridge. I never can decide which is worse, the dust or the wind. Little did I know the wind would blow, day in, day out. It never dies down, never rests. It brings sandy dust that fills the air and seeps in to the huts, covering faces, fingers, clothes and our belongings, even food. We put up with it, we must, but we grumble. I don't want anyone to know what I sometimes think.

The War Relocation Authority, the arm of the government responsible for the 10 camps, decreed camp residents would have the work and responsibility of running the camp. Despite a spate of hasty disagreements, committees have been formed and Manzanar begins to have a semblance of order. Each of the 36 blocks has 16 barracks, a mess hall, lavatories and administration buildings. We learned that about 5,000 acres lie beyond the residential area. People have even begun gardening right here in the Mojave Desert. Neighbors who'd farmed for a living vowed we'd be seeing greenery soon. That's difficult to believe yet they promise it will be so. "Your eyes will see the truth," they pledge. It's strange to have such hope but I felt encouraged by their certainty that they could transform the bleakness of where we are into what one told me would be an oasis.

Some families were able to avoid being put in the camps by moving away from the West coast. They are free to live in the world. Those of us from Bainbridge have friends beyond the confines of the camp, former neighbors and colleagues. They urge us to ask for what we need and we mail requests even though letters can be censored. Books and seeds and other things arrive. Each delivery is treated like treasure, which it is to us. Welcome visitors come from different church groups and often these kind people bring useful gifts and ask what else they may bring when they return.

Yoko closed the diary. Her aunt's words created a compelling picture. She looked over the stack of diaries by her chair. Which was next? The top one was also dated 1942. When she looked inside, she saw it had been penned in August. Yoko turned to the first page.

Ai Sasaki's Diary.

Manzanar War Relocation Camp.

August 1942.

Today the most amazing and wonderful happening. A truck arrived loaded with what looked like a ton of books. Even more exciting, the truck also contained two pianos. In no time, people surrounded the truck to help with the unloading. One of the first to line up was Dan Tanaka and he recognized the driver.

"This is Herbert Nicholson," Dan called out. "He says to call him Herbert-san. That Dodge pick-up was lent him by one of us." Mr. Nicholson smiled and nodded, never stopping in the heavy work of unloading the books. "He was a pastor at one of the Japanese Methodist churches for more than a year," Dan explained. "Before that, he and his wife Madeline worked in Japan."

"Here are books so you can start a library," our visitor told us.

What a cheer went up, as much for the fact that he spoke in fluent Japanese as for the books.

"The pianos, what are they for?" someone called out.

"A piano can be used in a Buddhist or a Christian church," Herbert-san chuckled. "Now, while we finish unloading the truck, will you please make lists of what you'd like me to bring on my next visit? When I have enough to fill the truck, I'll be back."

Such excitement! It lasted long after the man drove away.

We crowded around Dan Tanaka, who told us more about Herbert-san. "He's a Quaker," Dan said. "He knew the chief of Naval Intelligence when they were both in Japan. Herbert-san has been going up and down the West coast as far as Seattle, visiting homes and churches and making a list of the names of those in the Japanese communities who were picked up by the FBI."

"Why is he doing that?" someone asked.

"He's trying to document why people were taken into custody. He and another Quaker, Floyd Schmoe, went to Missoula, Montana, where the first 600 detainees were taken. They planned to visit with them. The Department of Justice was just starting hearings and

Herbert-san stayed to be an interpreter. He also testified in the hearings of those he knew from the West coast."

Faces in the circle around Dan grew grave at this solemn news.

"Who knows Kanjitsu Iijima?" Dan asked.

"The monk?" my Saburo questioned.

"Yes," Dan said.

One by one, people called out, "Yes," they knew the monk.

"In the summer of 1940," Dan said, "he and Herbert-san were on same liner traveling to the U.S. from Japan. It was Kanjitsu-san who recommended Herbert-san to be the pastor at the Methodist church. When Herbert-san was in Missoula, he saw Kanjitsu-san, who was one of the detainees and knew the monk had studied at the Hartford Theological School in Connecticut and after graduating had moved to Seattle, where he'd been preaching at a local Japanese community church.

"The FBI classified the monk as an opinion leader and detained him. Herbert-san spoke to the interrogating officer at the detention center, explaining that the monk was not a troublemaker but was a good man who was against the Japanese military aggression. Kanjitsu-san was not released although marked in the files as 'clean.' It took time but he was transferred to one of the internment camps where he was able to preach in its church."

Little by little, the crowd drifted away, walking back to their huts in groups, talking about the Quaker man of compassion and action.

"To think of bringing us books," I heard one say.

"And not one but two pianos," someone added.

"He brought something else, just as valuable as the books and pianos, Herbert Nicholson brought good cheer and hope," Saburo said quietly to me.

I nodded and smiled in agreement. Ben, who was walking ahead of us, hadn't heard what his father said and Ben spoke, crushing my happy frame of mind.

"All it takes to put you in detention is your looks," Ben muttered. "No matter whether you are a pastor or a student like me, born on

Bainbridge Island of parents born in the U.S. We look Japanese so the thinking is we must be dangerous."

My heart ached for my son, for all of us who have been rounded up like criminals and treated like cattle.

Yoko was reluctant to close the diary, caught up in journaling that opened with joyful news but closed with a wrenching reminder of the truth of those war years. When she glanced at the time, she was surprised to find how long she'd been reading. She didn't want to stop, even though it was almost time to think about a meal. Before she could decide what to do next, a call came in on the landline. The sound startled Yoko, who'd become used to the ring tones of the iPhone. Caller ID showed it was Dan.

"You're the first to know," he said cheerfully. "The chief and I are free of CT.* I'm outta here before they change their minds. Quick, where do you want to go for dinner?"

"Just when I thought I had time to myself to read through Auntie Ai's treasure trove," Yoko joked.

"How's it going?"

"Not bad. But it's strange, in one of Auntie's recent diaries, she made a few entries in kanji, you know, the Japanese writing?"

"Right. And?" Dan said.

"I'm waiting for a translator to pick up the copies I made of those entries. The question is, why would Auntie Ai use kanji in a few entries when she'd always written everything else in English?"

"That is strange," Dan said.

Yoko thought of something else. "I'm waiting for the diary Zoran and I found at Ben's. Zoran wanted forensics to check it over. When they're done, he'll have it sent to me. I'm not sure going out to eat is a good idea."

"What? Zoran wouldn't let you take the diary right then?" Dan was surprised. "When I think of the rules he bends or flat out ignores . . ." his voice trailed off.

---

* CT—Cop speak for counter-terrorism.

"It was a reasonable precaution," Yoko said. "I agree with Zoran. Who knows what forensics might find."

"True enough," Dan agreed. "Why don't I tell Zoran we'll be out for dinner? He can always call if something comes up. The translation and forensics might not be ready for hours, maybe not until tomorrow. After dinner, we'll go to your place and you can go back to reading—we both can because I've a lot of work to sort through. We'll be well fed and virtuous." Yoko smiled at Dan's oblique reference to an evening that would be companionable but less than romantic. "Meet me at Pete's Tavern in thirty? I'm leaving the one-three as I speak."

Dan was a tad optimistic. The minute he and the chief had walked in to the precinct after CT Dan called out goodnight and headed for the street door. But Zoran waved to him to wait. Never one to ignore his partner, Dan obliged by stopping short but tapping his hand on the door to signal his impatience.

"Will you call Dr. Nicosian about the Sasaki case?" Zoran asked. "Although I spoke to him this morning, at that time he did not have any news to report. Perhaps by now he will have discovered more."

"Okay," Dan said, relieved he didn't have to go to the morgue. He much preferred to make a phone call to the ME. It was nothing to do with Dante. It was because although the ventilating fans were heavy duty, they could never quite remove the odor of formaldehyde from the morgue. No one would describe the air in the precinct as fresh, though no one smoked at their desks any more or anywhere in the one-three. Ignore the formaldehyde odor you could not and Dan had always thought the morgue's air was tinged with the presence of death. That was an intangible you could never remove.

Dante answered the call at once and Dan relayed the request. He was still in a diplomatic mode after dealing with the mayor and other executives and didn't mention Zoran's name.

"It's a first for me," The medical examiner sounded exasperated. He sighed heavily. Dan visualized Dante in his office, waving in frustration at the white-tiled exam room that was visible through the only window in Dante's office.

"I've run a battery of tests but nothing has been conclusive."

"Still haven't discovered marks on the body?" Dan asked, referring to one of the early comments from the ME when Ben Sasaki's body first reached the morgue.

"I'll hold to that," Dante replied.

"You'll call when you . . . ?" Dan didn't finish the question, he didn't want to hear more sighs or the hissing that followed.

"It will be my pleasure to call you, *mystikos practoras,* though if I don't have any information, I will not be pleased."

Dante always called Dan *mystikos practoras,* his way of saying detective. Vinnie insisted Dante was flirting and it was true Dante regularly suggested he and Dan get together for a drink. Dan knew Dante was only being friendly because Dante had told him more than once he approved of Yoko and Dan's relationship with her.

Zoran didn't comment when Dan told him that there was no news yet. Dan watched as Zoran gazed into space. It was obvious he was reviewing an intriguing possibility: a poison that hadn't been detected, perhaps something that would never be identified? Dante would know and verify signs of a heart attack, an aneurism or a diabetic coma, those would have been ruled out at the start of the autopsy. No, this was a first, as the ME had stated with such despairing finality.

"Do you think it wise if I call the morgue in an hour or two," Zoran said, his face calm but his voice eager. "It is clear Dr. Nicosian is hard at work on this case."

Before Dan could answer, his phone rang again. To Dan's surprise, it was the ME calling back.

"Dante," Dan said and Zoran's eyes fastened on Dan's face with open interest. Dan angled the phone so Zoran could hear what the ME had to say.

"The analyses of all organs, stomach contents, blood, urine, anal and oral swabs are just this minute complete but I regret to say I still do not have any fresh information for you."

"Is that right?" Dan didn't hide the surprise in his voice.

"I report this terrible lack of information but offer one small hope. The slides of brain tissue are immersed in a chemical wash and it will take a few more hours for results to materialize. I'll call the minute I have news." The ME added, not able to resist, "No doubt Zoran would appreciate the call," and he chuckled though there was no real amusement in the sound.

"What sort of results?" Dan asked but he was talking to dead air, the ME had ended the call. "Death from natural causes isn't murder, is it?" Dan muttered.

"If and when natural causes are definitely ruled out," Zoran said, as if he and Dan had been having a conversation, "the challenge lies in finding the actual cause. That may take time. It is possible we may never find an answer. However, absent a ruling on the cause of death, we surmise that Ben Sasaki was murdered. Ergo, we need to ascertain the reason for the murder."

Dan hurried to the door, confident he could make his escape when he had yet another call from a disgruntled Dante.

"Nothing, I do not have any specifics for you," the medical examiner said, his voice low. "But I want to add one comment."

Dan shook his head. "Hmm," he said, rather than irritate Dante by repeating his earlier comment.

"In my opinion, the cause of death may be natural. I have strong doubts there is a poison that has been missed by the battery of tests I ordered."

"I see," Dan said. "If you . . . ." Once again, he was talking to dead air. The medical examiner had hung up. ". . . find anything, please call," Dan finished, shaking his head at Zoran, who frowned when Dan relayed the latest. Zoran didn't say anything but it was clear from his intense expression that he was thinking about the challenge of death where the cause had not been identified.

"Off I go, Yoko's waiting," Dan said and made a hurried escape.

Over dinner at the trendy eatery, as they shared the fried coconut shrimp with ginger apricot sauce before their pasta dishes arrived, Dan invited Yoko to tell him about the diary entries she'd read. He decided to wait until they had finished eating before telling Yoko about Dante's several calls. Dan had penne with shallots and a light cream sauce, Yoko had Prince Edward Island mussels with spaghetti marinara.

"So what have you read so far?" Dan asked, toasting Yoko with his glass of San Pellegrino sparkling water, which they'd chosen rather than wine, a nod to the need to keep their heads clear so they could work.

"Most of Auntie Ai's diaries, starting with the first when they arrived in the Mohave Desert." Yoko said. "Going through the ones written after the war didn't take long because I knew just about everything that happened in those years. Then there are letters between my aunt and her friend, Hana, who lived in New Paltz. Hana died a few years ago."

"What about Ben's diaries?" Dan asked.

"I've read the one when he was in the camp and another he wrote after the war about his experiences in the military."

"Let's hope the diary from the apartment has something that helps open this case," Dan said.

"Because Ben's death is suspicious?"

"You've got it in one," Dan said. "Ben's super was right to call in the police when he found Ben in the hall. Ben's death, coupled with his visit to the hospital the day before and the examining doctor's report, which is inconclusive about the cause of illness, sent up all sorts of red flags. Dante is working on the autopsy but our esteemed ME has yet to come up with anything to explain what caused Ben's death. Zoran and I were talking over what we know so far—lemme tell you, it was a short talk."

"When Zoran and I were leaving Ben's, Dante called me to explain he didn't have a handle yet on Ben's death." Yoko said ruefully.

"I'll give you all the details from Dante later—he called just now when I was leaving the precinct," Dan said. "More than once. He wants me to be the messenger to bring you the news ..." Dan paused and grinned at Yoko. "... that there is no news."

Yoko and Dan burst out laughing and the diners at the nearby tables smiled at the attractive young couple who were having such a good time.

"Are you serious? That's the message?" Yoko said, still laughing.

"Well, that and the fact he kept on sighing and the hissing makes me worry water would flood the phone line."

"I know," Yoko said. "Was that all Dante wanted, to ask you to tell me there's no news?"

"He had a lot to say about nothing," Dan said, shaking his head in amazement. "He's irritated he hasn't come up with an answer."

"So no news?" Yoko said.

"To be fair, Dante's report was full of plenty even if it boiled down to nothing."

"Do tell."

"Later. For now, I want to enjoy your company and this delicious meal."

They strolled back from Pete's arm in arm. It was all of two blocks but they prolonged it by leisurely laps around Gramercy Park. They settled down in the living room, Dan working on his iPad and Yoko browsing through more diaries.

"I'm finished for now," Dan said. "How're you doing?"

"I'm making mental notes about possible clues."

"Such as?"

"Too soon to say," Yoko teased.

"You're not going to share with me?" Dan sighed in his best theatrical manner. "I am a detective, you know."

"Not a word until I have a handle on it," Yoko said. "Wheedle all you want, you'll have to wait." She relented. "In all seriousness, nothing yet, I promise."

Dan's iPhone buzzed.

"Uh oh, a text from the chief," Dan said and read the message. "Thank God I've finished going over the notes. Tomorrow, I have to regurgitate their contents at an early meeting, so early it's disgusting. I think I'd better head home."

Yoko nodded. Dan's schedule had been the cause of friction and too many heated arguments between them. He didn't have control over what time of day or night he was called in but his erratic hours—not to mention it was rare for him to remember to call Yoko when he wasn't coming as planned—disrupted Yoko's days as well as her nights. Rather than continue to fight, they'd settled on a ceasefire.

"Let's plan on spending time together when we're both free?" Yoko suggested after one late-night argument. The solution worked. That night, Dan left, giving Yoko a long goodnight kiss that left them both anticipating when their free time would coincide.

*   *   *

Yoko was bleary eyed by the time she finished all of her aunt's the red silk-covered diaries. "Can't wait for the translation of the kanji," she murmured, yawning and stretching. The doorbell rang as if the universe was in sync with her desire.

"Dr. Kamimura?" the young woman standing at the door asked.

"Yes."

"I'm Andrea, a translator for the one-three. Detective Zeissing asked me to pick up some material, kanji writing?" the young woman said.

Yoko retrieved the envelope from the hall table and handed it to the translator.

"Would you prefer email or a paper copy?"

"A paper copy's best but email would work," Yoko said.

"Paper copy it is," Andrea said. "We're slammed right now but we'll do our best," and the courier hurried off. Soon, Yoko promised herself, soon I'll know the secret of the kanji in Auntie Ai's diary.

6 Hans Reiniger, Romani Extraordinaire

Sunday was busy though Yoko squeezed in a few hours more to read the diaries. Monday morning she worked in her office at SUNY. While she ate lunch—a deli sandwich liberally filled with sardines and onion and slathered with Grey Poupon—Yoko sorted through the papers strewn across her desk. She finished the last satisfying morsel of crusty bread and picked up the note with Hans Reiniger's phone number. She keyed the number into her iPhone and brushed crumbs off files without thinking as she listened to a generic recording asking her to leave a message. She'd expected this and had a simple request ready although when it was time to speak, she found it more difficult than she'd expected to explain why she was calling.

"This is Yoko Kamimura. We met some time ago." Yoko was annoyed with herself when she fumbled for words and tried to improvise. "Er, I was one of the first on the scene when your hot-air balloon crashed in Manhattan. I'm calling because I'd like to talk to you about . . . er . . . something that's important to me."

She worried that her words were awkward but felt reluctant to mention Ben's death in a phone message. Who knew how the Romani might react? It was possible that that he barely knew Ben and would wonder why on earth she wanted to talk about him.

Her iPhone rang almost at once, which meant calls were being screened. The question was, who was doing the screening? The answer was immediate.

"Dr. Kamimura, this is Hans Reiniger."

"Thanks for calling back," Yoko said. Interesting, she thought, he calls me "doctor." Does he remember I'm an optometrist?

"You said you'd like to talk. Do you wish to meet or can we discuss whatever it is over the phone?"

"I'd prefer it if we could meet," Yoko said.

"All right. I'm coming in to Manhattan to see a friend at six but I could come in earlier, around five. How does that sound?"

"That works for me!" Yoko gave the Romani directions to Good Eats and they arranged to meet at 5 p.m.

Yoko left the college just after 4:30, an hour or three earlier than normal. On the way to Good Eats, images of Ben flitted across her mind's eye. Why hadn't they spent more time together? They both lived in Manhattan yet saw each other more often in Brooklyn when Auntie Ai invited them for a meal, something that happened with religious regularity each month. Ben once summed it up. "We're workaholics, cut from the same cloth. I've got your back and I know you've got mine." He'd proved this by calling her when he took himself to the hospital. Yoko had to be content with that truth.

"Hello and welcome," Pete called out from his usual place behind the counter when Yoko arrived at Good Eats. "Someone's waiting for you," and he waved in the direction of the end booth where Hans Reiniger sat. Two women perched on stools at the counter were deep in conversation but other than that the place was empty, which suited Yoko.

Hans stood and greeted Yoko, a warm gleam in his striking blue eyes. In his late sixties, balding, dressed in chinos, a neat jacket and open-necked shirt, he looked relaxed, a man who had survived more daunting vicissitudes than most yet had made his peace with trouble and was content with himself and his life.

After they'd agreed to use first names and decided on bowls of borscht rather than tea or coffee, Hans said, "You look just the way you did when I first saw you, eyes full of compassion. Your shining hair was pulled back the way my beloved wife wore hers." He shook his head and stopped speaking. Yoko saw he was trying to hold back tears and she stared at the table, fiddling with her cutlery. "I was disoriented," Hans said. "I opened my eyes and looked at you and for a brief moment wondered if my hot-air balloon had drifted to Japan. Then you spoke and I knew you were American and I trusted I was on course in New York as planned."

Hans raised his glass of water in a grateful toast to Yoko. She raised her glass in return, remembering her shock at finding him in the wreckage of the hot-air balloon, how the man had struggled to talk. She'd seen the horrifying amount of blood when the ambulance men had started to move the unconscious man and asked herself if he would survive. Small wonder Hans Reiniger had been disoriented.

"Here's to you, Dr. Yoko, someone who helped me when I was in a crisis," Hans took a sip of water and added, "Perhaps I can be of assistance in return?" His voice was light but the look in his eyes was serious.

"I hope so," Yoko said, forcing a smile. She decided to plunge right in, the hell with subtlety or beating around the bush. "I believe you knew my cousin, Ben Sasaki?"

"Ah, I wondered if that's why you called," Hans said. "I'm so sorry for your loss. Ben was a good friend and I will miss him more than I can say."

"Thank you," Yoko said, taken aback. She had thought it probable the Romani knew Ben but had not anticipated that they were friends, good friends yet, and that the Romani knew of Ben's death. "How did you hear?"

"Ben's neighbor called me," Hans explained. "We three gathered now and then, sometimes with others. We enjoyed community as well as meals together. We're music lovers, people whose pasts were complicated, different from the norm."

Yoko understood. She knew that in the Romani culture, sharing food was a way to share success as well as largesse. Hans had used the word "complicated," and it was apt, whether for himself or for any whose heritage meant they were looked on as "the other." Arrested after he'd been found in the wreckage of the hot-air balloon, Hans Reinger had revealed he'd been on a mission to bring justice to his family name. The media seized on the story, playing up every angle of what they described as the Romani's "vendetta." The balloonist's background had been explored ad infinitum but with scant accuracy. Zoran summed up the articles in his succinct manner. "Commonly used labels like 'Gypsy' and 'traveler' obscure the heritage and true characters of the millions in the world who are Romani."

"Did you read the book, *The Living Fire*, by Ronald Lee?" Yoko asked Zoran, surprised when he shook his head. "Lee writes that the Romani migrated into Europe by the fifteenth century and their language comes from Sanskrit." Yoko smiled at the memory of the rare time she had shared a fact with Zoran. Then, in an effort to keep the conversation with Hans light, asked, "Did you play the violin when you met with Ben and friends?"

"Always!" Hans said with a wide grin. "Even if they didn't ask." He shook his head as if in shame.

"Ben would have enjoyed the music as well as the food," Yoko said. "We tried to go to most of the concerts in Central Park," and her heart lifted as she thought about the good times she'd shared with her cousin.

"One of Ben's specialties for the potlucks was the aduki bean loaf—he made sure we knew it was your recipe," Hans said.

Yoko was surprised. "Ben was the last of my family . . . ." To her chagrin, it was her turn for tears to fill her eyes. She fumbled for a Kleenex and stared at the table until she'd mopped her face dry of the stinging tears.

"I understand your feeling of being orphaned," Hans said. "My parents in Switzerland died two years ago within weeks of each other, which is why I no longer have a home in Lucerne. I passed the business to the next generation. It's the Romani way and what my wife, Brigitta, would have wanted me to do. We were blessed in our marriage. Brigitta and I enjoyed our time as impresarios of the hot-air balloon business as much as we enjoyed every day of the years before." He paused, eyes reflective as he considered the past.

"It was too much of a challenge," he continued, "trying to manage forty-eight balloons. Bookings flowed in nonstop from around the world. It was time for me to retire. I've always felt at home and comfortable in New York, it made sense for me to settle here. I have my music, close friends and golden memories from when Brigitta and I met and danced at the Cat Club with Frankie Manning."

"I'm glad to hear that," Yoko said. She recalled the newspaper stories about the Romani's beguiling violin playing and how Frankie Manning's family had been among the many who had come forward to vouch for the Romani's good character.

"May I ask a question?" Hans said, his voice low.

Yoko nodded. "Of course."

"Forgive me for being blunt but I ..." he hesitated, "... *all* Ben's friends, we are concerned about his sudden death. Even before I met Ben, I learned through my hot-air ballooning experience that even though you are an optometrist, you're associated with the police, a civilian consultant, yes?"

Yoko nodded.

"Do the police know what caused Ben's death?" Hans asked. "If so, can you tell me?"

"I'm sorry, the last I heard from the ME, the cause of death had not yet been identified," Yoko said, hoping Hans would accept her words but aware her answer sounded evasive and more like a non-answer.

"You mean the police are in the dark?" Hans sounded surprised.

"Yes." Yoko was relieved Hans had taken her answer for the truth it was.

For a moment, the Romani was silent, considering what she had said. Then he asked, "Did you want to talk to me about Ben?"

"I was curious about how you met Ben," Yoko hedged.

"Mutual friends, we had mutual friends," Hans said. Yoko saw a twinkle in his eyes and couldn't help smiling in return, even though she was concerned about where the conversation was headed. "It was amazing, the connections we uncovered, your cousin and I." He laughed then added, "I hope you are free next week, Monday evening? It is my pleasure, no, my responsibility to invite you to a special gathering, a celebration of Ben's life. You might call it a memorial."

"A memorial?" Yoko echoed. "For Ben?"

"Yes. We'll have his favorite dishes and share memories of Ben. You'll meet Ben's friends and speak about him if you wish to do so. Will you come?"

"Yes, of course," Yoko said. This time, when her eyes filled with tears, she didn't mind.

Hans reached across the table and put his hand on hers. "Tears help heal the heart."

"Thank you," Yoko sniffed, dabbing her damp cheeks with the soggy Kleenex.

"Ben said you had a friend, the name was Dan, if I recall." Hans grinned. "Ben approved of your friend. Dan's invited, too."

"Thanks, Hans. That's very thoughtful of you but right now, Dan's on a special project, he's a detective with the 13th Precinct and won't be free for a few days."

"So we'll see you at the wake at seven p.m.?"

"Where?"

"We're gathering at Bernie Perette's, Ben's neighbor," Hans explained. "It happens to be Bernie's turn to play host."

"Will there be many people?"

"Six or seven, maybe a few more. I'm not counting one or two who live in New Jersey, they visit when they can. Mind you, it's rare for more than three or four of us to be together at any one time," Hans explained. "Monday is special so everyone will make an effort to come. The common bond is a love of community, music, poetry and good food." His sigh was one of pure contentment. "We always enjoy such smorgasbords, what you call potlucks here." A sad look crossed his face. "It is our way to say farewell to Ben."

"Perhaps you could tell me a little about the people I'll meet at the memorial?" Yoko kept her voice light. What a simple way to get in touch with Ben's friends. Was it possible the notes in Ben's apartment had come from one of them? Yoko knew she might be on a wild goose chase but it came with the chance to join in a celebration of Ben's life. It would fill a void she hadn't acknowledged until now.

"Other than yours truly, unless a visiting Romani is in town, the group is American," Hans said, breaking into Yoko's thoughts. "Ben had Japanese ancestors, others have British or Italian heritage. Anna and her husband Bert are my neighbors in Brooklyn. We've lost a few over the years." His face was grave. "Another of my Brooklyn neighbors will pass soon. When doctors told the widow Emiko she had a tumor that was inoperable, she was determined to keep on with her work until she had to stop. No one knows how long she has." He sighed. "Last week, she talked of hospice."

Yoko couldn't stop a surprised gasp at hearing the name Emiko. She'd heard that name only once before but it had stayed with her. "Do you know if it was the same Emiko who was in the camp where Ben and his family were during the war? My Auntie Ai mentioned that name once."

"Yes, it *is* that Emiko," Hans said. "Not that the two of them talked much about their incarceration. It came up once when there was an article in the *New York Times* about other camp survivors."

Ah, Yoko thought, the hospice number and the E on the note at Ben's. Why hadn't Ben ever mentioned Emiko?

"Emiko is a very private person," Hans said as if in answer to Yoko's silent question. "Not what you'd call a hermit, but since the diagnosis, she pours her energy into her art, doesn't go out much, other than to the corner deli."

"She's an artist?"

"Emiko turned to sculpting after a career as an architect—her medium is stained glass."

"She lives in Brooklyn?" Yoko asked. She held her breath, waiting for the answer, hoping it would be yes.

"She does. She lived in Arizona for years but moved here to help an in-law who was ill. After the woman died, Emiko stayed. She liked being able to walk to the stores instead of driving places. She found the perfect place, large enough to double as her living space and studio."

"Does Emiko have children?"

"No," Hans said.

"Hans, do you think Emiko would let me visit?"

"I believe she'd be glad to see you," Hans replied. "Phone first. You know, to check when's a good time to go." He didn't wait for Yoko to ask but tore his napkin in half and scribbled a phone number on it.

Yoko sat back, pleased at what she'd learned. Wait till Dan and Zoran heard she'd discovered the identity of E.

They sipped the borscht and Hans told her about the people she'd see at the wake. "These are just snapshots," he said. "This way, you'll know a little about each person." Yoko paid careful attention. She didn't have an eidetic memory like Zoran but she'd be meeting everyone soon and could add her own perceptions to what Hans shared. When she got home after meeting Hans, Yoko called Zoran. She was able to repeat, almost word for word what Hans had told her. First she told him about Emiko.

"Zoran, I found out the identity of the E in the note at Ben's."

"That is a simple way to accomplish your detecting." Yoko heard the smile in Zoran's voice.

After she finished talking with Zoran, Yoko checked her watch. Now was as good a time as any to call Emiko.

"Hello, Yoko. Hans told me you'd be in touch." The speaker laughed and added, "There are no secrets with Caller I.D."

Thank you, Hans, Yoko thought, you didn't waste time paving the way. She was about to ask if she could visit but once again, Emiko beat her to it.

"When would you like to come to see me?"

"I wonder . . . is tonight possible?" Yoko said on an impulse. The answer was immediate.

"Perfect. I've worked enough today on my art. The trains are frequent in the evening and my place is a short walk from the subway."

It was dusk by the time Yoko arrived at Emiko's studio. The petite woman who opened the door greeted her with a warm smile, brown eyes filled with pleasure and, Yoko noticed, interest. Yoko followed the woman in and saw Emiko touch the furniture she passed to help steady herself. It was possible the brain tumor had caused vision problems if there was swelling in Emiko's optic nerve. The woman's rather stiff, slow walk in all likelihood meant movement was painful.

"Welcome. I'm so glad you're here," Emiko said, waving Yoko to a seat at the small table in the kitchen area. "I just made dessert, my own recipe, will you join me? After, if you like, I can show you around the studio."

"I'd love to see your work," Yoko said. "And I never refuse dessert." She glanced around the high-ceilinged space. The wood floors were scrubbed and clean and Yoko wished she had wood rather than the deep blue carpet at her place. Tall windows were open to the sky, no curtains or shades. Yoko smiled, it was how she left her windows, except those in the bedroom, where she had floor-length, room-darkening curtains. Benches filled with neatly organized tools and piles of glass lined the walls and two stained-glass sculptures that shimmered with color towered almost to the large skylight they were positioned under. Nearby were three smaller, partially complete sculptures. The walls were covered in photographs, most were framed, most were of buildings.

Yoko's qualms at disturbing someone Hans had described as not quite a hermit vanished. Emiko had the rare quality of putting people at ease almost as soon as they met her. Soon Yoko and the woman sitting opposite her at the table were chatting as if they'd been friends for years.

"Ben and I were close from the time we met in the camp when we were teens," Emiko said, her voice low. Tears started to build in her eyes. "You must have been shocked, we all were, at his sudden death." She brushed away her tears and there was a hint of mischief in her smile. "I will have my own memorial here for Ben at the same time you gather in Manhattan tomorrow." She laughed ruefully. "That's if I remember. These days I'm more and more forgetful." Her smile disappeared when she stared at the largest sculpture. "In all seriousness, I dare not work with glass any more," she said. "My hands are no longer steady and my vision is not good, but I'm one of the lucky ones, it's rare that I have a headache."

Yoko wasn't sure what to say. She settled for a simple, "I'm sorry, Emiko."

"Where was I?" Emiko said.

"Your own memorial for Ben, a lovely idea."

"Ah, that. I will start with a meal and a glass of wine. Then I will sit and think back over the years. You know that Ben and I met as youngsters in the camp?" Yoko nodded. Emiko looked directly at Yoko, and said, "Ben and I were close but it was platonic—once he got over his puppy love for me." Her gaze slid away as she looked back at her memories. Yoko waited. She wasn't impatient, whatever time the artist had left, now was precious.

"Ben left Manzanar, which was where my family and I were, when his family transferred to the Minidoka camp. After that, he was able to go to college. He enlisted the minute he could and went to war." She shook her head at the memory. "We didn't see each other for years and our letters were few. When I moved to Brooklyn, it was wonderful. We picked up as if there hadn't been decades since we'd seen each other. When I was diagnosed with a tumor, I thought I'd be the first to go," Emiko sighed. "Yet here I am, surprising the doctors and confounding their predictions." Her mood changed as if she was deliberately brushing away the sadness. She reached across the table and took Yoko's hand, "I'm grateful you are here. Happy, too."

"Thank you, I'm so glad to meet you," Yoko said and the two smiled at each other. Yoko felt a stirring of sorrow at the loss that was inevitable. She resolved not to mourn Emiko now but take joy in her company. Life was handing her another lesson. She would learn how to deal with more grief. Perhaps find the recipe for tear soup and cook up a storm.

"Now for a treat. At least, I hope you think it's a treat." Emiko stood and walked to the refrigerator, grace in her movement, despite the stiffness. Had the woman talked to her doctors about her pain? Hans had mentioned hospice and Ben's note had the hospice phone number. Yoko shut her mouth in a firm line. She was not going to ask questions. Emiko would talk to her if and when she was ready to do so. Until then, Yoko was determined to stay in the present.

"Here's where East meets West," Emiko said in a cheerful tone. She put two small bowls on the table. "Noodles with coconut cream and blueberries. This," she explained, "is my variation of what the corner deli makes. I hope you enjoy it." For a few moments, there was silence only broken by spoons clicking against the bowls and sighs of enjoyment.

"Delicious!" Yoko said as she scraped the last trace of cream from her dish. "Is it a difficult recipe?"

"It's complicated ... not," Emiko said, laughing. "Add coconut cream or ice cream and fruit to cooked noodles or rice, plus a drop of vanilla and a sprinkle of cinnamon for instant delight. Now, if you like, we can start the grand tour. It'll take at least five minutes."

"Let's start with my favorites," Emiko said and led the way to the two largest sculptures. At first, Yoko thought she was looking at esoteric geometric patterns. In one smooth millisecond, her focus shifted and she saw vivid foliage, swirls of leaves floating in harmony. She looked at the second sculpture and realized it too was an exuberant portrayal of nature, with a humming bird hovering by the red berries on the spreading branches of a tree.

"My passion is to show the power and light of nature," Emiko explained. "When I was in the camp, it was so different from what I took for granted when I was free. The Mohave Desert was bleak and the mountains overwhelming." She turned and pointed at a large, framed photograph on the wall. Yoko walked over for a closer look.

"The huge wall of the Sierra Nevada rises on the West," Yoko read the caption and asked, "What a marvelous shot, is it your photo?"

"No, that's one Ansel Adams took when he came to Manzanar," Emiko said. "I might never have learned to look beyond the manmade barriers imprisoning us if Ansel hadn't come to the camp. He taught me how to appreciate where I was, to watch Mother Nature morph through the seasons in the desert. It was different from what we saw on Bainbridge Island but it was the life of nature. He took photos of the land as well as the camp and us. We teens followed him around and he helped us see the beauty in our surroundings, even if the land was arid."

"Ansel Adams was at Manzanar?" Yoko was surprised. Had Auntie Ai's diaries mentioned the famous photographer—was she forgetting something she'd read?

"He stayed for two or three months." Emiko put her hand to her head, wrinkling her forehead in concentration. "I think it was in 1943, in the autumn. He was friendly, a real people person. He had a genuine interest in our lives." Emiko stared into space for a long moment. "Somewhere, I have his book. *Born Free and Equal.*"

"I'm amazed a photographer was allowed in the camp," Yoko said.

"He was invited," Emiko explained.

"Invited? Who invited him?"

"The camp director was his friend . . . what was the man's name? Oh, Ralph Merritt, a decent man," Emiko said. "The War Relocation Authority, the government agency that organized the camps, had to approve Mr. Adams' visit." She frowned. "Let me think, a woman photographer visited before Mr. Adams. Her name isn't coming to me right now. Toyo

Miyatake, one of the men in the camp, created his own makeshift camera from a lens he smuggled in. He was a well-known photographer before the war. His camera was confiscated when someone informed on him, but after a while it was returned and Toyo was allowed to take photos," Emiko said. "A lot of trouble was caused by informants—to be blunt, we called them spies."

Yoko struggled to take in the news. Photographers? Smuggling? Spies? She searched her memory. "My aunt wrote about traitors, she used the word *inu* in one of her early entries. From what I've read in the diaries so far, life calmed down after a riot at Manzanar in December 1942. Was there trouble after that? I'm sorry, this will sound naive but I'm wondering what was there to spy on?"

Yoko's question brought a quick response from Emiko. "No need to apologize, how could you know? Life in Manzanar had a strange rhythm, it was all so different from anything any of us had experienced." She shook her head and gave Yoko an intent look. "Do you really want to hear about that time? It's not pretty."

"Yes, I do. My parents never spoke about their lives in the camp and so far my aunt's diaries haven't touched on anything like what you just told me," Yoko explained. She listened almost in disbelief to the torrent of words from Emiko. At last, after decades, Yoko was hearing firsthand from someone who'd been in one of the camps.

"What happens when you have too many people crammed into too small a space? None of us had ever been behind barbed wire or had armed guards watching us round the clock. Our lives were so uncertain and the stress and strain led to tension and frustration," Emiko said. "People in Manzanar were from such different backgrounds and had different ideas. Now that I'm an adult, I can understand how resentment, prejudice and struggles for power triggered trouble. Radios, the shortwave type, were banned but people were desperate for news so radios or parts were smuggled in and used in secret until someone found out and informed for whatever reason, perhaps fear of repercussions from the authorities. Such is human nature, there was the perhaps inevitable retribution from the person or people who'd been using the radio.

"When you've experienced such trouble, you want to put it behind you," Emiko said. "Do you want me to go on?"

"If you're sure you don't mind."

"I don't believe I've ever talked about this with anyone. You know, it feels good to let it out," Emiko said. "It's been buried in my subconscious all these years. I was a teen when we were in the camp and not what you'd call worldly. I remember hearing the word 'paranoia' for the first time when my parents were discussing a neighbor who reported someone for being 'subversive.' My father talked about political intrigue, 'It's insidious,' he said. 'Wreaks havoc.' My mother explained to me that there were academics at Manazanar doing fieldwork and research. She was an academic, she'd taught graduate students at Seattle College, which is what Seattle University was first called. Like so many, she lost her position as a professor when we were sent to Manzanar.

"I can still hear the disbelief in her voice when she said that people in the camp believed academics were planted by the government to spy on us. She and Dad talked about Tamie Tsuchiyama, a doctoral student in anthropology at Berkeley. My mother knew the family, the father died when Tamie was young, but the mother and her siblings were so proud when Tamie was hired in 1942 for Berkeley's Japanese Evacuation and Resettlement to research a camp in Arizona, Poston. It was common knowledge the FBI had grilled her and some said it proved she wasn't working for the FBI but others were convinced Tamie and other researchers, close to thirty, were in the camps to spy on them."

"That's incredible," Yoko said.

Emiko shrugged. "It's in the past. Not what you want to see in the rearview mirror." She gave a wry laugh. "For now, let's finish the tour. We can talk more about the camp another time, if you want." She waved a hand at the sculpture they were near. "This was Ben's favorite."

"It's beautiful," Yoko said. "Did you always sculpt? Hans told me you were an architect."

"In the last decade of my career, I studied sculpture when I wasn't designing buildings. After I retired, I decided to work in stained glass. Not traditional stained glass. You can see the raw materials, *dalles de verre*, slabs of glass," and Emiko nodded at the benches against the walls.

Yoko wandered past the benches, examining the tools and orderly piles of slabs and squares of colored glass.

"When Hans said you wanted to visit, I was pleased for more than one reason. Ben planned to bring you over but ..." Emiko shook her head, not finishing her sentence, staring at the sculpture for a long moment. Yoko was startled at what she said when she broke her silence. "I need to talk to someone outside Ben's circle of regulars. I hope you won't mind if I bounce my questions and ideas off you?"

"Not a problem, I'd be glad of the chance to talk," Yoko said and her mind raced over the possibilities. What did Emiko want to discuss?

"Good, thank you. I've been puzzled by a dilemma. Your arrival is timely," Emiko said.

"Whatever I can do, I'll be glad to help." Yoko wondered what Emiko needed. Support with a move to hospice? Help disposing of the studio's contents? Yoko looked at the two finished sculptures that towered up almost to the skylight. No way could she move those, she wouldn't even be able to help with the smaller, unfinished pieces, they were taller than her by a foot or so. Serious muscle would be needed. Still, if nothing else, she'd be able to help pack the material on the benches.

Emiko followed Yoko's gaze. "Don't worry, I've made arrangements for the equipment and the art. A fellow sculptor will work on any pieces that need to be finished. That one," and she inclined her head toward the tallest sculpture "is going to a residential setting in Montana. It will be placed to the left of a masonry fireplace, a few feet away from the original mountain ash tree that inspired the design. The others have homes waiting when the finishing touches are made," and she waved in the direction of the small sculptures. "Now to my dilemma—what to do with the letters Ben wrote to me over the years."

"L-L-letters?" Yoko stammered.

"Yes. They're few and far between but Ben wrote from the time he went off to college, even after he enlisted. After the war, we remained in touch—my husband was very understanding. Sometimes it might only be once a year but we shared our news." Emiko laughed at the look on Yoko's face. "Ben told me how pleased you were with what you found in the box at his mother's place. He said you'd always wanted to know about life in the camp." A shadow crossed Emiko's face. "Hans explained it's possible you may find clues about . . . Ben's death in the diaries."

Before Yoko could speak, Emiko spread her arms wide.

"Dorothea," she said in triumph. "The photographer who came to the camp before Ansel Adams was Dorothea Lange. I've read reviews of her photos, haven't seen them, they're considered dark, perhaps because the camp hadn't been open long and it took some time before there was order. And it took time before we settled in to some sort of reasonable routine. We were forced to became accustomed to the confinement, to accept the injustice." Emiko shrugged and said, "That's what Dorothea Lange's photos captured, those early, darkest days in the camp." She paused then added, "Sorry, where was I?"

"Ben's letters."

"Ah, letters. If you want them, you may have them but there's one caveat—we talk about everything after you've read them."

"Thank you, I do want the letters and would like to talk to you about . . . about everything," Yoko said.

Emiko gave Yoko a hug and tears welled up in Yoko's eyes. "Don't, you'll make me cry," Emiko said.

"Okay." Yoko mopped tears from her face with her hands and hic-cupped, which brought rueful laughs from both women.

"Fine. It's settled. Look at the time. It will be late when you reach home. We'll talk more another time, all right?"

"Yes," Yoko said. "It will be good to talk again."

"I'll fetch the letters." Emiko made her way with slow caution to the other side of the studio to an area with a desk and several small filing cabinets and came back in a few minutes with a slender briefcase.

The two women hugged again.

"You'll come back soon?" Emiko invited.

"I promise. I'm away at a conference for a few days, police business. I'll call you when I return."

Yoko took a taxi home, the leather briefcase resting on her lap. She could feel the bulge of the letters under the soft leather. She felt drained but with the fatigue was a sense of gratitude. Little by little, Yoko was learning about her family's past.

7 Stolen Time

"D'you need the defibrillator, Doc?"

"What?" Yoko Kamimura stared in surprise at the sergeant on desk duty at the 13th Precinct.

"Thought you were gonna have a heart attack when the lieutenant said he didn't fancy taking the trip to Philly." The desk sergeant grinned to take the edge off his gloomy words. His grin faded at the look on Yoko's face.

I know what I'd like to do with a defibrillator, Yoko thought. Up to now, she'd never regretted following in the steps of her mentors, Drs. Forkiotis and Bertolli. Each of those distinguished optometrists had lectured at the Connecticut State Police Academy for decades and Dr. Forkiotis had been an Expert Witness for most of those years. Yoko had a wealth of support from her colleagues when she accepted Chief Mark Sander's invitation several years ago to become a civilian consultant with the NYPD.

Until this moment, the experience had been great, yet here she was at an early morning start at the 13th Precinct that had flipped from normal to serious, deadly serious. Bad enough it was 4:30 a.m. though Yoko wasn't feeling any pain, just sleep fog when she arrived at the station seconds ahead of Zoran. Until, that is, the OCD detective aired his dissatisfaction, picking through his grievance in his unique pedantic way with an added fretful tone.

Before Yoko could think of a snappy retort to the sergeant, Zoran spoke again. "I do not see any reason why I have to go to the conference. Chief Sanders is going. Lieutenant Riley is going. You, Dr. Kamimura, are going. I am sure that is enough people." Zoran's voice was quiet but firm. "Besides, there is a specific reason why I need to stay here."

Really? What did *that* mean? What a downer so early. Yoko thought about the research Dan had done in preparation for the trip. Philadelphia in the spring, perfect time to explore the town in whatever time they could steal to sneak away from the conference. Now Zoran threatened to throw a massive spanner in the works. Small wonder the desk sergeant asked if she needed a defibrillator.

"If you observe my eyes, Doctor, you will note that I am annoyed," Zoran said. It was rare for him to use sarcasm but there was no doubt he was being sarcastic this time with his oblique allusion to Yoko's work at SUNY. Yoko shook her head. Did she want to agree with Zoran? Why argue with the master of logic? She could say, "True, your annoyance is clear," but that didn't feel like the best way to handle Zoran's hissy fit. Where the hell was Dan Riley? He was wise in the ways of dealing with Zoran after years of partnering with the sometime cranky detective. Called by the chief on official business seconds before midnight, Dan had left her warm bed in a hurry, taking his suitcase with him.

"See you at the precinct tomorrow, darling." That was the total of his goodbye.

Yoko sighed. Right now, rather than worry whether Dan would make it to the one-three in time, she had to try to calm Zoran so that he wouldn't carry out his threat to stay in New York and skip the conference. Zoran's declaration was unsettling, although Yoko had witnessed many a mind-boggling event courtesy of Zoran. What were the odds the trip would be cancelled if Zoran pulled out? He was the department star. Everyone knew the award was mostly because of his decades of brilliant detective work. Besides, how would it look if Zoran did not attend the conference?

Zoran began venting as soon as he walked in and spotted Yoko in the lobby. After his wisecrack, the desk sergeant listened in the background, deadpan, but Yoko knew the conversation would zip through the one-three like a YouTube video gone viral.

"Zoran, it's official business," Yoko said, choosing her words with care. It wouldn't do to sound placating or, heaven forbid, pitying. The truth was that sometimes Zoran just didn't perceive what was obvious to everyone else. His obsessive-compulsive disorder could obscure nuances, major and minor, in what other people said or did. True he was a brilliant detective whose record of solving cases was second to none, but Zoran was quirky, thanks to the OCD, although he kept it under tight control. Still, at times, it could create issues. This was one such time.

"You were present, we all were, when the chief explained he submitted the department's name to the Police Chiefs months ago. The award is an honor for the one-three and it's for the department's record for solving crimes—it's the best in the country and that's due to your work. How wonderful to have your work recognized by the Police Chiefs."

Even in the middle of a major hissy fit, Zoran's need for accuracy was ratcheted up on the highest notch. "The name is the International Association of Chiefs of Police," Zoran said, his voice close to petulant. Yoko decided he had to be feeling sleep fog as much as she was. She sighed. Zoran was the only person in the world who would quibble over a correct name when a trip was at stake. She snuck a glance at the large suitcase at his feet. Hadn't he'd signaled his intention to go by bringing the suitcase to the station? She hid a wry smile at the thought of the news flashing around the precinct when Zoran had arrived with the bulky suitcase in a firm grasp. The odds would be in favor of the suitcase being packed with shirts and underwear in individual plastic bags as well as bottles of water—glass, not single-use plastic bottles—and sanitary wipes. Everything arranged with meticulous care.

Eyeing the large suitcase, Yoko decided Zoran could be persuaded to go, even though he sounded ready to back out and claimed to have a "specific" reason. The lieutenant was a stickler for following the rules unless he decided he knew better. That had happened the last time they'd worked together, when Zoran had known, as he often did through some uncanny instinct, how to solve the case nicknamed Eye Witness. Zoran brought criminals to justice by bending rules so far they were in danger of snapping. His unusual methods were overlooked by the authorities, who had every reason to appreciate Zoran's maneuvers despite the fact that they might be outrageous and far beyond standard protocol.

"Why do *I* have to go? Surely the award could be given to Chief Sanders or accepted by someone who lives in Philadelphia?" Zoran nodded, satisfied with his suggestion. "Someone there, yes. That would be logical." Zoran was the prince of logic. He was also irritating. Always was. Today even more so.

"This has been arranged for months," Yoko said. "The four of us are taking a flight from Newark and we'll be met at the Philadelphia airport and driven to the conference."

"They could give me the award without my being there, could they not?" Zoran mused, ignoring Yoko's comment. Vinnie Baldoni sauntered past.

"Hey, a large suitcase for a short visit? Last I heard, Philly had water and wipes."

Yoko winced at Vinnie's breezy comment as well as the officer's next comment that floated down the hallway, "Hey, Dude, get an eyeful of what Monk came in with for a short trip. Looks like what me and the wife take when we go on vacation for a coupla weeks."

Vinnie was the officer who coined nicknames for everyone at the one-three, even suspects and criminals. Vinnie had named Sophia Fellini the Dragon Lady in the Eye Witness case. The TV show, "Monk," starring Tony Shalhoub as an obsessive-compulsive detective, was the source of Zoran's nickname but Vinnie had the grace not to use it in front of Zoran. The Dude, Brian Watson, strolled into view. Dreaming of retirement, less and less interested in day-to-day police work, Brian was a Big Lebowski lookalike in a rumpled uniform that strained over an imposing belly. He took one look at the situation in the lobby and turned on his heel, true to his belief in avoiding anything that might mean he'd be asked to think or, heaven forbid, act.

"Yoko, perhaps you will ask Chief Sanders if someone else can accept the award for me?"

"Zoran, the chief named you to accept the award," Yoko said. "You have to go."

"Are you trying to wriggle out of this trip, Zoran?" The question came from Detective Dan Riley, who had just breezed in. Dan dropped his small suitcase on the floor and grinned when he looked at the large case in front of Zoran. Yoko breathed a sigh of relief. If anyone could extract sanity out of this mess, it would be Dan.

"You know I neither asked for an award nor . . . ." Zoran stopped in mid-sentence when Dan looked at him, eyebrows raised in query.

"He doesn't want to go," Yoko said to Dan, her voice low, avoiding Zoran's glare. "He says he has a specific reason not to go."

"Zoran, the department will have egg all over its face if you don't attend." Dan's voice had the brisk, no-nonsense tone of a teacher talking to a fussy student. "As soon as we reach the conference center, before the lectures start they'll make a video of us receiving the award. That'll be shown during the conference when the department is named the winner. We'll be away for a coupla days. New York can manage without us."

What did Dan mean, "manage without us"? What trouble was brewing now? Yoko wondered. Zoran was not placated.

"They could make a videotape here in New York. We are all here. Why do we have to travel?"

"The locations are different each year." Yoko put in her two cents. "The award is for the department. You don't want to let the department down." She felt a twinge of sympathy for the brilliant detective who worked hard to keep his obsessive-compulsive disorder in check. She wondered if she'd do better zipping her lip. Few people at the one-three bothered to try and change Zoran's mind about anything. Had they learned it didn't make a difference? Dan was the only officer who often tried and often succeeded in persuading Zoran to go along with something that he first tried to resist. Behind Zoran's back, the desk sergeant rolled his eyes.

"You're not worried about flying, are you, Zoran?" Dan asked.

Yoko squashed a smirk. Dan knew Zoran wasn't afraid of anything except disorder and hospitals, places he called germ factories. Zoran was huffing in annoyance and staring in indignant outrage at Dan when Chief Sanders arrived.

"You look exhausted, Chief," Zoran said, eyeing the chief. He switched his attention back to Dan Riley. "You too, Dan, look rather tired."

"See tee business, Zoran," the chief said.

CT was cop shorthand for counterterrorism. The chief didn't need to say more. Zoran was never involved in any of the frequent trainings or activities of the CT unit. He was kept separate from this facet of police work. That way, if New York ever experienced the catastrophe of a deadly twin-header—a major murder case and a terrorist attack—Zoran would be assigned to lead the investigation of the case and the cops trained in CT would focus on the terrorists. If it was a case where Zoran thought he'd like her on board, Yoko would be assigned to work with him. So that's what Zoran meant, Yoko thought. CT business is a legitimate reason why he'd have to stay in New York in anticipation of any trouble that might fall into his bailiwick.

"Security is vital," Zoran said. "We must be careful that we do not win the war and lose the peace . . ."

Before Zoran could rev his theory up to full throttle, the chief interrupted him when a tall, lanky man in a dark suit strolled into the station.

"Morning, Mac," the chief said. "Cutting it short, aren't you? Did you remember we've a flight to catch?" Chief Sanders clapped the newcomer on the shoulder. "This is Terrence MacCauley. I'll brief you all in my office."

The group filed into the small office and Dan closed the door. Chief Sanders strode behind the desk but didn't sit. He straightened his signature bow tie and waved at the man he'd called Mac.

"This is Terry MacCauley, our local CT liaison." The chief gave a dry chuckle. "We have a possible tripleheader and I don't mean baseball. It's not verified yet whether the threats are real. Our investigations haven't come up with specific or useful information." Sounds as if the chief is making an end run round Zoran, Yoko thought.

"The first threat we received warned us of bombs dropping from the sky onto the Pan Am building."

The Pan Am skyscraper had squatted over the historic Grand Central Terminal since 1963—what New Yorker didn't know that? The building of it and the location had infuriated most residents of the city and not just because it obscured the view of Park Avenue. "Sale of air rights for an ugly behemoth," blared the *Post*.

"The Metlife Building," Zoran clarified.

The chief nodded, "Correct, Zoran, Metlife, but those huge Pan Am signs stayed up until the 1990s." He shook his head. "My dad was on duty when they scraped up the suicide in February of 1975."

"The person committing suicide was the CEO of the company that is now Chiquita Brands International," Zoran clarified. "He jumped to his death on Park Avenue from a window on the 44th floor."

"True, Zoran," the chief nodded. "Back to the present! Within hours of the bomb threat to the . . . ah, Metlife building . . . more threats were received, this time targeting TV stations and the mayor's place, Gracie Mansion."

All eyes swiveled toward Zoran when he murmured "Archibald Gracie Mansion." In uncanny unison, all eyes turned back to the chief, who glanced at his prize detective but plowed on, a slight sigh the only indication he'd registered Zoran's correction.

"It may be one group or one nutcase. No ownership claims have been made yet. Bottom line, our trip will go as planned. The message we're sending, in case anyone or any group is watching, is that we're in control. Mac will keep tabs on the situation until we return." The chief paused. "Questions?"

Yoko held her breath but no one spoke. Zoran was silent. Airing his grievance to Yoko must have been enough to vent his irritation. Then she twitched in alarm when she heard Zoran take a deep breath. Drat, it was obvious he was about to speak.

"Chief Sanders, are we at Code Yellow or Code Orange?" His question brought an approving nod from the chief.

"We're at Code Yellow," the chief said. "Elevated. Corroboration of specific potential threats has not yet been received. Might be a crank caller or callers." Chief Sanders exchanged a look with Dan Riley as if thinking, "We should be so lucky."

"Everyone ready to head to the airport?" Chief Sanders beamed at the group.

Minutes later, the four left the 13th Precinct. Three in the group anticipated the change of pace from their daily routine. Thoughts percolated in the minds of all four about what they'd face when they returned to New York. More threats? Bombs? Or would the trouble fizzle into oblivion?

*　　*　　*

The video taping of the award ceremony was short and simple. The four attended morning workshops as scheduled and as soon as it was over, they took off around the city in the down time, which had also been scheduled. At Zoran's request, the group took the 72 stone steps up to the front entrance of the Museum of Art, panting their way to the top in triumph. The chief and Zoran went into the museum but Dan, exchanging complicit smiles with the chief, spirited Yoko away to a destination he refused to identify until they arrived.

"Welcome to lunch at the Moshuli, the only square-rigged sailing vessel in the world that's a restaurant," he told Yoko. They stood in front of a four-masted barque that floated at the dock in Penn's Landing.

"This is a surprise," Yoko said. When they were seated, the waiter gave them time to admire the spectacular view of the waterfront then took their orders—miso-glazed salmon for Yoko, jumbo crab cake for Dan. After the meal, as soon as they left the restaurant, Dan hailed a cab.

"Old City," Yoko heard him say to the driver but she didn't catch the rest of the address. It sounded like something about an elf. What now?

"Sure, I know the place, round the corner from Elfreth's Alley," the driver said, clearing up that puzzle. Yoko decided not to ask questions but to go with the flow and enjoy whatever surprise Dan had in store, perhaps a museum or art gallery. Minutes after they drove over cobblestones that rattled her teeth, the cab pulled up outside a venerable three-story house, its tall windows flanked by shutters that were a luminous white against the brick walls that weather had faded to a warm rose. Dan paid the driver and guided Yoko across the sidewalk to the bright yellow front door.

"Welcome to our hideaway," Dan said, his voice muffled because he was bent over, retrieving the key from a key box at the side of the door. "If this is as good as the info I read on Airbnb, it will be a treat." He led the way in and they walked around the ground floor, exploring the place.

"What do you mean, 'our hideaway,'" Yoko asked. "Aren't we due at the conference soon?"

"The chief and Zoran will cover for us, we're not expected back."

"What *are* you talking about?" Yoko was baffled.

"Hey, you're the one who wanted alone time without work

interruptions. Come on," and Dan led the way up the stairs. He didn't stop on the second floor although as they passed the open door to a large bedroom, he tilted his head in the direction of the king-sized bed and grinned. He kept on going up the next flight of stairs to the top of the house. Opening a door with a flourish, he invited Yoko to step out onto the large rooftop deck.

"Look, dear heart, panoramic views of the Old City and over there the Ben Franklin bridge." He pointed to the graceful arc of the suspension bridge over which traffic was streaming. "That's the way to New Jersey, if you're so inclined."

They leaned on the deck railing, shoulders touching.

"We're here for two whole days, you, me, walks, restaurants, museums, anything you want—no work calls whatsoever. I can guarantee that I won't disappear at a moment's notice."

"You've thrown your cell phone away?" Yoko teased. "Isn't that a criminal offense?"

"Why do you think the chief brought in Terry MacCauley?"

"To have backup in place? Oh, you mean . . . to give you time off?"

Dan slid his arm around Yoko's waist. "Correct and correct. The chief promised he won't call me until we're back in the Big Apple."

Yoko turned to face him and they kissed, a long kiss.

"That's not one of those quick pecks you plant on my cheek when you're running out the door," Yoko said when they came up for air. She was right, it was a deep, lingering kiss. Followed by another. They linked hands and headed back down the stairs to the second floor and the king-sized bed. Words would have been superfluous.

"That was blissful. Time off together and not a single work distraction, so relaxing," Yoko said to Dan. They were in a cab en route for the airport.

"Tell me, any *thoughts* of work cross your mind?"

"Maybe," Yoko countered. "What about you?"

Dan laughed. "I turned off that switch in my brain. The one-three didn't cross my mind once." He turned serious, "I did think about Ben."

"So did I," Yoko said, eyes unwavering on Dan's face. She sighed. "SUNY and the NORA conference didn't cross my mind but I did think about Ben. I tried to tease sense out of what happened. The incredible thing was, my thinking wasn't stressed. I was able to be more objective than I have been up to now."

"And did you? Tease any sense out of the situation?" Dan asked.

"Yes, but Zoran would say wait."

"Whatever he'd say, I'm hearing you have less stress. Do I have your permission to dream up another escape?"

"Let me think about that," Yoko said, making her voice cool. She relented. "One word, Yes."

Dan put his arm around her and planted a light kiss on her cheek. The cab driver eyed them in his rearview mirror and decided he knew a happy couple when he saw them. It was early in the morning. Very early. But Yoko didn't mind the sleep fog. Once she was back at SUNY, deskwork would clear the fog and focus her mind.

Minutes after they landed, they were walking through the Newark terminal when Dan's phone rang. He checked the ID and rolled his eyes. "The chief kept his word, no contact until we're back in the Big Apple." He listened to the short call. "Yes, sir. It was, thank you. 34th and Fifth, right, I'll see you there." With that the call ended and so did their bubble of serenity. Dan hailed a cab.

"Do you want to take the cab on to SUNY?"

"I'll get out when you do and walk to the college from there," Yoko said. "It'll help me get back into work mode." When the cab slid to the curb at 34th and Fifth, they got out. "Later, cupcake," Yoko said, hugging Dan goodbye and they set off in opposite directions. Yoko didn't need to ask, Dan and the chief were off on CT business.

Welcome news circulated: the triple threat alarm had been bogus. The culprit had been identified and had learned prank calls didn't end with a light tap on the wrist, not when it involved Homeland Security.

Rumor at the one-three had it that Yoko and Dan were surviving their strange relationship.

"Who knew it would last?" Vince grumbled. He was buying Charlie lunch at a diner they often frequented. It was the price of betting Yoko and Dan were finished when news had circulated that the two were only going to spend time together when work couldn't interrupt. "Never heard of such goings on. How did they manage down time?"

"Depends on how much the relationship means, doesn't it?" Charlie said, digging into his meatloaf.

8 Revelation

That night, Yoko's sleep was deep. She'd spent the day at SUNY at her desk, working feverishly to straighten files and catch up. She woke up early. Staying in bed was not an option. She had two hours before she needed to leave for the college so after a mug of green tea accompanied by buckwheat toast smeared with almond nut butter, strawberry jam and a dusting of flax seed, Yoko opened the briefcase Emiko had given her and pulled out the bundle of letters. It was a long shot that any would have clues to the cause of Ben's death.

Yoko hadn't found anything even though she'd gone over Ben's diaries a second time. He'd started the first in Manzanar, pressing his pen heavily into the page, rage fueling his words, "Guards with guns watching us 24/7." She'd read with care, taking it slow that second time, searching for meanings behind the words. Nothing jumped off the pages to signal problems brewing for Ben, who'd been a teen.

"Ben wasn't a troublemaker. What could he have done in the camp or in the military to cause someone to wish him harm decades later?" she complained to her brother cats, which were sprawled next to her on the couch. They raised their heads and stared at her, their gaze sharp. When Yoko didn't say anything else, the cats resumed their grooming.

Yoko had pored over the other two diaries Ben had written after WWII. Even though it was years after he'd left the military, some entries described his experiences in the war.

Ben Sasaki's Diary.
Manhattan, 1999.
   Memories flooded over me last night when I watched the movie, "Saving Private Ryan." The 442nd had high jinks south of Rome

and they are picture perfect in my mind's eye, even though it happened in 1943. How can I ever forget the time a tanker bounced on landing and its tires blew? The fuel tanks ruptured and flooded the ground under two rows of armed bombers. Man, nothing gets you moving quicker than fear of an explosion, we hustled to lay down thick foam from the fire trucks. If even one bomb went up, explosive material would be hurled far and wide, dangerous around bombers or fuel tanks. We called for ambulances but the officer of the day was tight-fisted, refused to send more than one. Said he didn't want all the ambulances exposed if there was an incident. That made sense but we grumbled. Sam said we might as well draw straws to see who'd be carted off in the ambulance. Koichi warned of a lethal chain reaction if bombs were detonated.

No explosion this time—the evening ended with us vacuuming up the foam. The TUFFs, the Tough Ugly Fat Fuckers—who comes up with these names?—squatted on the field like nothing had gone wrong. They're something else. You can't believe one will take off, it's so heavy, it lumbers down the runway. Airborne, it's an elegant, man-made bird.

What on earth was Ben doing around bombers? He'd transferred to the 442nd Regimental Combat team when it was formed—was the 442nd tasked with aircraft maintenance? Puzzled, Yoko read on and learned that Ben had been part of the 442nd's antitank company.

Ben Sasaki's Diary.
Manhattan, 1999.

Around mid July, the antitank company was pulled from the front line and placed with the 517th Parachute Infantry Regiment, 1st Airborne Task Force. It took us a few weeks to learn to load and fly the gliders. They were 48' long and 15' high and could hold a jeep and a trailer filled with ammo or a Brit antitank gun. Still, we were ready for the August invasion of southern France. When we learned the airfield near us was low on manpower, we volunteered for fire-fighting duty, just for the hell of it. We were sick of gliding into trees or being hit by enemy flak. We were there for two months, guarding the right flank of the Seventh Army and protecting the 517th Parachute Infantry. We also played firefighters when there were urgent calls for man-power. Most of the time, we cleared mines, captured Germans and guarded roads and tunnels. Late October we got back to the 442nd and saw heavy action, murderous for many.

Yoko sorted through Ben's letters to Emiko. Some were short, some were intense and personal when he described his agony over the loss of friends. "How did I survive? Why? Good, brave men, lives ended by war. Yet here I am." He wrote how therapy helped him. "I learned there is no shame in survival." Yoko winced at the exposure of his demons and regrets. Tears filled Yoko's eyes as she read his words. "Emiko, know that I will not squander the time I have. We who survived the camps suffered from shock and apathy. Some were bitter yet you and I recognize life always has meaning. Our salvation is through love and in love."

The tone of the letters changed as Ben wrote about his patients—never by name but about their progress.

Ben Sasaki to Emiko.
Manhattan, 2001.
In some of my younger patients, I witnessed what Jung believed, that the politics of war will jaundice us. Yet even though we were in-carcerated because of our ancestry, 33,000 Japanese Americans served in WWII, 6,000 in the Pacific Theater. No one of Japanese descent was ever charged with espionage. Of the 18 Caucasians charged with spying for Japan from 1942-44, 10 were convicted.

Henry Steele Commager wrote in *Harper's Magazine* in 1947,"It is sobering to recall that though the Japanese relocation program, carried through at such incalculable cost in misery and tragedy, was justified on the ground that the Japanese were potentially disloyal, the record does not disclose a single case of Japanese disloyalty or sabotage during the whole war . . . ."

The cold truth is that women and men of Japanese ancestry who enlisted in the military served as translators, cryptographers and language instructors, some in military intelligence in the Pacific Theater. They traveled in combat zones with combat teams and questioned prisoners. They were Americans in enemy territory yet were not allowed to carry arms.

One of life's ironies, the US government planted spies in the camps. Hard to believe but we discovered that these spies were informants whose jobs were to weasel out potential or actual troublemakers.

What the hell did Ben mean about spies in the camp? Yoko shook her head in disbelief, remembering what Emiko had told her. It was way too early to call Zoran to ask what his memory banks held about this. She Googled, "Spies in Manzanar Camp in WWII." The Wikipedia article didn't have anything about spies or informants. Scrolling down, Yoko found the *Densho Encyclopedia* and read that the FBI had started spying on people of Japanese origin in Hawai'i, the Philippines and the continental US as early as 1916 and "at least through the 1930s." The Office of Naval Intelligence (ONI) also employed Japanese Americans to spy on their fellows at Navy bases and where there were Japanese American commercial fishing fleets.

Yoko put the search for spies aside and opened another letter.

Ben Sasaki to Emiko.
Manhattan, 2005.
You'll remember George Fujita? He was determined to win your heart. I could not understand how you, such a tender young woman, didn't see through his braggadocio. My parents warned me. "Why tangle with George?" my father asked. "His perspective is different from yours." Hindsight is a balanced 20/20, but back then I was young and headstrong and couldn't hear the advice.

I don't think your parents or mine or George's ever knew what went on. God, the fistfights. We guys pulled our sleeves over bruises. The name calling and taunting stayed hidden from plain view. The young crowd knew but kept mum.

You did not know but trouble ramped up big time when the three men from a family of Italians arrived in Manzanar. It was obvious there'd been an appalling mix up, they were in the camp about three months. We learned that Italians were moved from camp to camp. It was harsh enough to be forced into a camp but to know you'd be subjected to frequent moves, that was draconian. In striking contrast, my family was allowed to choose our move from Manzanar to Minidoka.

The Italians were sent to Manzanar by the government because the three males in the family worked for a small magazine—the dad told anyone who'd listen, "It was a newsletter for Italian workers, nothing subversive." The government claimed the guys were "intellectuals gathering information for the enemy." That was about as believable as saying our farmers on Bainbridge Island were poisoning vegetable.

You'll not have forgotten Enrico. Such a pleasant, outgoing guy, unlike his brother, Antonio, who avoided people and sat alone, brooding. From what I know now, the younger brother must have had Asperger's. Back then, we thought he was awkward, didn't have social skills. Remember how the father was protective of Antonio but let Enrico go his own way?

You and Enrico met within hours of the Italians arriving and it was clear to anyone with eyes that you two were smitten with each other. Looking back, I understand the attraction. Enrico was easy going and good-tempered, a natural charmer. I tried to grasp the truth of it and glimpsed why there was such chemistry between you two. You did not know how much George despised me and any others who dared have feelings for you. When Enrico arrived, George plain loathed him. Here was a serious rival, four years older than George and me, quite a man of the world. He'd even had a job.

Such was my luck that I was removed from the scene. Torn from you, the object of my puppy love. First, my family decided to transition to Minidoka, then the Quakers, the American Friends Service Committee arrived. I was one of the students offered the incredible opportunity to leave Minidoka and go to college, not that I lasted long at Earlham. As you know, the minute I was eligible, I enlisted. After the war, I learned Quakers were responsible for more than 4,000 students leaving camps and going to college. Other religious organizations stepped up, helping in many ways, often so people could get work permits. You and your cousins were released to farms, picking sugar beets, harvesting crops. Anything was better than being behind barbed wire.

We hadn't started writing to each other yet but Mom and Dad wrote me while I was in the military. Letters were delayed because our battalion was always on the move. When a batch of mail would arrive, I'd not have time to read them all at once.

That was the end of the entry. George who? Yoko searched her memory. Had Ben or Auntie Ai ever mentioned a George or a family whose last name was Fujita? She came up blank. What about Enrico and his family? Would it be possible to locate them after so many years? Perhaps Emiko would be able to fill in the blanks.

Yoko had set her alarm and she twitched when it shrilled. The two hours had disappeared. If she didn't leave now, she'd be late for work.

9 Harsh Reality

Yoko struggled for breath. It felt as if someone was trying to smother her. What the hell was going on? She rolled over in bed, wriggling free of the weight pressing on her throat. The heavy book she'd been reading when she fell asleep at midnight tumbled to the floor. She was jolted into a gray predawn and an awareness of the relentless hammering of her heart. It felt as if it was trying to escape from her chest. Groggy but awake, gulping in air, she put shaky fingers on her pulse and counted. Good grief—110 beats a minute? Damn, way past her normal 70. It took many minutes but at last the furious pulsing eased. She lay watching mist move in sluggish swirls across the pewter sky outside her bedroom window, wondering if anything other than the cumbersome book almost throttling her had triggered the frightening awakening.

Was it the sight of the visiting professor at the college the other day? The woman must have been fourth-generation American of Japanese descent. Yoko searched her memory, what was fourth generation called? Ah, Yonsei, that was it. Yes, that brief encounter summoned up the nightmare that torments my sleep and all too often sets my heart racing frantically.

It wasn't her worst nightmare, Yoko consoled herself, the one where she was still married to the passive-aggressive man until the welcome release of divorce. No, this was her second worst nightmare, the one where her family was incarcerated in the Mojave Desert. In the hellish distortion of sleep's thinking, Yoko was an adult living in the camp with her parents although in reality, she'd been born years after they were released. This time, Ben, her cousin, wove a ghostly way through the nightmare. He'd been a teen in the camp but in the terrible dream he was an adult, the adult he had been when he died. Yoko lay in bed, hearing again what Ben had whispered in the nightmare, "Revenge is a dangerous dish."

Did those words mean anything? Was her mind playing tricks? It was a year or more since she had gone with Auntie Ai on the pilgrimage to the camp but Ben's death just last week was tangled up in her nightmare about the WWII incarceration of Japanese Americans. God, Queen Elizabeth had complained about her *annus horribilis,* she ought to have had my last year, Yoko thought, it's been damn *horribilis.* My family is all gone. That makes me an orphan. She shook her head, annoyed at her self-pity. Why was she bitching? She wasn't homeless or living in a war zone like so many places round the world, from the Ukraine to Syria. Right now she was dealing with a bizarre dream. Could she believe in the message of the dream?

Yoko eased out of bed. Her sleep hadn't been restorative, far from it. After breakfast, two mugs of caffeinated green tea and a toasted bagel topped with cream cheese and plum jam, she felt close to normal. "Should I take a walk?" she asked her brother cats. The doorbell rang. "It's not even 7 a.m., who can that be?" Yoko said. The cats blinked and looked wise but withheld advice. Was that because they knew she never paid their words of wisdom any heed?

Andrea was at the door, a large envelope in her hand. "Here you are, Dr. Kamimura, a twofer." Yoko stared at the visitor, not understanding the comment. "Detective Zeissing wanted you to have the translation as soon as possible," the young woman said. "He asked me to tell you he has a copy of the translations and also that forensics didn't find anything out of the ordinary in the item from the apartment." She grinned. "I'm not sure what that means but there's a package that feels like a small book in this envelope beside the coupla pages of kanji translation you requested."

"Got it," Yoko said. "At least, I think I understand." She signed for the envelope and thanked Andrea, who said as she left, "Back to the one-three for me, we've a mountain of work."

Yoko hurried to her study, ripping open the envelope on the way. She shook the contents onto her desk. As promised, out tumbled two pages stapled together and a small package. "Ben's diary," Yoko breathed and sat down, staring from the diary to the translation, dithering over her choices. "Which do I open first?" she asked herself. Curious to discover the meaning of the kanji, she picked up the two pages, leaving the diary until she'd read what her aunt had written.

Translation of Kanji to English in Auntie Ai's Diary.
Brooklyn, New York.

Something is bothering Ben. He insists he's fine but a mother can tell. Is he concerned about one of his patients? Years back, when he opened his practice, he said he'd learned not to carry the problems of those he counseled beyond the office walls.

Brooklyn, New York.

Ben is worried. At dinner the other evening, he said, his voice bitter, "People can't let go. The past doesn't die."

"What do you mean, the past doesn't die?" I asked.

"Nothing." He gave a fake laugh. "I guess my subconscious has been working overtime," he said. "Bothersome memories." He saw doubt on my face and said, "You remember the years behind barbed wire. The unexpected rears up." Ben wouldn't look at me and I chose not to challenge him. Was it something that happened in the camps?

Does whatever's going on with Ben now have anything to do with the No Noes? The questionnaire the government sent around caused such trouble, violent reactions in families and between neighbors and friends. Ben sided with those who wanted to enlist in the military even though some of his closest friends were on the other side of that decision. He doesn't want to confide in me yet.

What did Auntie Ai mean when she wrote about the No Noes? Yoko didn't have a clue. She searched her memory. Had Auntie Ai written something in her diaries about the No Noes? Was it from the time the family was in Manzanar or Minidoka? Would she find anything helpful in Ben's diary that forensics had just released?

*   *   *

Yoko riffled through the diary, disappointed to find that most of the pages were blank. The first entry confirmed her suspicions—Ben had looked to his past to try to understand why he was receiving threats.

Ben's Diary, Found in His Apartment.
Manhattan, 2015.

Another of the wretched anonymous letters arrived. Only a coward sends mail without signing it. The stupid message from the first two is repeated. Are the words meant to make me shake in fear? As if! Someone pieced together scraps from a magazine to read: *A wrong will be made right. Your time will come.* How can I take this at face value? If I've done something wrong, whoever is writing this needs to brave up and face me, man to man. My gut instinct is it's not a woman but I could be wrong.

I'm sorry I threw out the first ones. Ought I to show this to Yoko? She and Detective Dan might have suggestions though I can't imagine how they'd be able to help or find out who is sending this much. Is it someone I've counseled? I saw veterans, just veterans, in my practice. Most ask if I served in the military. When someone learns I'm a veteran and experienced war, a bond is created. Does one of my patients think I've done him or her wrong? Is someone holding a grudge? Who? And for what? I refuse to believe it's anyone from the 442nd, we were a tight unit. Our motto was, "Go for Broke." We didn't risk life and limb then carry grudges after the war. At our few reunions, everyone was friendly, glad to see each other.

The most serious conflict I recall when the government put us behind barbed wire wasn't personal. It was what happened when the government's outrageous questionnaire was sent round to the camps. Ours arrived when my parents and I were in Minidoka. I wanted to join up and fight as soon as I was old enough. The government helped when they changed the age of enlistment from 21 to 18 in November 1942. When I was 18, I signed up. Plenty of my friends in Minidoka did, others didn't. Rancorous statements were hurled around. I stayed the hell out of it. If the government had wanted to cause problems, they couldn't have chosen any better way than the damn questionnaire. It turned families against each other, siblings fought, neighbors fought. Utter turmoil. Looking back, I can discern why there were such extreme reactions. I remember heated quarrels and epic fights.

Questions 27 and 28 caused the uproar. Osamu Hasegawa's parents answered No, but they had their reasons and with hindsight, I understand. These days, from what I read, it's obvious Osamu and the others who were in the No group have found that as the years rolled by, membership in the No Noes cast dark shadows over their lives. Wherever they live, whatever their community, they find they are often viewed with suspicion.

Yoko groaned. Here was another mention of No Noes. What were Questions 27 and 28? She recalled the names of two of Ben's closest friends, men he'd kept in touch with until they died. Shigi, short for Hiroshigi, and Steve. No one named Osamu. Rather than ferret around on the Internet for information about the No Noes, she decided she'd ask Zoran. Yoko paged through the diary again and discovered she'd missed a short entry written on the back of the page where Ben described the problems of the No Noes. The entry was shocking and sent her blood pressure up a notch or two.

Ben's Diary, Found in His Apartment.
Manhattan, 2015

Hard to believe but I'm damn sure my phone calls are being monitored somehow. I know I can trust Hans. I'll call him and arrange to meet at Molly's for a burger so we can talk face-to-face about what to do. I think I need to set a trap.

That was one hell of an eye opener. Yoko leafed through diary again, this time with slow care. Had she missed another entry? Nope. Ben had written two entries, one about the No Noes and the other about a problem with his phone calls. Time would tell if anything helpful would come from learning about the No Noes but if Ben thought someone was tapping his phone, it was important. She felt uneasy but also excited.

Why would someone tap Ben's phone? And who? Her first impulse was to call Dan. Damn, it was no good trying to catch him, he was off somewhere on CT. She had no way to track him down and even if she did, he might not have privacy or time to talk. Yoko felt like screaming in frustration. She didn't, it would scare the daylights out of the cats. Should she call Hans and find out what was discussed when he and Ben met to talk about the problem? Yoko decided she had to talk to Zoran.

She was about to pick up her iPhone when a sudden thought stopped her. If Ben's calls had been bugged, were hers? One call vivid in her memory in the past few days was Ben's call to say he was going to the hospital. Then she remembered the lovey-dovey nonsense she and Dan exchanged over the phone before and after the trip to Philadelphia. She felt the heat of a flush and didn't need to look in a mirror to know her face was bright red. Too creepy to think someone might have been listening to her calls. Yoko cringed. If her phone was tapped, every conversation she'd had must have been overheard. This had to include calls with Dan and Zoran. After a moment's careful thinking, she had a plan. Without hesitating, she made a call.

"Zoran, I know it's early but it's the nicest weather we've had in ages. The other day you said you'd like to walk in Gramercy Park rather than peering through the railings at the flowers. Care to join me and visit the park before the work day starts?"

Yoko smiled as she waited for an answer. She could almost hear the cogs and wheels in the detective's mind running over the meaning behind her request. She doubted he would be baffled for long.

"I was considering going out for a walk," Zoran said. "A turn or two around Gramercy Park's inner sanctum would be most agreeable. You are fortunate that your building has a key for the gate."

"How about we meet in fifteen minutes in front of my building?" Yoko said. It would take Zoran less than five minutes to walk from his apartment on 28th and Lexington—the place no one had seen but which everyone knew was spotless and formidably tidy. She left her apartment a few minutes later and picked up the key to Gramercy Park from the doorman. Zoran was waiting for her outside the park gate.

"Good morning again, Zoran."

"Good morning, Yoko. I wonder, does your key work on all four gates?"

"I'm not sure. I've never tried to use it on any other gate, just this one because it's closest to my building." They crossed the street and Yoko unlocked the gate. "Sometimes, a passerby will rattle the gate and ask to be let in. I often used to sit on one of the benches and read but I don't like to do so now, it's embarrassing to have to tell people you can't let them in."

"That is understandable," Zoran said. "Now," he continued as they strolled along the gravel path, "I doubt if anyone is monitoring our conversation inside the park although there is equipment available for that purpose. I believe it is safe to discuss the reason for this meeting."

"Was I that obvious?" Yoko asked, smiling. She'd known Zoran would understand why she'd suggested they go for a walk.

"Not at all," Zoran said. "Your maneuver was skillful."

"First," Yoko said, "thanks for the translations that Andrea delivered this morning. She told me you've a copy of what the kanji meant. Have you read it and the diary we found at Ben's place?"

"Yes."

Yoko took a deep breath to help herself focus and mirror Zoran's calm attitude.

"I've gone over Ben's other diaries, the ones I found at Auntie Ai's, but I didn't find anything helpful. What's your reaction to Ben writing he thought his phone calls were being recorded?"

"It is significant, Yoko," Zoran said. "It is possible that in the time since that was written, Ben uncovered more details. Hans Reiniger may be aware of what developed. Perhaps, if we are fortunate, he will know who is the perpetrator or at the very least have suspicions about who is doing this and, if we are fortunate, why. When we have the name of that individual, we may have a promising opening in the case of the death of your cousin. Do you agree?"

"I do." Yoko allowed herself to feel something akin to relief that at last there was a break or as Zoran put it, a promising opening. The OCD detective wasn't done yet.

"I have asked the head of surveillance to resolve the situation with the phones, cell and landlines of yours, Detective Riley, mine, Dr. Nicosian and certainly that of Hans Reiniger. Do you consider there are others whose phones ought to be checked?"

"Perhaps Emiko and everyone in Ben's group of friends?"

"Those will be included. I understand all these phones will be secure within twenty-four hours," Zoran said, his voice confident.

"Something can be done?"

"A variety of possibilities exist," Zoran said. "Perhaps you have heard of the Five Eyes surveillance program?"

"Echelon? The program that was so secret it didn't exist until Edward Snowden released documents to the Intercept?"

"That is the program," Zoran said. "In actual fact, various reports had been made before by some of the five governments involved, the US, UK, Canada, Australia and New Zealand. Encryption is of value, although I am told it is not foolproof because in the long run it can be broken. It is normal for SIM cards to be reprogrammed but again, they remain vulnerable. However, there is no need for encryption or reprogramming because I am assured by our experts that the Thirteenth Precinct has a failsafe unit. It is the S Box."

"S Box?"

"The grapevine has it that S may mean Secret or Squawk. The surveillance team is not answering questions. I suggest that the S stands for Surveillance." Zoran looked serious but Yoko saw the twinkle in his eyes before he stopped walking and turned for a closer look at the park's Calder sculpture, Janey Waney.

"Security that works can be called any name," Yoko said.

"Yes," Zoran said. "I agree that S Box is an acceptable name though the name of this sculpture, Janey Waney, smacks of childhood."

"Baby Jane Holzer was in Warhol's films. She asked Calder to make the sculpture from a model she saw in his studio. Hence the name."

"Is that correct?" Zoran asked in surprise and Yoko hid a smirk. For once, she knew something the detective didn't. She'd have to share that tidbit with Dan.

"Did you have any queries about the material you received this morning from the courier?" Zoran asked.

"I don't know anything about the No Noes and the questionnaire Ben wrote about. Can you clue me in?"

"Ah, the infamous government questionnaire," Zoran said. "It was issued by the War Relocation Authority to assess the loyalty of those imprisoned in the ten camps. At first, it was circulated among draft-age men whom the military hoped to conscript into service if they were found 'American' enough."

Did Zoran snort after he said that? Yoko didn't risk looking at him or, heaven forbid, asking, but she was certain that was the derisive sound the detective made.

"Before long, the questionnaire, which was cobbled together in an ignorant and contradictory way, became mandatory for all adults in the camps." Zoran stopped to admire the flowers in the border of the path they were following. Yoko waited, knowing more helpful details would arrive when Zoran was ready. "Question 27 asked, 'Are you willing to serve in the armed forces of the United States on combat duty, wherever ordered?' Some young men resisted this question even though they were not opposed to military service. They felt that because their rights as citizens had been stripped from them, it was insulting to ask them to risk their lives in combat. Many answered, 'I'll serve in the Army when my family is freed.'

"Question 28 asked, 'Will you swear unqualified allegiance to the United States and faithfully defend the United States from any or all attack by foreign or domestic forces, and forswear any form of allegiance or obedience to the Japanese emperor, or any other foreign government, power or organization?'"

"What awkward wording," Yoko said.

"Awkward is one way to describe it," Zoran agreed. "Both questions stirred up confusion and unrest. Internees felt insulted by Question 28 because for some it implied that they had allegiance to a country they had left decades before. For those who were U.S. citizens, most had never even visited Japan. Others, especially the Issei, who were not U.S. citizens, feared deportation regardless of their answer."

"What I don't understand is how would the government's questions have affected Ben? He enlisted, he couldn't wait to do so," Yoko said.

"Perhaps someone held a grudge over his reaction to the questions or something else and the feeling festered over the decades until revenge was the only action and became the trigger for the threats and the monitoring of phone calls," Zoran mused.

Yoko's shoulders stiffened when Zoran used the word, "revenge." Ben's ghost had whispered that word in her nightmare but Yoko was reluctant to mention it to Zoran. What would he think if she told him the impact on her of a ghost's words? Better to zip her lip.

"I too wondered if revenge might be a motive." She kept her voice matter-of-fact, avoiding mention of ghosts or nightmares.

"Consider the list of reasons why people threaten or kill others," Zoran said. "Hate, love, those jostle for first place. Revenge is wrapped in hate and gives the perpetrator the desire to wreak havoc on someone believed to have caused harm, whether this is true or not. Then there is power and anger and cruelty and we would do well not to forget sheer madness." Zoran paused, no doubt reflecting on bruising encounters with those issues. He shook his head and returned to the discussion of the No Noes.

"The immediate repercussions if people did not answer, 'Yes' were severe. Whole families were sent to Camp Tule Lake. It became the most heavily guarded of the camps. Its director was notorious for oppressive management. Tanks were added around the bases of the twenty-eight guard towers and the height of the barbed-wire fence was increased."

"It sounds terrible," Yoko said.

"When the war ended, the aftermath was no less troublesome," Zoran said. "It was difficult for the No Noes to find a place in society. They were regarded with suspicion and ostracized by others of Japanese ancestry who felt their pledges of loyalty might have been threatened by the action of the No Noes.

"Many of those incarcerated felt guilt even though they were not guilty of anything but they were ashamed they'd been in Camp Tule Lake and forbade their children to talk about it. As it was, they faced rampant racism in the country. In recent years, those who were sent to that camp have begun to speak about their decisions to answer, 'No.'

Their stories reveal they were thoughtful people who considered the implications and possibilities with care."

"Thank you," Yoko said. Had her parents felt guilt and shame at being sent to Manzanar? Did that explain their resolute silence about the devastating experience? Whatever the reason, Yoko felt sure that uppermost in their minds was the desire to put the life-changing experience behind them and move on with their lives.

"I am glad to share what information I have," Zoran said. "You have your valuable insights, I have my nickel knowledge. Let me know when you have finished reading the other diaries."

Did the cerebral detective from the one-three make another subtle joke about Yoko's work in optometric vision therapy? Yoko smiled. Dan would enjoy the latest of Zoran's quirky comments.

10 New Faces

Yoko paced through her apartment, Zoran's comments echoing in her ears. He'd given her plenty to think about but she was restless and nervous anticipation of the wake crowded out everything else in her mind. She stopped by one of the windows overlooking Gramercy Park and leaned her forehead on the cool glass, gazing at a street empty of traffic until the traffic light at Park Avenue changed and two cars drove by. A lone pedestrian walked a small dog. The landline rang and Yoko waited until she heard a voice. It was Dan.

"What's up, buttercup?"

Yoko hesitated. Dan didn't know there was a strong chance the phone was tapped. She chose her words with care. "I'm gloomy."

"Why?"

"It's the wake tomorrow. I'm anxious about it. And there's the frustration of not knowing the cause of Ben's death. It was different when Auntie Ai died."

"I get that," Dan said. A voice in the background called his name and Dan groaned. "Damn, sorry, sweetie. I thought I had more of a break." He ended the call.

Airing her concerns to Dan was an improvement over chasing the thoughts round in her mind, even though she had not talked to Dan about everything. Yoko smiled grimly, even if she had told Dan more, he didn't have time to talk. What relationship was perfect? Yoko knew that the wake was more than the opportunity to air the heartache of loss, it was the chance to meet Ben's circle of friends. Was it too much to hope she might discover who sent threats to Ben or who was monitoring phones? She laughed out loud. Was she deluding herself? Ben told her more than once, "You're the most optimistic person I know." Maybe

Ben was right. When she had another chance to talk to Hans, she ought to learn more. He hadn't mentioned anything on their first meeting at Good Eats, perhaps because the wake was on his mind.

Yoko was up early the next morning. She hadn't slept well and moved on autopilot, putting together the ingredients for a recipe she knew by heart, a spinach-tofu quiche for the evening. After a simple breakfast of oatmeal sprinkled with nuts and slivers of dried papaya, she showered while the quiche baked. By the time she'd dressed, the quiche was done. She set it to cool on a shelf in the pantry and closed the pantry door to thwart her brother cats, a lesson learned from the time the cats had found the crab quiche she'd labored over. They'd gobbled most of the quiche. Evidence of their enjoyment was splattered over the kitchen counter and floor. Ever since that fiasco, Yoko put anything she baked on a shelf in the small pantry and shut the door tight. She was about to leave for work when a text came in from Dan.

> Hey, sweet pea, sorry I didn't have time to talk last night. Looks like I may be tied up a bit longer, ain't that a surprise? Hope you aren't overworking like me. Not sure when I can spring free. When that happens, I ought to be due serious time off. Let's plan on having some fun.

Yoko texted back.

> A big fat yes to fun! With you. That's a double yes from me.

> Can't remember, did I tell you, Hans included you in the invite to the wake but I explained you're tied up, as you often are. Remind me to untie you soon.

Dan sent another text. The tone switched from joking to serious.

> Are you sure you're OK going by yourself to the wake? You won't try to go it alone, will you, if it looks like there's a problem?

Yoko's first reaction was a rush of irritation at Dan's query. Was that sexism or what? Then she felt a sense of gratitude for his concern. Of course he'd have a knee-jerk reaction to the idea she might be in danger. Not to mention that the detectives at the one-three were constantly warned not to play heroes and never, ever to try to go it alone.

She texted Dan.

> Thanks, I did think about this in the wee hours when I really, really

wanted to be sleeping. I trust I'll be safe with Hans there. He and Ben were close and Ben's nose for fakers was quite foolproof.

Dan replied promptly.

Fair enough. Your instincts are good.

Texting helped move Yoko's mind away from brooding about the evening. She decided to play it safe and telephone Zoran from the office rather than her iPhone or her home landline. She doubted the college phones had been breached and congratulated herself that she was out-maneuvering whoever might be tapping the phones. Yoko didn't make a habit of crossing the line into police work when she was at SUNY, even though her involvement with the police was supported by the dean of the college. Yoko was following in the august footsteps of many practitioners, including Drs. Forkiotis and Bertolli who'd consulted with the police for decades. Except for murder and mayhem at the college a few years back—the situation that had brought her to Zoran Zeissing's attention in the first place—Yoko had been able to keep optometry and sleuthing separate.

The morning was mild and Yoko enjoyed the walk to work. She was waiting to cross the street at 40th and Park when she was startled by a slight cough right behind her. A familiar voice said, "Good morning, Dr. Kamimura." It was Zoran. A dark blue Honda was idling at the curb and Yoko saw that Dan was the driver.

Why was Dan with Zoran when earlier Dan said he was tied up, a code he often used for CT work? As if he'd followed her thought process, Dan lowered the window and said, "Morning, Yoko. The chief was whisked off to a meeting with the powers that be and generously gave me an hour or two free. Some free time! Zoran didn't waste a second and snagged me for a rendezvous with you. Not that I object." He wiggled his eyebrows more suggestive of romantic playtime than work.

Zoran cleared his throat. "If we might consider the matter at hand? I realize you are on your way to the college, Doctor. Could you spare a few minutes?"

"I'm early, we don't have to worry about time. I'm glad of the chance to talk to you both."

Zoran opened the rear door of the car and gestured to Yoko to get in. He followed.

"Decision time, folks," Dan said, turning round and winking at Yoko. "We could let the car idle and sit here or we could drive and drop off the good doctor at the college."

"I'd just as soon walk," Yoko said.

"We are not blocking traffic or access to any building so we could remain here but please turn off the motor, Dan," Zoran said. "You indicated you wish to talk to us, Doctor?"

The two detectives listened as Yoko shared what Hans had explained to her about the personalities in the group of Ben's friends.

"Perceptive insights," Dan said.

"That was my reaction," Yoko said. "Hans told me he couldn't claim credit for most of the details. He said comments Ben made over the years added to his own understanding."

"Hans Reiniger is an honest man," Zoran said. "That is the opinion I formed when interviewing him after he was apprehended for flying his hot-air balloon over the city." In his need for accuracy, Zoran added, "Apprehended for that and other charges. I value my instincts and experience as much as those of the forensic psychiatrist who examined Hans Reiniger and determined he was someone of sound mind and fit to stand trial."

"Yes, Dr. Bronner was . . . well, positive is the word that comes to mind when she testified as the expert witness for Hans," Dan added and Yoko nodded agreement. Zoran's *Hmm* was quiet although he didn't agree or disagree with Dan.

"A further question," Zoran began. "Am I correct in thinking that people understand there cannot be a funeral for Mr. Sasaki until Dr. Nicosian, our Chief Medical Examiner, releases the body?"

"Yes, Hans told me he and the others know that," Yoko said. "As for a funeral, whenever that happens, Ben arranged to have green burial like his mother. The most he and I ever discussed for ourselves was that we agreed it didn't matter what happens to one's body after one dies. It often boils down to what the living want. Hard for the dead person to object."

The second the words left her mouth, Yoko hoped she wasn't stepping on Zoran's sensibilities. It could be tricky to find the most diplomatic way to talk to him, not that Zoran was any more sensitive than the next person, it was more that his perspective was unique and nowhere close to the norm.

"Most people leave specific instructions," the OCD detective said, not disclosing whether he had decided to leave any. "If large sums of money are involved, often the wishes of the deceased are honored. If Mr. Sasaki chose green burial and did not feel any need to plan further, that was his prerogative."

"To recap," Dan said, jumping into the silence that followed this statement, "Ben's regular circle of friends has two couples and four single men, one of whom is Hans. It seems certain all will be present at the wake."

"That's right," Yoko said.

"Everyone's retired," Dan continued. "Two of the group, Vincent Gee and Tom Toppour, rarely attended the gatherings with any regularity and although Ben and Hans did not consider these men threatening, we will have thorough background checks of everyone. Bernie Perette was a cop before he retired. Never anything amiss but we'll still check on him."

Yoko and Zoran murmured approval. Yoko was sure she knew where Dan was heading but just as she was congratulating herself on getting the hang of the detecting business, Zoran surprised her.

"Do you have questions, Yoko?" he asked. "You look thoughtful, what is it?"

"Nothing really," Yoko said. Zoran watched her, not speaking. Yoko knew he had the patience to outwait her so even though she was reluctant to speak, she said, "It's a random thought. It occurs to me we never have charts and photos of suspects. All we ever do is discuss a case."

Zoran's eyebrows raised a fraction and his lips curved in a half smile that took away the sting of his comment. "Perhaps you have been influenced by the portrayal of detective work on television and in motion pictures? Do you feel the need of such props?"

"No, it was a random thought."

"When you and Detective Riley and I work together, I have yet to see any reason to spend time creating charts or displaying photos. We consider possibilities and a coherence develops from our talks as it will now," Zoran explained. "In confidence, on the rare occasions when I have been part of a group that resorts to the use of charts and photographs, I feel it interferes with the mental process. Does that make sense?"

"It does," Yoko said, appreciating Zoran's ability to understand and to answer her. "Sometimes I make notes. If only I had an eidetic memory like you, Zoran."

"To continue," Zoran said patiently, acknowledging the compliment with a slight inclination of his head, "We are justified in considering the possibility that Ben Sasaki was murdered. What we have learned so far is that Ben received threats and he thought his phone was being tapped. The wake offers Yoko an opportunity to spend time with the people who knew Ben. She may be able to find out more about them and anything else that might be pertinent."

"That's my hope," Yoko said.

"Are you comfortable in following through with this line of enquiry alone?"

"I am." Yoko wondered what prompted Zoran's question? Had Dan mentioned his concern to his partner?

"I was sure you did not have a problem but needed to ask," Zoran said, satisfying Yoko's unspoken query and she thought, not for the first time, she was glad to be working with Dan and Zoran. She knew from the rumor mill that not all the detectives at the one-three were as reasonable or as considerate as the two men with whom she was always partnered.

"Thank you," Zoran said. "Unless you have questions, Dan, I believe we have taken enough time. This was a most satisfactory talk."

"Agreed," Dan said. "Most satisfactory." He winked and Zoran smothered a sigh.

Yoko rolled her eyes at Dan, who grinned. He waited until Yoko got out of the car before starting the engine. She watched as the car pulled away from the curb then walked the few blocks to the college.

Yoko spent the day at SUNY catching up with deskwork. When she left the college, she swung by her apartment to pick up the quiche and headed downtown. Had Ben ever made the quiche for the group's pot-lucks, she wondered? He'd asked for the recipe when she'd taken it to their monthly meal at Auntie Ai's but they often swopped recipes. Yoko thought about Quaker Meetings she'd attended to celebrate the lives of Friends who'd died. Those memorials helped ease the distress of losing loved ones. It had been a terrible shock to lose Auntie Ai. Ben's death added to Yoko's grief. When she opened up to it, her feelings were raw, tinged with anger. Yoko knew she couldn't push through the grief, she wasn't going to get to the other side. She would adjust. Accept. Grief wasn't to be endured, it was a new way of seeing.

It was a wrench to enter the building where her cousin had lived and know he wasn't there, that she would never see him again. Yoko felt the all too familiar deep ache at the loss and was aware of a reluctance to reach her destination. Her steps became slower and slower as she walked up the familiar flights of stairs. The handwritten note on the door of the apartment next to Ben's place was simple, "Welcome. Don't knock, come in." Stifling a sigh, she shifted the container with the quiche to her other hand and grasped the doorknob.

The strains of Magyar music flooded her ears when she opened the door and her mood lifted. Hans was standing by the window, playing his violin. The vivid red shirt he wore was an eye-catching splash of color in a room of people in somber clothes. He grinned when he saw Yoko, not missing a note in the complicated harmony he was creating. She smiled back, remembering what he'd said.

"We wear black or red to a wake, it can depend on your tribe. I will wear red in celebration of Ben's life. And you, Yoko, what is your tradition?"

"People in Japan wear black to funerals these days like Westerners," Yoko had told him. "Generations back, white was worn to funerals in Japan because white signals sorrow in Buddhism. My mother and Auntie Ai wore dresses, black ones, to funerals. I have an outfit, a black jacket and skirt, for memorial services."

Yoko had taken a few steps into the room when a slender woman with long, shiny brown hair hurried up to her, holding the skirt of her floor-length black dress away from her feet so she wouldn't trip.

"Are you Yoko? Am I right, you're Ben's cousin? Hans told us you were coming," the woman said, her English accent strong. Yoko nodded and held the quiche up, out of harm's way when the woman pulled Yoko into a warm hug. "It's good you could join us, I'm so sorry for your loss, for our loss. I'm Anna Balducci. Don't be fooled, we're not related to Balducci's fab food emporiums, sad to say. My husband Bert—that's short for Umberto—is over there, pouring wine," Anna laughed. "Bert always wanted to be a sommelier, he's in his element now. He just retired, he was a waiter at Pete's Tavern for years."

Yoko glanced at the would-be sommelier who was filling glasses with an air of confidence. She recognized the wiry man from Pete's, although she hadn't seen him there for a while.

"Did you make a quiche?" Anna asked, eyeing the dish Yoko held. Yoko nodded but before she could speak, Anna continued, "I'll put it with the other dishes," and took the container from Yoko.

Another woman, curly blonde hair tied back with an enormous black bow and wearing a black top and short gray skirt, bustled up. "Anna, is this who I think it is?"

"You're right, Pansy, this is Yoko, Ben's cousin," Anna called over her shoulder. Yoko smoothed her shoulder-length black hair, wishing she'd put a ribbon in it.

"Welcome, wonderful, we hoped you'd come," Pansy said and Yoko had another hug. "I'm Pansy, this is Thomas, my husband," and Pansy gestured to the burly man behind her. "We miss Ben, everyone does, he was a good soul."

Pansy turned away from Yoko and pulled out a smartphone from a pocket in her skirt and in seconds was engrossed, eyes fixed on the small screen. Yoko smothered a smile, Hans was right. "Pansy's smartphone might as well be welded to her ear," he'd said. "She may ask for it to be buried with her."

"Thomas Hardy," Pansy's husband said. "I'm more formal than Pansy and Anna. My condolences." Yoko shook hands with him, keeping her gaze casual as she scanned his eyes, thinking about what Hans had told her.

"Hardy was in the Marines toward the end of the war in Vietnam.

Pansy says he was awarded a ton of medals plus he was the sole survivor of a helicopter crash. Ben said it'd be strange if he didn't have TBI* and he suspected Thomas was taking tranquillizers, maybe not legit pills. Once or twice Ben raised the subject, in a diplomatic way, mind you, and Hardy turned nasty, quite belligerent. Ben said that kinda confirmed his suspicion."

"What sort of problems did Hardy have?" Yoko asked.

"Pansy said he had difficulty driving at night and sometimes had dizzy spells. She said he hated working on the computer, said his eyes got tired."

Yoko didn't say anything, she knew those were among the classic signs of TBI.

As she stood looking at Thomas Hardy, Yoko noticed his eyes jerk. It was a small movement few would notice but unmistakable to someone who worked with the vision system. It was a nystagmus if ever she saw one, an uncontrolled movement of the eyes although in Hardy's case it was low key. It was possible the ex-Marine was indeed on some sort of substance, which might be the cause of his nystagmus. Short of asking pointblank, it was impossible to know if he had a legal prescription for medications. She wished she could check Hardy's vision but there was no way to do so without him knowing. Even a simple vision test would involve asking the man to watch a moving target. She could use a finger as a moving target though a flashlight would be better.

Pansy's husband dropped Yoko's hand and turned away but not before she registered something else, the look in his eyes was a mix of guarded attention and, yes, hostility. Why? Right then, Bert Balducci arrived with a tray loaded with glasses brimming with liquid. Most were filled with red wine, some had juice. Yoko admired the way he balanced the tray, somehow managing not to spill a drop.

"I know who *you* are, glad to meet you, Dr. Kamimura. This is a sad time, we've lost one of the best." Bert and his smile were upbeat, even cheery. He lowered his voice and his tone switched to sharp when he spoke to Hardy. Yoko didn't catch what he muttered to the ex-Marine, who took the tray from Bert in a way that was grudging, his face set close

---

* TBI, traumatic brain injury. See Citation in back matter.

to a scowl. "Welcome," Bert said and shook hands with Yoko. Despite Bert's cordial greeting, his smile was strained and his eyes watchful. Was that the hallmark of a waiter, even one who was retired? Hans had said these days it was rare for Bert and Thomas to be on good terms. Was it normal dislike? Something deeper? Whatever was going on, hostility was obvious in the body language of the two men. It was coupled with irate looks and hissed comments between them when Thomas passed the tray back to Bert, who didn't look Thomas in the face.

Bert moved away, offering people drinks and Yoko saw that most everyone chose wine. She decided to follow in Bert's steps and walked around the room, chatting with people, her theory being that too much information was better than too little. She was careful how she asked questions, adding them as if they were an afterthought when she'd introduced herself in a way that was open and friendly. Time and again she responded to the inevitable query, "No, we still don't know what caused Ben's death."

She saw concern in people's eyes and sorrow on their faces. She managed to include a loaded question, "When you last saw Ben, did he seem worried about anything?" The answers were variations on a theme and given without hesitation.

"No, he was his usual self."

Often there was consternation in the eyes of those she talked with, even bewilderment. It's a dead end, Yoko thought, wincing at the upsetting image she conjured up by those words.

Hans ended his playing in a wild crescendo that had everyone applauding and the time for casual chatter was over. Hans flourished his violin and bowed to acknowledge the clapping and with care returned bow and violin to its case. The applause was still strong and he bowed again. Picking up a glass of wine from the table where Bert had put it for him, he tapped on the glass with a fork until the room was quiet.

"Friends, it's time for a toast. Before we eat, let's share memories of our dear friend Ben." Raising his glass, he said, "To you, Ben, missed but never forgotten."

Glasses were raised and the room echoed with the words, "To Ben."

Hans threaded his way across the room to where Yoko stood. "Glad you're here," he said and they stood side by side, listening as people spoke about Ben. The reminiscences were poignant, sometimes humorous, and smiles were dampened by tears. Bottles of wine were passed around and glasses refilled. Voices grew louder and more confident as inhibitions loosened. Yoko listened and watched, aware that she was being watched. Sometimes the looks were open, sometimes, surreptitious.

Hans was still standing next to Yoko. In a sudden silence, she heard him take a long sip of his wine. Hans swallowed then took a deep breath and launched into the account of how, although he lived in Brooklyn, he maneuvered his way into meeting Ben, who lived in Manhattan. "I kept bumping into our host, Bernie," and Hans waved his glass in Bernie's direction, somehow not spilling a drop. "Always at the shop of the guy in Chinatown who repairs musical instruments. Bernie tantalized me with his tale of the tasty tapenade dip his neighbor made as well as reports of other good food."

A murmur of appreciation ran around the room. "I begged to be invited and Bernie, kind soul that he is, caved. He was right. Ben's tapenade was delicious." Hans chuckled and added, "I wheedled that recipe out of Ben. Truth be known, I think of each of you by the dishes you bring." He pointed to Bernie. "You sir, are Mr. Fruit Cobbler. The thought of your baking makes my mouth water."

"And you, Hans, are Mr. Marinated Kale," Bernie replied.

Laughter broke out then the room became quiet and people listened to what Hans had to share. In the pause after Hans finished his comment, Yoko was aware all eyes were on her. Everyone else had spoken. On her way to the wake, she'd sorted through her memories and decided on a favorite story from family lore. "This happened when I was an infant and home with a sitter but my dad told the story so often, I began to think I was there," she began. "Ben and Jack, his college roommate, invited their families, Ben and Jack's parents, mine too, to homemade spaghetti carbonara. What could go wrong with eggs, cheese and bacon? But they cooked so much pasta, every pot and dish, even the bathtub was overflowing with noodles."

Loud applause erupted until someone called out, "Anna, did you bring your spaghetti bolognese?"

"Yes," Anna said. That was the signal for the meal to begin.

Plates and casseroles had been scraped clean. Chatter in the room subsided to a low murmur as people collected their empty dishes and prepared to leave. Yoko looked into the faces one by one as hugs were shared and subdued goodbyes exchanged. She'd spoken to each person. No one remembered Ben being worried. Everyone assured her Ben was his normal, calm and good-tempered self when they'd last seen him. In the face of death, had the group closed ranks? Yoko sensed more than one person was hiding something, not necessarily guilt, perhaps they were tamping down emotion? Yoko felt fatigue wash over her, she was more than ready to go. She waved goodbye to Hans who was on the other side of the room talking to Bert.

"Will you take your time walking down so I can catch up with you?" he called out. Surprised, Yoko nodded. She was closing the apartment door behind her when she heard what sounded like the start of an argument.

"I'm sick of trekking out there. You can bloody go by yourself." The voice was shrill but it was Anna, no mistaking the English accent.

"You can't back out, you know Alfredo is sick. Besides, they like to see us both," Bert said, his voice none too pleasant.

"Don't throw a wobbly," Anna fired back. "He's always sick and if it isn't Alfredo, Maria is under the weather. Umberto exists to boss everyone around. The one reason they want to see us is to put us to work. We're supposed to be retired, remember?"

Yoko closed the door and walked down the stairs wondering what the argument was about. Where was "out there" and who put Anna and Bert to work? Hans caught up with Yoko and she asked, "Anna sounded upset. Family problems?"

"Oh, you heard," Hans said, embarrassed. "Anna doesn't want to visit Bert's family, they're out on Long Island. Most of the time she's even-tempered but wine darkens her mood, which is ironic."

"Why do you say 'ironic'?"

"Bert's grandparents started a vineyard on Long Island and Anna is never against a glass or three of wine, more so when it's from the vineyard, it's quality wine. Still, you have to laugh when Anna talks about throwing a wobbly."

"Cricket term?" Yoko ventured.

"You'd think so but no, it means someone's upset. She accuses Bert of being upset but she's the one having the wobbly!" His chuckle was forced.

"What does Anna mean, they have to work when they visit?"

"Well, the family is proud of the business but they just had a major setback. Bert was close-mouthed about it, wouldn't say whether the grapes had a virus or if it was something else. What he did say was that the season's wine had to be thrown out. Since then, it's been desperate, they're paddling hard to keep their heads above water." Hans said, his voice low. "It's a real small family affair, somehow they scrape by. Bert grew up out there and is so knowledgeable and Anna's learned a lot over the years. Still, it sounds as if she's had enough and they did retire a few months back."

"The wine tonight was good," Yoko said. "Was it from Bert's family place?"

"No," Hans said. "The vineyard doesn't have wide distribution and someone would have had to go out to Long Island to pick it up though I'm not sure if any is available right now."

They reached the building lobby and Hans held the street door open for Yoko and followed her out.

"Which way are you headed?" he said.

"Up to Gramercy Park, I'm walking. Aren't you getting a ride back to Brooklyn with Anna and Bert?" Yoko asked.

Hans shook his head. "Not tonight. They were going to leave for Long Island right after tonight's gathering. That was the plan," he said. "Who knows? I'll catch the subway at 14th Street. How about we walk and talk?"

"Fine," Yoko said. "Thanks again for including me tonight."

"We made our farewells to Ben, yes?" Hans said as they started off at a leisurely pace.

"We did," Yoko agreed.

"You circulated and chatted with everyone. Gathering information?" Hans raised his eyebrows, his look quizzical.

"In a way." Yoko didn't say more although it was obvious the Romani hoped for a longer answer. When it was clear she wasn't going to say anything else, Hans spoke again.

"When the cause of Ben's death is determined, you'll let me know?"

"I will," Yoko said.

"Look, I know it's late but now that you've met the group, I want to share some . . . er . . . something." Hans glanced at Yoko and didn't stop but slowed his walk and said, "You know, Ben was a good *gadjo*."

"Excuse me?"

"It's a compliment, *gadjo* is a non-Romani." His sigh was heavy. "We've lost a fine man."

Yoko saw the concern on the Romani's face. She matched her steps to the slower pace Hans was setting and asked, "Do you want to stop in somewhere?" She waved at the cafes and bars they were passing.

"No. It's best to keep walking and look casual."

"All right, let's walk and talk," Yoko said, wondering why it was good to look casual. Was someone watching? Another thought crossed her mind, was the Romani paranoid?

"I want you to know that I haven't let my imagination run wild," Hans said. "This is something Ben and I mulled over."

Yoko nodded.

"We talked about going to the police because we had more than an inkling, it was closer to a full-blown suspicion." Hans hesitated then said, "Look, first I need to tell you something personal, something Ben accepted." Hans stopped walking and faced Yoko. Looking her straight in the eye, he said, "It's traditional for Romani women to be 'seers of future events,' yes?"

"Yes."

"When I was young, I discovered my great-grandmother's abilities had touched me, though the occasions are rare," Hans said. "When they do happen, I am able to predict what is going to happen." He started walking, a look of relief on his face as if freed of a burden. Yoko fell into step beside him.

"Are you telling me you're psychic?" Yoko felt a tingle of excitement at this unexpected twist.

"I confess." The Romani's voice was mock serious. He grinned then continued, "What I see of the future comes when I least expect it, in small waves, with vast spaces of time in between. From what my family's told me, it's nothing like that of my great-grandmother, Floritsa, who was a true seer. Ben described it as acute premonition."

"Ben and I talked about premonition once," Yoko said. "He changed my thinking. I said I didn't believe in it and he told me that when he was in the military, too many times men in his battalion described with scary accuracy what was going to happen. Ben said at first he discounted the stories but they came true so often he accepted there's such a thing as second sight."

Hans nodded. "Yes. Second sight. Thank you. I had a premonition something serious was going to happen to Ben. He'd received the threatening notes and we knew his phone was being tapped. Then, when he was ill and had to go to the hospital I thought that was all my premonition meant."

"About the phone tapping . . ." Yoko began but before she could say more, a voice cut across hers.

"Hey, you can't keep Ben's cousin to yourself, Hans." It was Pansy. She and her husband had come up behind Yoko and Hans. "Why don't we stop somewhere for a nightcap?" Pansy tugged on Yoko's arm. "Come on, Anna introduced me to Guinness. Wow, it's the best."

The look on the Romani's face was enough to let Yoko know she wasn't going to hear anything about the phone tapping or anything else from him, not with Pansy and Thomas in tow.

"Thanks, but I've an early start tomorrow," Yoko said, hiding her irritation at the couple's arrival.

Pansy would not take no for an answer. "Come on," she wheedled. "I want to know how you and Hans met. Something tells me it wasn't because of Ben."

What, Yoko wondered, did Pansy mean by that? Was Hardy's wife flirting? Hans and Thomas Hardy were opposites, one pleasant and outgoing, the other with a steely reserve under a brusque manner. Did his pleasant ways make Hans appealing to Pansy?

"If you want to hear about my exploits before I turned model citizen, I can tell you any time." Hans gave a small laugh.

"We're buying," Hardy said, his voice firm. He spread his arms out as if to shepherd them along to where he wanted them to go. "Spare a few minutes, wind down after the wake?"

"Why not? One drink then," Yoko said, changing her mind. Why pass up an opportunity to learn more about the ex-Marine and his wife.

"Let's go to the Winslow," Pansy suggested.

"Too far," Hardy harshly dismissed the suggestion and Pansy pouted. He steered the group into the bar they were standing outside. The place wasn't crowded and to Pansy's loud delight they carried Guinness.

"Righty ho, Hans, tell us how you and Yoko met," Pansy said when they were seated and drinks ordered.

"I thought you all knew about the . . . journey . . . I made in the hot-air balloon," Hans said. "The newspapers were full of it. I was famous for the requisite fifteen minutes." He shrugged. "My quest wasn't revenge, it was a search for justice for my family. When my hot-air balloon was downed, me with it, Dr. Kamimura happened to be first on the scene," he tilted his head toward Yoko, who nodded in silent agreement and sipped on her ginger libation.

"You know she's an optometrist?" Hans didn't wait for an answer but continued, "Did you know she's also a civilian consultant to the police? Anyhow, the law caught up with me when I was in hospital. Turns out I broke a whole raft of rules."

"A journey in a hot-air balloon," Pansy said. "How exciting even if you ended up in the clutches of the police and Yoko." Hardy didn't speak, narrowed eyes trained on Hans.

The Romani hadn't finished. "Ben asked me once if I'd learned my lesson. I told him I'd make that balloon flight all over again." His voice was low and he kept his eyes on his drink, not looking at anyone. "The dark secrets of Marco Fellini, the object of my quest, were exposed.

Never could I have accomplished that through the courts. Fellini outweighed me in every respect, money, connections, reputation, whatever it takes to pervert the course of justice, something he'd done with great success for years."

Hans emptied the beer in his glass in one swallow and glanced around the bar. His gaze stopped on Hardy and lingered. Yoko wondered if she was reading too much into what was going on and decided her emotions were raw, too close to the surface after Ben's memorial.

"What a story," Pansy said. "I'm glad I asked. I didn't know any of it, did you, Thomas?" Her husband grunted. It might have been a "No." Out of the blue, Hardy turned to Yoko.

"Did your cousin Ben ever tell you that Bert Balducci had family incarcerated in one of the WWII camps?"

Yoko stared in surprise at the revelation. "No," she mumbled. "I didn't know that." Why, she wondered, had Hardy trotted out that piece of news? Had Ben known?

Hans shook his head when Hardy suggested another drink. "Time for me to take the subway to Brooklyn."

"It's been a long evening, tomorrow is a busy day for me," Yoko said when Hardy held up her glass and looked at her. Outside the bar, they stood for a few moments in an uneasy group then parted company. Pansy called a loud goodbye as her husband steered her over to the cab he hailed.

"Did you know that Bert Balducci had family in one of the camps?" Yoko asked Hans.

"No, I did not," Hans said. "How the hell did Hardy find that out? I don't think Ben knew, he certainly never mentioned it." The Romani shrugged. "It's late. I'm brain dead. Let's meet at Good Eats soon? We can talk then." He looked exhausted, not ready to pick up the conversation he'd started before Pansy and Hardy arrived.

"Sure. Any time. Give me a call," Yoko said and they walked the few blocks to 14th Street in silence.

Hans clattered down the subway steps, waving a silent farewell.

At her apartment, Yoko listened to a brief message from Dan on her answering machine. "I hope you survived the wake? Guess you're not back yet. The chief and I are off on a project any moment now so thought I'd leave you some good vibes. Mega hugs, dear heart."

"That's nice, thanks, Dan," Yoko said aloud as she erased the message. The cats looked up at her with interest as they wove their way around her legs, purring and welcoming her home. Yoko busied herself changing the water bowls for the feline brothers, adding treats to their food dishes. While her hands were occupied, her mind went over what Hans Reiniger had said about having premonitions before Pansy and Thomas arrived and interrupted the conversation. What else did he have to share?

"Too many questions," Yoko muttered. The cats, busy lapping water, paused to stare at her. "It's okay, boys," Yoko said, "I need to make a list." She left the kitchen and the cats wandered after her, jumping up to settle on the living room couch but watching as Yoko headed for her study. It didn't take long to compile the list and Yoko walked back to the living room to sit on the chair opposite the couch.

"Listen up, you two," she told the cats. "Let's see if you can earn your keep." Busy grooming themselves, the brother felines swiveled their heads and looked at Yoko, who read from her list. "1. How did Hardy know Bert had family in the WWII camps and what was his motive in dropping that bombshell? 2. Did Ben know? If so, why hadn't Ben mentioned it to Hans? 3. Is there a connection between Ben's death and the internment of Bert's family?"

"That covers it, right?" Yoko asked the cats, who blinked then resumed their grooming. "I'll be giving you a quiz later, boys, I hope you'll be ready." Yoko studied the list and when she was satisfied the queries were in her memory, she tore up the sheet of paper. She really wanted to talk Dan and Zoran but it was too late to call Zoran and Dan was on assignment. Then there was the issue of the phone being tapped. How would she know if that problem had been resolved? As if on cue, her phone rang and she heard a man's voice. "This is to let you know your phones are clear. If you've any question, call Detective Zeissing." Yoko recognized the speaker, it was Earl, one of the one-three's IT staff.

That was welcome news. She decided it was time to put thoughts of the list aside. The minute she did, something struck her—how strange that Hans said *he'd* call *her*. It felt as if Hans was warning *her* not to call *him*. Yoko shook her head, now who was having a premonition? She yawned and stretched and decided she needed to unwind. Yoko unrolled her yoga mat and slipped off her shoes. Some stretches followed by yoga would ease her aches and help quiet her mind before bed.

11 A Walk in Central Park

Yoko cursed as her hand groped for the phone ringing so loudly in her darkened room. Such a tranquil dream, now quickly fading. Three hawks circling overhead, wings spread as they soared on thermals, the red in their tails vivid as she strolled near the Hudson River glistened by the sun. A yacht sailed against the Manhattan skyline.

"What?" she demanded, not caring that her voice wasn't even halfway pleasant. Convinced it was predawn and not bothering to check caller ID, she was certain it was just another robocall. But a robocaller this early?

"Want to run away with your sweetheart?" It was Dan. "Remember the cottage we rented last year on the Sound in Connecticut? It's available next month, which gives us plenty of time to arrange for time off. How about it?"

On the verge of agreeing with enthusiasm, Yoko caught sight of the time and her eyes widened in alarm. "No," she moaned.

"No?" Dan repeated. He sounded surprised. He also sounded hurt. Yoko didn't have time to reassure him he was her sweetheart and she did want to go back to the cottage where they'd made love on the couch with only the moon to see them.

Words tumbled out. "Not you. I overslept."

"It's 8:15. What's the hurry?"

"The NORA*conference the college is hosting, I've a ton of work to do for it."

"No!" Dan imitated Yoko's moan. "You mentioned you'd be helping

---

* NORA—The Neuro-Optometric Rehabilitation Association, International.

with NORA when we were in Philly but I thought it was a ways off. Is it out of town?"

"No, you goof, it's for two days right here in Manhattan."

"That's more like it! Any chance of dinner tonight?"

"Doubt it," Yoko grumbled, jumping out of bed and shucking her pjs.

"At least a phone call? We can plot about sneaking off to the cottage. Besides, we need to talk, you were going to fill me in on Ben's wake."

"Dan, I gotta go but before I forget, I had the strangest dream." Yoko sat down abruptly, her hurry forgotten as the images from her sleep flooded back.

"I'm listening," Dan was all patience this morning.

"First I saw three hawks soaring above me. I was walking by the Hudson River, it was so peaceful," Yoko said.

"Hmm," Dan grunted. He sounded dubious but he was trying to keep his options open. "Tell me more. Did you go anywhere else in this dream?"

"The scenery melted," Yoko said. Her throat constricted. "Up to then, I felt tranquil. All at once, I had a sense of dread."

"That's not good. Why d'you think you were worried?"

"Hard to say. I was standing by water so shallow I could see the skinny stretch of legs of two herons motionless a few feet from me. It was Turtle Pond in Central Park where we walk sometimes. You like that place."

"Yeah, Turtle Pond, love it," Yoko hoped Dan wasn't just being agreeable.

"What does it mean, Dan, with the water and the birds?"

Dan made what he might have meant as a flip comment but it startled Yoko wide awake. "Maybe you and me and Zoran are the hawks, keeping our beady eyes out for trouble. Those two herons could be the bad guys?"

Yoko didn't tell Dan he was right or wrong but settled for a pragmatic, "That's an intriguing theory."

"Wait," Dan said, aware Yoko was ready to end the call. "Experts say the brain keeps working when we're asleep. If you felt a sense of dread, you must have sensed danger in something you're involved with in your waking hours." He took a quick breath and plunged on. "I'm willing to bet it's something to do with Ben's death."

"Call you later, I'm outa here," Yoko said. Dan was hitting close to home.

She dressed at speed and dashed around the apartment, gathering what she needed for the day, dodging the cats as they wove around her legs. She skipped breakfast at home in favor of yoga, abbreviating her usual practice, knowing it was better than nothing. She was on her way to work scant minutes after talking to Dan. Outside, on the street, cabs zoomed past, full, not a bus was in sight. Muttering under her breath, Yoko decided the walk would give her time to consider the difference between dreams and premonitions, if there was any difference. Was it ridiculous to think the dream had any meaning other than her subconscious searching for answers? She was a scientist but she hadn't ruled out the premonitions Hans said he had.

Yoko had been willing to accept the Romani's explanation that there were times he could see the future. She'd have to ask Hans if his premonitions were as cryptic as her dreams. She'd not reached any resolution on the difference between premonitions and dreams by the time she arrived at SUNY at a respectable nine minutes before nine although often she arrived at the college well before eight.

"Morning, Yoko, the NORA conference is almost here, remind me what you offered to do." It was Dean Kate Grant, who was right behind Yoko. They entered the college lobby together. Yoko swallowed the last bite of the donut she'd grabbed from a food cart on 23rd Street on her hurried walk to work and smiled.

"Morning, Dean. I signed up to match attendees with a city visit—not the most serious part of any conference but popular."

"What will our visitors see?"

"The top choices, Grand Central Station and Times Square were snapped up quickly so we added a tour that Clint Davis organized, some of Central Park's lesser known gems. That's almost full."

"Sounds good. Any idea how many we're expecting at the conference?"

"Last I checked, ninety-five had signed up. A mix of practitioners, optometrists and neurologists as well as educators and occupational therapists."

"Bob Williams is coming, I heard from him yesterday," the dean said. "He was Executive Director of NORA for about four years."

""Great, I haven't seen him for a while. Wasn't he running the OEP Foundation at the same time he was NORA's director?"

"That he was. A man of many abilities and a multitude of hats. He'll be here representing Western U's College of Optometry."

They started up the stairs and Yoko sighed in relief when the dean waved goodbye at her floor. By the time her computer was up and running, Yoko had located the bulging NORA Conference file on her desk. Emails had arrived from five people, including Bob Williams, all interested in the morning activity with the ambiguous name, "A Hike, an Arcade and a Castle." Yoko scrolled through the rest of the emails, stopping to reread one from Clint Davis, the young optometrist who'd volunteered to guide people on the hike.

> Apologies, Yoko, but I just learned I'll be out of town for a week, starting tomorrow. Here's info on the hike-arcade-castle activity. It's a "walk in the park." Ha, ha. You could handle it with one hand tied behind your back if you can't find anyone else. I recommend you take a walk a day or so before the event to get the lie of the land. Go to the arcade first, it can get crowded. The name, Belvedere Castle, means beautiful or panoramic view in Italian. You can wow NORA visitors with that snippet.

Yoko grumbled to herself as she read through Clint's directions. What a smartass with bad jokes yet and he looked so innocent. Still, Clint was right, the activity was simple enough. It might be time wasted trying to find someone to take Clint's place, Yoko was one of the few SUNY staff who lived in Manhattan. During the NORA conference, she wasn't on rotation at any of the vision clinics, which would give her time to go to conference workshops and, she realized, lead the tour. Yikes, the park tour was close. Clint's suggestion to take a dry run to check on the route was smart. Yoko worked out the timing for the actual day of the hike. If she got up by 7:00 a.m., she'd have time for the full morning yoga, energizing stretches and Downward Dogs, the multivitamin of yoga. After breakfast, she'd be ready to walk to the subway, the quickest way to travel though the ride might take close to an hour.

Yoko knew everyone who'd signed up for the tour, it would be easy to find them at 9:00 a.m., at the meeting place on 5th Avenue at East 59th/60th Street, the Grand Army Plaza entrance, which was closed to motor traffic. They'd start with a pleasant walk, not really a hike, up to the Arcade that ran under Bethesda Terrace, which was located mid-park around 72nd Street. She looked over the map Clint had included and saw it was a reasonable distance from the Arcade to Belvedere Castle, which opened at 10 a.m. Yoko had visited the castle and knew Bethesda Terrace, which was considered the heart of Central Park, but had never walked through the Arcade, a passageway that ran under Terrace Drive.

Wikipedia photos showed a stunning tiled ceiling and gracious arches at the Bethesda Terrace Arcade. Her annoyance at Clint faded, he'd designed a good tour. After the group had admired the fountain at Bethesda Terrace and the plantings, they'd walk through the underground arcade and on to Belvedere Castle. Yoko decided she'd take the visitors on the tour, partly because it would be tricky finding someone else, partly because she wanted to see the Arcade though they might be too early for any of the performers who used the arcade because of its superb acoustics.

"If the Arcade is deserted, we'll call out our names and listen to the echo," she said and was startled when someone at her door said, "Talking to yourself?" It was Clint Davis. "Thought I'd stop in and see if you had any questions about the info I sent you for the park tour," he said. "Sorry I had to bow out. Have you found someone to take over?"

"Your info's helpful, thanks," Yoko said, "I decided to do it myself." The phone on her desk shrilled and Clint waved a hasty goodbye.

It was Hans Reiniger on the phone. "Are you free to get together today, perhaps a bite to eat at our favorite place? Or is this too short notice?"

Yoko thought about her day and made a snap decision. "Does six o'clock work for you?"

"See you then."

Seconds after the call ended, Yoko realized she'd assumed Hans meant they should meet at Good Eats. Strange he hadn't said the name. Still, they'd met there once and for sure he didn't mean the bar Pansy had dragged them to after the wake. The arrival of Pansy and Thomas had interrupted Hans as he was about to tell Yoko something important. Yoko hoped it was the name of whoever was tapping Ben's phone. It was intriguing that Hans had premonitions and Yoko was eager to meet with the Romani to learn more. Dan and Zoran would be interested also, though just how receptive the OCD detective would be to news of premonitions was anyone's guess. Yoko hadn't decided whether to share the Romani's unusual personal news even with Dan. She'd delay that decision until she heard what else Hans had to tell her. Lunch was a hasty but hearty sandwich at her desk and she was powering through a mountain of deskwork when Dan called again.

"Got a minute for an official call? Thought you'd like to know the results of our background checks," Dan said and he ran down the list. "The two guys, Vincent Gee and Tom Toppour, are squeaky clean. Never in any trouble. As for Bernie Perette, he was in security, exemplary career. Record still spotless. As you know, Hans was monitored after his arrest for flying the hot-air balloon over Manhattan. Like Gee, Toppour and Perette, these days he's your model citizen. The Balduccis, husband and wife, are clean, no arrests or rap sheets per se, but the husband is involved with his family's vineyard out on Long Island and the history there is murky."

"What do you mean, murky?"

"Neighbors have complained about strange comings and goings. The local detectives made discreet inquiries and ran surveillance on the property for a brief period but nothing illegal was discovered. One theory is that someone may want to buy the vineyard but the Balducci family doesn't want to sell even though they're struggling to keep going."

"An attempt at a hostile takeover?" Yoko said.

"Could be."

"Hans told me the vineyard had a bad season last year, something wrong with the wine and sales slumped," Yoko said. "Why would any-one want to buy the place? Bert Balducci goes out to help, has for years.

He knows a lot about the business but his wife isn't willing to keep on spending time out on Long Island."

"Okay. Now on to Thomas Hardy and his wife, Pansy. We're still digging. At first, it looked as if they were clean but after in-depth searching, we found information about them had been scrubbed."

"As in removed?"

"Right."

Yoko whistled.

"Yeah, the experts can go right behind what is seen on the computer screen and unearth the trail. It'll take time to discover just what was scrubbed but it's a red flag," Dan explained. "I'll let you know as soon as more is uncovered."

"Thanks, Dan, let's talk later. Right now, I'm off to meet Hans," Yoko said.

Hans was chatting with Pete when Yoko arrived at Good Eats.

"You've kept your friend waiting." Pete wagged a reproving finger.

"She's early." Hans tapped an imaginary watch on his wrist. "I'm earlier. Greetings, Dr. Yoko. Pete has recommended the borscht."

"Best in town," Yoko said.

"Two bowls? I'll bring them over." Pete waved them to a booth.

"Full service? Quite the honor," Yoko said. They settled themselves in a booth and she asked, "After we eat, d'you have time to go to Central Park? I need to go over the route of a mini tour for out-of-towners coming to a conference at SUNY. We'd have time to talk as we walk."

The Romani looked doubtful and Yoko was relieved when he said, "Rain's predicted but not till around midnight—let's go after we finish our soup."

12 In the Gloaming

Yoko and Hans arrived at the Grand Army Plaza entrance to Central Park after a tooth-rattling subway ride. The noise of the subway as it clattered uptown made it impossible to talk. That didn't bother Yoko although she was anxious to hear what Hans had to say. They'd have time to talk when they walked the route of the tour. Low clouds obscured a sun thinking of setting but dusk and the threat of rain didn't deter New Yorkers and the Fifth Avenue sidewalk was crowded. Yoko could see the park was just as busy with walkers and joggers. Safety in numbers, she hoped, although it was years since the time she'd been caught in a murderous tangle in the park. She'd been saved at the last moment by the arrival of a mounted policeman. That trauma had faded but it was embedded in her atavistic memory. As happened on other visits to the park, ice trickled along her spine.

Yoko and Hans left Fifth Avenue and entered the park. She didn't waste a moment. Keeping her voice casual, Yoko said, "You were about to tell me something last night when the Hardys arrived and interrupted you."

"Ah, you had more than a healthy walk in mind?" the Romani teased. "Yes, you're right. I want to share with you what was going on in the weeks before Ben died." They walked in silence while Hans gathered his thoughts. Yoko waited, curbing her instinct to start asking questions. She knew it would be wise to let the Romani tell her what he had to say in his own time and way.

She glanced at the slip of paper with her scribbled notes about the tour route. The entrance to the park for the Arcade at Bethesda Terrace was 72nd Street, a modest walk from where they'd entered the park at 59th Street. They'd start by going through the Arcade, which might be crowded at this time. Then they'd head to Belvedere Castle, which was close to 79th Street. The castle closed at 5 so she and Hans wouldn't be able to go in tonight, but if all went well on the morning of the tour, the NORA group would reach the castle around 10 a.m. when it opened. A Victorian folly dating from 1869, the castle had the highest and most superb views of the park as well as a number of interesting exhibits and had been the official weather station for the National Weather Service since 1919. How often had Yoko heard the radio forecast start, "Right now, the temperature in Central Park is . . . ."

Yoko was congratulating herself for inviting Hans to join her when his voice broke in on her thoughts. He moved closer to her so she could hear his quiet words.

"You chatted with everyone last night, so you have some measure of the various personalities. I didn't want to talk too much about any single person before you had a chance to meet them all. Did I tell you that Vince Gee was a New Jersey Poet Laureate?"

"You did. You said he's in another world when he's creating poetry."

"That's true. Vince is passionate about haiku. Besides, Ben and I agreed it was totally out of character for Vince to send Ben or anyone threats. Bottom line, Vince wouldn't hurt anyone. The same holds true for Tom Toppour. He's a retired NYU professor of mathematics. Tom plays the accordion, which is how I met him and why I invited him to our get-togethers. Bernie Perette is also retired, he was head of security at the German Consulate, so he's okay."

"That leaves the two couples, the Balduccis and the Hardys," Yoko said, wishing Hans would get to the nitty-gritty. "Oh, and you," she joked.

"Me, the Balduccis and the Hardys." Hans glanced at Yoko and she saw the glint of amusement in his brilliant blue eyes. "You can keep me on the list but Ben counted me on the side of all that's good."

"If *you* say so," Yoko said, putting disbelief in her voice. Hans broke into laughter and she added, "In all seriousness, I'm sure Ben was right."

"I thank you, though Ben once suggested I had FOMO," Hans said.

"That's a psychological term?"

"In a way. It means Fear Of Missing Out," Hans said. "Seniors are often infected with it though we maintain we're trying to have fun and keep busy."

Yoko grinned, glad the Romani had a sense of humor. She was about to tell him about the background checks when Hans started speaking.

"So, the two wives, Pansy and Anna," Hans began. "Both worked at P.S.41, the Greenwich Village School. Pansy taught 3rd grade, Anna was the assistant to the principal. Their husbands also worked in the city and the two couples went dancing now and then. Sometimes they persuaded Ben to go with them. Bingo night was another favorite. The women retired within months of each other and Bert left Pete's Tavern. Now, because Anna and Bert live in Brooklyn, they don't come in to Manhattan often."

"Would you say the couples were good friends?"

"Yes and no," Hans said. "When the wives worked in the same place and Bert worked in town, it was easy enough for them to get together. They were friendly but I do not know if they were good friends. The past four or five months, Ben and I noticed tension between the men and to a certain extent between the wives. We weren't entirely sure what might have caused this though we had theories."

"What about Hardy? Is he retired?"

"Not really. He runs his own business and has what he calls an open schedule."

"What's his business?"

"Surveillance equipment. Ben was able to dig into Thomas's military background and discovered that after he left the Marines, Thomas was a rep for a business that makes surveillance equipment. A year or so ago, he went into business for himself."

Walking as Hans talked, they reached Bethesda Terrace. They stopped to admire the beautiful arches that led to the Arcade's walkway that ran under the Terrace then threaded their way through the crowd. They paused to watch a juggler flinging a dizzying array of vegetables higher and higher. Farther on, they lingered by a trio playing jazz. The fiddler, sax player and guitarist had a circle of admirers, some dancing to the music.

"Hans, look up," Yoko said and the two craned their necks to stare at the stunning tiled ceiling.

"I wonder if there's any place where it's better to view the ceiling," Yoko said. They walked on in silence, stopping now and then to look up at the intricate design of the tiles. "Perhaps it would work if the group looks up at the ceiling at the beginning of the arcade and again at the end of the walk through the Arcade," Yoko said.

"Makes sense," the Romani said.

"Hope you don't mind if I try out my tour guide talk on you," Yoko joked. Hans smiled and she continued. "The gorgeous designs in the tiles come from the use of clays of different colors. These tiles were made in England by the famous Minton Tile company. This type of tile was often used on the floors of European cathedrals and Minton tiles are on the floor of the U.S. Capitol building."

"Really? But why are these on the ceiling?" Hans asked.

"That, I regret to say, I do not know. But I did read that this is the only place in the world where the tiles have been used on a ceiling."

They reached the end of the Arcade and came out into twilight, to find a few walkers, a jogger or two, and one or two couples arm in arm, heads close as they strolled by.

"What now?"

"Let's see," Yoko consulted her notes. "On to Belvedere Castle." They moved at a relaxed pace, almost an amble, merging with the stream of people on the path. Yoko touched Hans on the arm and said, "You mentioned tension between Balducci and Hardy?"

"Yes," Hans said. Yoko saw he was struggling to speak. When he did, he chose his words with halting care. "I thought ... Ben thought ... these two men were our friends. We spent many hours with them over the years. But in the past months we began to question if either was to be trusted. It was obvious the two men were having differences although we didn't know the reason. When we discovered that Ben's phone was being tapped, we agreed Hardy had the expertise. We couldn't discount the possibility that Balducci had picked up the know-how from Hardy, unlikely though that was."

Two suspects, Yoko thought. Did not anticipate that. A second later she remembered the jarring comment Dan had made about the two herons being the bad guys. How weird.

"Were you certain it was Hardy tapping the phones?"

"Yes. Ben suggested he call me and we'd talk about going to one of the concerts in the park." Hans waved around him. "Right here in Central Park."

"And did you?"

"We did. And almost as if he wanted us to know he knew our plans, Hardy asked at the next potluck if we'd decided to go."

"So it was confirmed Hardy was tapping the phones?"

"For sure. Even though we suspected Hardy was the culprit, Ben was reluctant to believe it without this proof," Hans said. "Ben was compassionate, he knew Hardy had to be struggling and was denying he had repercussions from service in Vietnam, TBI."

Hans stopped walking. Yoko hesitated then stopped. The Romani stared around, a puzzled look on his face. Yoko followed his gaze, wondering what he'd seen in the stream of people around them that had brought him to an abrupt stop.

"Are you all right?" Yoko said.

"I thought I sa . . ." Hans broke off in mid-word. Just as Yoko realized the deafening crack of noise in her ears was the sound of a gunshot, she watched astounded as Hans floated back away from her. He crumpled to the ground, limbs splayed in a grotesque semblance of relaxation. A trickle of red seeped through a small round hole in his jacket high up on his left arm. Had the bullet been meant for his heart?

Yoko dropped to her knees beside Hans. "No," she whispered. "No." She put her fingers on his jugular and was relieved at the strength of the pulsing. This was a bizarre replay of the first time she'd met the Romani years ago when he'd been lying on 23rd Street in the wreckage of his hot-air balloon. She hadn't seen blood then, not until the ambulance people moved him, but she'd feared he was close to death. This time, when Hans opened his eyes, Yoko breathed a deep sigh of relief. The pupils of the Romani's eyes although dilated did not show the severe level of trauma from his horrific injury when his hot-air balloon was downed years ago. Since then, whenever they met, she'd noticed the diameter of his pupils—it was instinctive to Yoko, an optometrist who worked with the vision system, a habit she couldn't break. Until today, the normal range of the Romani's pupils was some 3 mm. Now, those pupils were 5 mm, an increase but not one that indicated severe injury.

"This is not a dream," he gasped and Yoko knew he too was remembering that time when he'd asked, "Is . . . a dream?" Then, as if uncomfortable on the uneven ground of the Central Park path where he lay, the Romani shifted his legs a fraction, groaning at the effort. "Martya," he gasped.

"What?" Yoko felt a chill that had nothing to do with the evening's temperature.

Had Hans seen someone called Martya? Had she shot him? Did Hans stop walking because he'd had a premonition?

"We're in Central Park," Hans said, his voice low but clear and steady. "I've been shot, it knocked me down, it hurts but . . . ." That was all he said. The Romani's eyes closed as if rubbed shut by a giant thumb.

Yoko pulled out her iPhone but before she could make a call, a voice near her said, "EMTs are on the way with an ambulance." Yoko slipped the phone back in her pocket. The same voice said, louder and with authority, "People, let's give this man breathing room, excitement's over. Medical help is on the way." The speaker, a woman of about forty, was on a mountain bike, one foot rested on the ground, the other on a pedal. The onlookers backed away and one by one moved off, reluctant to be involved in any investigation. "I'm Diana Bandler, one of the medical technicians with the park unit," the speaker introduced herself to Yoko. "I saw you check the victim's pulse. Are you a . . . ?" She didn't finish the sentence but Yoko knew she was being asked for her credentials.

"No, I'm not a . . ."Yoko said but the rest of the sentence was drowned by the sound of brakes squealing. An ambulance had arrived.

"You know this man?" Diana said.

"Yes, I do." Yoko scrambled to her feet to get out of the way of the EMT crew.

"His name?" Diana asked.

"I am Hans Reiniger," the Romani said, surprising them both. His eyes were open and he winced as he tilted his chin slightly, giving Yoko the universal signal to come close. She bent down beside him. "I had a premonition Martya was near," Hans whispered, trembling. "Martya is the angel of death." Yoko knew he was in shock, his reaction to being shot, but his voice was calm as he added, "It is not my time."

While Hans had been speaking to Yoko, Diana and the EMTs had been in quick consultation. One of the EMTs bent over Hans.

"May be best if I cut the sleeve off your jacket, okay?" the EMT asked.

"Can you just take it off?" Hans said. "It's new."

"You sure? It's gonna hurt."

"Be quick." Hans gritted his teeth as his jacket was removed.

"Hey, there's a bonus." the EMT was astonished. "The bullet hit your arm below your short-sleeved shirt so the shirt is intact. You'll need your jacket patched but you are lucky."

"Right, lucky me."

The EMT held up the jacket, looking for someone to take it. Yoko put out her hand and accepted the jacket, zipping the pockets shut so nothing would fall out then draping the jacket over her arm.

A second EMT crouched down beside Hans to examine the wound now that it was exposed. "Your humerus is intact, bullet missed the bone by a fraction," he said in surprise. He lifted the arm with practiced gentleness, peering at the back. "Clear exit wound. Means both sides of your arm will need to be treated. The good news is no one has to probe around for a bullet." He got to his feet and said with satisfaction, "Vital signs strong, minimal bleeding staunched. Let's get to Mount Sinai." Hans was lifted onto a stretcher and moved to the ambulance.

"I wonder if we can find the bullet?" Yoko said. Had she only heard one shot? She searched her memory. Hans only had one wound although that wasn't any guarantee a single shot had been fired. She eyed the area where Hans had been standing when he was hit. He'd been on the edge of the path, which was bordered with low bushes.

"I've filed the coordinates of the location," Diana said. "Maybe it was someone firing a gun for the heck of it. It happens. If the police want to investigate, they'll check our files."

Yoko left that comment alone. Perhaps there would be an official investigation. Even so, no need to spread the news that Hans might have been deliberately attacked.

"Can Dr. Kamimura come to the hospital with me?" Hans asked, startling Yoko and Diana. Yoko looked at Diana to check her reaction.

"Yes," Diana said, returning Yoko's glance with open curiosity. "That's okay, the doctor can ride in the ambulance."

"I'm an optometrist, not an M.D.," Yoko clarified. Hadn't she explained that somewhere the other day? Where had she had been when she'd said that? Her heart skipped a beat when she remembered it was at Beth Israel where she'd rushed after Ben called. Tears filled Yoko's eyes as she thought of Ben and Diana's curiosity turned to concern. Yoko shook her head. "I'm okay." Diana relaxed and smiled.

The ride to the hospital was swift. Once there, Hans was transferred to a gurney and whisked into the ER. One of the EMTs from Central Park hurried alongside the gurney, explaining the extent of the injury to the nurse who was taking over. The park medical help had been thorough, they'd called ahead and paperwork was waiting for Yoko to fill out. She was completing the task when an aide brought her a plastic bag.

"These are the clothes and belongings of Mr. Reiniger. He's just gone into the OR."

Most of the seats in the waiting room were occupied. Yoko found a quiet space in the hall nearby. About to telephone Dan, she heard a phone ringing from the bag. She fumbled through the clothes and located the phone. The call was from Emiko. Rather than talk to Emiko before Hans was out of surgery, Yoko let the call go to message. And that's what happened when she tried Dan's number, her call went straight to his messages. This meant Dan was with the chief and might not be free for some time. She tried Zoran, who picked up on the first ring.

"I'm at Mount Sinai Hospital with Hans," Yoko said. Before Zoran could say more than, "Yes, Yoko," she continued, "We were walking in Central Park and he was shot in the left arm. He just went into the OR. The bullet exited and I don't know if it's possible to recover it."

"I will leave the precinct at once and join you as soon as possible," Zoran said. "I know Ben Gurley, the Deputy Inspector at the 23rd. I will arrange it so that you and I will be allowed to sit in with the detectives who will be sent to interview Hans when he has recovered from surgery. After that, if Hans is able to continue, we will spend time with him."

Minutes later two men arrived who didn't look as if they needed the ER. They surveyed the crowd in the waiting room then walked over to where Yoko leaned against a wall. "Dr. Kamimura?" the older man said. He held out his hand when she nodded. "I'm Ned Raymond, Good to meet you, Zoran Zeissing called from the one-three. Said to tell you he'll be here soon."

"Frank Jenkins." The second detective shook hands with Yoko. "So you're the civilian consultant the one-three added to their squad. We've heard about your work with Zoran and Dan. My pleasure."

"Thanks," Yoko said.

"We have the use of a room, more of a broom closet, down the hall," Ned Raymond said. "We can talk there until the victim is out of surgery." He led the way. He was right, the room was tiny. Cleaning supplies filled the shelves and folding chairs were stacked against one wall. Frank Jenkins pulled out chairs, "Make yourself comfortable."

When they were settled, Jenkins said, "What can you tell us?"

Yoko gave the two detectives a quick summary of what had happened in the park.

"Strange only one bullet," Raymond said.

"I heard a single shot. Hans was hit once," Yoko said.

"We checked—there are no reports of attacks or gunfire in the immediate area or anywhere else in the park for the hour before or after the shooting," Raymond said. "Do you know any reason why someone might be gunning for this man, this Reiniger?"

Yoko was debating how to answer when the door opened and Zoran came in. He listened without comment as Yoko filled him in on the shooting, looking relieved when she added, "The EMTs said the wound was clean and that Hans was in reasonable shape." Yoko sat back and watched in admiration as Zoran fielded the queries of the detectives from the 23rd.

Ned Raymond's cell phone rang. The message he received was short. He thanked the caller and shut off the phone. "Mr. Reiniger is out of surgery, turns out it was straightforward, simpler than expected, an unusual wound that missed the bone and arteries," he said. "The surgeon's given permission for us to see him. Time to go talk to the victim."

Surprise filled Hans Reiniger's eyes when four people filed into the hospital cubicle where he lay. Zoran introduced the two detectives from the 23rd. "They are here to talk to you about the shooting in Central Park."

Hans answered the questions without hesitation, even the last one. "No, I don't know why anyone would want to kill me." His puzzlement sounded genuine.

After a short silence, Ned Raymond, no doubt thinking the answers weren't as informative as he would have liked, said with a resignation he didn't try to hide, "We have taken enough of your time, Mr. Reiniger. We'll leave you in the capable hands of your friends from the one-three." The two detectives from the 23rd left.

"Hans, do you feel able to continue to talk with us now?" Zoran asked.

"Definitely," Hans said. "Where were we?" he asked Yoko. "Have you had time to tell Zoran about our conversation up to the point when I was knocked off my feet by a stray bullet?"

"No, why don't you tell him?" Yoko said, thinking it interesting Hans called it a stray bullet.

Zoran sat in silence while Hans explained the conclusions Ben and he had reached about Thomas Hardy and the possible involvement of Bert Balducci. When the Romani was done, Zoran glanced at Yoko but before he could speak, a nurse bustled in.

"We have a room for you now, Mr. Reiniger," she told Hans.

"I don't want to stay," Hans said.

"The doctor has not discharged you," the nurse began.

"I can discharge myself, can't I?"

The nurse pursed her lips. "You really need to stay. For one thing, you ought not to be alone tonight."

Hans looked from Zoran to Yoko, the appeal on his face clear as he assessed the possibility of an invitation to stay with one of them. Yoko cleared her throat and all heads swiveled to stare at her. "Mr. Reiniger could stay with me," she said. "That's if you'd like to do so, Hans."

Hans beamed like a man pardoned from prison and thanked Yoko. The nurse left, mumbling in disapproval about paperwork.

"We have a reasonable compromise," Zoran said. "It will be easier to talk in private, Hans, unless you need to rest?"

"Don't tell the nurse, but I could use a nap," Hans said.

"We can resume our conversation in the morning. I will drive you to the apartment where Yoko lives," Zoran said. "Traffic at this time of night is not severe but it will take time. I am sure the nurse would agree that a quiet evening and early night would be good."

Zoran was correct.

"If you insist on discharging yourself, I hope you will at least rest," said the doctor who arrived to sign paperwork. "I see it's useless to persuade you to stay." Behind the back of the departing doctor, Hans flashed a triumphant thumbs-up sign to Yoko and Zoran although by now he was drooping with fatigue.

"Here you are, Hans," Yoko said, giving the Romani the bag of his belongings. She and Zoran waited outside while Hans changed out of the hospital johnny. Minutes later, Hans was free to leave and escorted to the hospital front entrance in the obligatory wheelchair by a cheerful orderly.

It didn't take long to settle Hans in the guest bedroom. Dan's sweatpants were a decent fit and a baggy T-shirt slipped over the bandage on the Romani's arm. Yoko took him a cup of ginger tea and a plate of chocolate chip cookies and found him perched on the windowsill, staring into the night.

"Did you check your messages? You may have one from Emiko," Yoko said.

"Thanks, I heard it." Hans didn't turn from the window. "Emiko wanted me to know she's moved to the hospice residence because she needs inpatient care. I called back but was switched through to someone in the office. No one wants to guess how much longer she has but they said she is eating and that's a good sign. Emiko left word I could visit, I'll call in the morning."

"I'm so sorry," Yoko said.

"We've expected this," Hans said. He turned and faced Yoko and tried to smile. "I saw Emiko a few days ago and she asked me to give you her love. Said she was glad you'd visited and seen her studio."

Yoko's eyes filled with tears. Mingled with her sorrow was the stark truth that Emiko would welcome the release from illness. "When you call Emiko, will you ask if I can visit her?" Hans looked at Yoko, inquiry clear on his face. "When I saw her," Yoko continued, "Emiko said she wanted to talk more about Ben's death but it was late."

Hans sighed. "What if I ask if we can visit together?"

"That would be good," Yoko said. "I'll say goodnight. I hope you sleep well." Yoko wiped tears from her face with her sleeve, too tired to search for a tissue. She made her way slowly down the hall to her bedroom. It was 9:45 p.m. but Hans was not the only one who needed an early night.

Loud rapping on her bedroom door woke Yoko from a deep sleep. "Yes?" She scrambled out of bed, amazed the clock showed it was barely 11 p.m.

"It's Hardy's wife. She needs help."

"What?" Yoko flung open the door and saw Hans heading for the front door, talking over his shoulder as he hurried down the hall.

"Pansy was on the phone with her sister venting about Hardy's mood swings. He overheard and flew into a rage. She locked herself in the bedroom but he's threatening to shoot himself or her. Coming?"

"Be right with you," Yoko said, horrified. She wriggled into clothes, calling Zoran as she searched for her sneakers. She and Hans snagged a cab cruising Gramercy Park East. Light traffic and a cab driver with a heavy foot on the accelerator meant they arrived in minutes at LaGuardia Place where the Hardys had a loft.

"I don't remember the number." Hans sounded panicked.

"S'okay, pal," the driver said, "LaGuardia Place is all of two blocks long. Will you recognize the place?"

"Um, not sure," Hans said.

"Didn't Pansy say they lived opposite the public flower garden, over a store?" Yoko said.

"Oh, that's right," Hans said.

"We're opposite the garden," the driver said, "This it? Uh oh, we're not the first. Looks like trouble."

"This is the place," Hans said.

Yoko's heart sank at the sight of two police cruisers, a fire engine and an ambulance outside the small building. Police tape was strung up to prevent pedestrians from walking on that side of the street. Onlookers were milling around on the sidewalk opposite. Yoko shivered. Her nerves were stretched tight. Would Hardy really shoot himself or his wife? Yoko felt ill at the thought of more death.

Zoran, who was standing next to a tall man talking into a cruiser's radio phones, beckoned Yoko and Hans over.

"Although we are outside the official boundaries of the one-three precinct, we have been invited to liaise with Commander Garnham." Zoran indicated the tall man, who was now listening to a message that crackled over the radio. "We have this courtesy because Hardy is a subject in one of our ongoing investigations. I will introduce you to the commander when he is free. It is possible that one or both of you may be able to offer helpful suggestions in this situation."

"What's going on?" Yoko asked.

Zoran was not to be distracted by the frenzied activity around them. He started at the beginning. "The police had a call from Mrs. Hardy's sister. As you know, she had been on the phone with Mrs. Hardy when Mr. Hardy started threatening his wife. Andrea Smythe, a mediator, is upstairs trying to talk to Hardy, who is still raging and vowing to shoot someone. There are only two loft apartments and they are on the second floor of the building over the ground-floor store, which is closed at this time of night. The lofts have a separate entrance from the store. One loft is rented by Hardy, the other belongs to the owners of the lofts who are out of town."

"Is Pansy all right?"

"A policewoman reached Mrs. Hardy by phone. She is scared but so far nothing has happened despite her husband threatening harm."

"I've known Hardy for years. What if I went upstairs to speak to him?" Hans asked.

Zoran shook his head. "Thank you. At this stage we have someone who is armed and has the potential to be violent. It is impossible to predict how events will unfold. We cannot allow a civilian to become involved in such a dangerous situation."

"Besides, you've already been wounded," Yoko said.

Uneasy minutes passed. One of the police cars received a radio message. Yoko couldn't make out the words. Two of the uniforms got out of the car, bulletproof vests snug over their chests. Another car arrived with police reinforcements. One of the men who emerged from the second car had a red object tucked under one arm. It was obvious it was heavy and Yoko recognized it as a battering ram. She felt dread at the confrontation that looked inevitable. Police poured into the building. Outside, people fell silent and strained to hear what was happening. Another car arrived and parked next to where Commander Garnham stood. Yoko recognized the woman who stepped out.

"That's Dr. Roz, she's a psychiatrist," Yoko told Hans in a low voice. "She counsels officers who've been involved in major trauma like gang warfare and gunfights."

"Another mediator?" Hans was puzzled.

"No," Zoran replied. "Commander Garnham informed me he called for Dr. Roz. He is willing to try the non-confrontational tactic she wrote about in her latest article in *The Police Chief*."

Yoko swallowed hard, hope mixing with her surprise. "I read that article. You mean Hardy's place will be flooded with tranquilizing gas?"

"Yes."

"How?"

"The owners of the loft apartment adjacent to where Hardy lives have been located. Officers have permission to enter the place and pump the gas through the heating vents."

The non-confrontational tactic was a wild success. While gas was being pumped in from the adjacent loft, a policewoman had Pansy Hardy on the phone, giving her instructions.

"Block the vents in the bedroom then open the window and stand by it."

"What's going on?" Pansy asked, her voice shaky.

"Hurry," the policewoman said, "We'll be able to rescue you soon."

Andrea Smythe, the mediator, was able to keep Hardy talking. He was in the main loft area and his rants, interspersed with impressive strings of curses, didn't make much sense. Psychotic, the mediator thought, he's having a massive meltdown. She countered Hardy's threats with calm answers. Hardy began to slur his words. Within minutes, the mediator had the satisfaction of hearing a thud and a clatter.

"Mr. Hardy," she said, face pressed close to the door. "Mr. Hardy, talk to me. Are you all right?" She listened to silence. When Hardy did not answer, she felt sure the thud she'd heard had been Hardy falling down, anesthetized by the tranquilizing gas. It was possible the clatter was his gun hitting the floor. The mediator moved out of the way and the officers who had been standing behind her, surged forward to break open the door. The wood splintered and the door flew open. Pulling oxygen masks over their faces, the police, followed by Dr. Roz, entered the loft with slow caution.

Hardy was flat on his back in the middle of the room, a gun near him. Dr. Roz knelt beside him and felt his pulse. "He'll be all right," she said. Hardy stirred and Dr. Roz gave him an injection to stem off nausea from the tranquilizing gas that had flooded his system and a second injection to keep him docile in the event the effects of the gas wore off sooner than expected.

Officers spread throughout the loft, opening windows and setting up fans to help remove the residue of tranquilizing gas.

Next to arrive were EMTs, who were also wearing oxygen masks. They had two stretchers, which they adjusted into chairs. "The elevator's small, it will only hold a single chair stretcher and two EMTs at a time," one told Dr. Roz. "Handcuffs for him? Do we need an officer with us?"

"No, he won't regain consciousness immediately," Dr. Roz said.

"Good," was the answer. "We'll be right back for the other person." Hardy was wheeled onto the elevator and taken down to the street where he was loaded into one of the waiting ambulances.

The policewoman who had been on the phone with Pansy Hardy tapped on the bedroom door and called, "Mrs. Hardy, it's safe to come out. I have an oxygen mask for you. Your husband has been taken downstairs to an ambulance. A doctor is here, waiting to see you. Can you unlock the door?"

"I feel woozy."

"Why don't you come out? The doctor can help."

Pansy Hardy emerged from the bedroom, swaying and clutching her head. The policewoman helped settle the oxygen mask on Pansy's head and guided her to the hallway where Dr. Roz gave her an injection to ward off nausea.

When she reached the street level, Pansy Hardy pulled off the mask. "Hans, Yoko, you came," she called out when she saw them and opened her arms wide. Commander Garnham nodded to Hans and Yoko, who walked over and took turns hugging Pansy.

"Is Thomas all right?" Pansy asked. "I thought he was going to kill himself. Or me."

"He's all right," Yoko said. "How are you?"

"It was hell on wheels but stiff upper lip." Pansy giggled, a raucous sound. "I'm not hysterical," she said. "It just sounds that way. What's going to happen now?"

"You'll be taken to the hospital."

"I'm exhausted. I could sleep for a week. Can you two visit me tomorrow?"

"Yes," Hans and Yoko chimed together.

They stood with Zoran and watched as the ambulances drove away. Zoran and Commander Garnham had a brief talk that ended in a hearty handshake, then Zoran drove Yoko and Hans back to Gramercy Park.

"Tomorrow, when the hospital and Dr. Roz give permission, I will interview Hardy," Zoran said. "Do you want an officer with you when you talk with Mrs. Hardy, Hans and Yoko? Perhaps the policewoman who escorted her from the loft?"

Yoko thought for a moment. "Thanks, I don't think that's necessary."

"I agree with Yoko," Hans said.

Home at last, Yoko closed the front door of her apartment and leaned against it, smiling in relief at Hans. He had walked in ahead of her and gave a great sigh as he said, "I hope not to repeat any of this evening's activities."

"Oh, good grief, how are you? You were supposed to have an early night."

"LaGuardia Place was okay. No one shot at me," Hans said, sounding surprised. He was wearing the jacket that had the bullet hole in the sleeve, the jacket he'd not wanted cut. In the drama at LaGuardia Place, no one had noticed or if they had, no comment had been made. Surely it didn't get past Zoran's eagle eye. Yoko wondered if Zoran would ever mention it.

"How about some warm almond milk? I'll add a shot of brandy," she offered.

"Straight brandy for me," Hans said.

Yoko settled for warm almond milk.

13 Decisions, Decisions

The next morning, Yoko was up early. After a shower, she checked her SUNY email to review what needed to be done for the NORA conference. No new requests had arrived so she was up to date for the conference. This meant she had free time to visit Pansy Hardy that morning with Hans. Later, if Emiko felt like a visit, they'd travel to the assisted living place where someone from Caring Hospice in Brooklyn was helping Emiko. Yoko wasn't surprised to find Hans in the kitchen, sipping herbal tea. He was relaxed and did not look like a man who'd had a bullet go through his arm less than twenty-four hours ago and witnessed what was too close to a catastrophe at LaGuardia Place. Oatmeal was bubbling on the stove and a dish of slivered almonds and a jar of maple syrup were lined up on the table.

"I hope you don't mind but I thought food to stick to our ribs might be a good idea."

"Great minds think alike," Yoko said. "How are you and how's your arm?"

"I'm doing well. The arm was quite sore last night so I took some of the Arnica you gave me and slept through the night. The arm felt pretty normal this morning, no pain."

After breakfast, Hans telephoned Emiko and Yoko called Zoran. And, like all plans, the circumstances had changed so their plans had to change as well.

"Emiko says this morning would be good for us to visit," Hans said. "Is that okay?"

"Better than okay—we can see Pansy Hardy in the afternoon. Zoran will let me know the time."

The subway was the best option for them to reach Brooklyn and

Hans knew which trains to take. When they entered the building where Emiko was staying, the front desk receptionist directed them to her room. Their tap on the door brought an immediate response.

"Hello and welcome." The pleasant greeting was from the woman who opened the door. She stepped outside and pulled the door shut after her. "I'm Maria from Caring Hospice. You're expected. I'll give you some privacy." She ushered them into the room, whispering quick advice. "Best not to overstay. Don't be surprised at long pauses when Emiko talks, it's a result of the illness."

"How good to see you." Emiko's smile was wide. "Make yourselves comfortable." Emiko pointed at two chairs placed one on either side of her bed. She was pale and her speech was slow but the warmth in her voice was strong. "Look," she said, and her visitors followed her gaze and saw that hanging on the wall opposite the bed was the Ansel Adams' photo of the Sierras. "I brought this from my studio because I love it and not just because it's by the person who helped me choose my life path. I love it because it shows how we learned to see beyond the barbed wire when we were in Manzanar." Her eyes were reflective as she remembered those years. Emiko looked at Hans and Yoko saw that even that slight movement was made with caution as if it was painful.

"You'll remember, Hans, how puzzled we were over Ben's sudden death when the hospital could not explain the cause?"

"Yes," Hans said.

"Has that changed? Is anything new known?"

"I'm sorry, Yoko tells me there's nothing new," Hans said.

One of the long pauses Maria had warned them of came. Emiko gazed into the distance and was silent. After some minutes, she looked at Yoko and again it was obvious even that slow movement was painful.

"Ever since you visited me, Yoko, I've been resurrecting memories, thinking back to the time in Manzanar. I remembered something strange that happened after Ben and his family left the camp and wondered if it might help understand more about his death."

Yoko and Hans waited.

"Ben's family, like most of the families from Bainbridge Island, transferred from Manzanar to the camp in Minidoka," Emiko said, her voice low. "No sooner had they left than rumors started that Ben was an informant. Claims about traitors caused such terrible unrest and arrests were frequent. George Fujita spread the word that Ben had spied on others, turning them into the authorities." Emiko sighed and stopped speaking. Minutes went by before she spoke again and it was apparent she didn't know she'd been silent for a stretch of time.

"We knew George hated Ben and were sure George was lying but Ben and his family weren't in Manzanar to deny what George said." Emiko sighed. "I don't know if this is useful but I had to share it with you."

"Thank you, Emiko, it's a starting point. Someone could have carried a grudge over the years," Yoko said. "We'll see what we can unearth."

"It might be a wild goose chase," Emiko said.

Hans shifted in his seat. "Thank you, Emiko. It's very possible someone kept a vendetta alive. I've known of families where ill feelings festered for generations."

Emiko closed her eyes for a moment. Yoko and Hans glanced at each other. They stood without needing to speak.

"We'll let you rest," Yoko said.

Hans cleared his throat yet his voice was husky when he spoke. "I'll call you tomorrow."

"I'm grateful you both came." Emiko held out her hands and Yoko and Hans linked hands with her in a silent parting.

Maria was waiting outside Emiko's room and walked with Hans and Yoko to the main entrance. "I'm glad you could visit. Emiko was looking forward to seeing you. She is still eating and that's a good sign."

They were headed for the subway when Yoko had a phone call from Zoran.

"The doctor has suggested you and Mr. Reiniger could visit Mrs. Hardy at three this afternoon."

Yoko glanced at her watch. "We'll be there."

"How was your visit with . . ." Zoran hesitated, ". . . the architect who was in Manzanar?"

"Emiko made an interesting suggestion." Yoko said, supplying the name Zoran had avoided using, knowing Zoran was reluctant to use a first name when he hadn't met the person.

"Yes?" In his typical way, Zoran was brevity itself.

Yoko filled him in on their talk with Emiko.

"It is worth exploring," Zoran said, "although many of those incarcerated have passed on."

"The older generation has gone, even some of the younger generation," Yoko replied.

"I trust we can meet later today to discuss what we have learned?"

"Sounds like a plan," Yoko said.

On the way to the subway for the return trip to Manhattan, Yoko and Hans were quiet, each thinking about the visit.

Yoko broke the silence. "I'm glad we were able to see Emiko."

"Yes," Hans agreed. "She is brave, never a complaint, no bitterness. She's just thinking about how to help."

"Do you think there's anything to her suggestion?"

"It's possible. It may be tricky to find out more."

"Pizza?" Hans suggested, spotting a Famous Ray's. They were back in Manhattan and had walked a few blocks from the subway, enjoying the change of pace from switching from one train to another and sitting through frequent station stops. Hunger satisfied by hot slices of pizza topped with broccoli and red pepper, they decided to go to Stuyvesant Square Park, which was close to Beth Israel where Pansy Hardy was recovering. They sat on a bench near the dog park, watching dogs romping and running. It was relaxing, knowing they were within walking distance of their next appointment. Yoko put thoughts of anything related to work out of her mind.

"Time to breathe," she said. "We've almost an hour before we're due at Beth Israel."

The afternoon sun was warm and Yoko dozed off. A child ran past, calling to a friend and Yoko shook herself awake. She snuck a look at Hans. His chin was lowered to his chest. He deserved forty winks. Was it really only yesterday he'd been hit by a bullet? The yipping of dogs tangled in fun brought Hans upright. He checked his watch.

"Time for us to move on?"

"Just about," Yoko agreed.

"What's next after we visit Pansy?"

"Zoran wants us to touch base with him so we can share what we've learned from our meetings. He said Pansy Hardy had a visit from detectives at the 23rd precinct this morning but because she's part of our ongoing investigation, they're leaving the in-depth work to us. Zoran's meeting with Thomas Hardy this afternoon."

"I'm invited to a debriefing? I'm coming up in the world," Hans laughed.

"It's more like connect the dots," Yoko said.

"If we find out why Ben's phone was tapped, that might take us a long way toward understanding what happened." Hans said. "You know, I'm not surprised that Thomas Hardy had a mega meltdown. Ben believed Hardy had anger that ran deep. The man often made generalized comments, talking in a casual way about terminating someone or a group of people who're ticking him off. You know what he called Ben behind his back? A 'wet nurse,' said he'd never go to one, never needed one."

"Maybe Zoran will discover what meds Hardy's been on, legal or otherwise. The man must have TBI."

They had ample time to stroll the short distance to Beth Israel and still reach there by 3. As they entered the building, Yoko thought of her frantic rush to the hospital the night Ben called. It was the last time she'd seen her cousin and being there again dredged up the pain of that loss. She consoled herself with her sense of anticipation that answers might be close.

Hans raised his eyebrows in surprise at the sight of a policewoman seated outside the door to Pansy's room.

"Standard procedure," Yoko assured him and she knocked on the door.

"Go right in," the policewoman said, "Mrs. Hardy is expecting you."

Hans glanced at Yoko with an amused "I told you so" look when they found Pansy Hardy sitting in a chair by the window, chatting on her cell phone. She ended the call as soon as she saw them and gave a limp wave. Pansy had dark circles under her eyes and looked as jumpy and nervous as she had when she was brought out of the loft building at LaGuardia Place.

"How are you, Pansy?" Yoko asked.

"I've been better," Pansy said, pointing at the two chairs that had been placed near her. "Have a pew. How is Thomas, that bastard? If he had as restless a night as I did, he won't be a happy man. I've called more than once but haven't been able to get any information out of anyone except that he's doing as well as possible."

"That's all I know," Yoko confessed.

"I suppose you want to know why last night happened?" Pansy shuddered. "I still can't believe it."

"Your husband overheard you talking to your sister about his erratic behavior and went ballistic," Hans said.

"Right," Pansy nodded. "Thomas never used to get so cranky." Her eyes flicked away and Yoko wondered if Pansy was going to hide the truth. "No, this was about something way worse than his mood swings." Pansy swallowed a sob but squared her shoulders and took a deep breath. "I wasn't snooping but I stumbled across a file online." The emotion that filled her face was outrage. "My husband was keeping secrets, terrible ones. He was buying drugs." Words poured out in a steady stream. "I couldn't understand where the money was coming from. It wasn't out of his business account—you know he runs surveillance for companies? Industrial espionage." She snickered though her face was serious. She waited until she was sure Yoko and Hans understood then went on.

"His business is small but keeps him busy. At least he's out of the house a lot. I do the books, file tax returns, everything. No, the online file I found was secret. It showed a huge lump sum credit in a separate bank account, one I'd never seen, that dated back years. I was furious he'd kept this from me. He told everyone he had to start his business because our expenses kept going up and our savings didn't grow at the same rate."

Pansy paused. Yoko bit her lip to stop from saying, "Tell us about the drugs. What about them?" She knew better than to ask now, any comment might break Pansy's mood. Did Pansy know where the money came from? Lottery winnings? The stock market?

"I researched the hell out of that file," Pansy said. "It took hours but what I discovered was mind-blowing."

Hans allowed himself a small sound. "Hmm." It spurred Pansy on.

"It is so humiliating." Pansy's hands twisted in never-ending motion in her lap. "Thomas has always calculated the odds in his favor but this was outright theft."

"Theft?" Yoko repeated.

"It goes back to the war, the big one in the forties." Pansy glanced at Yoko. "You of all people must know the government in their infinite wisdom locked up people from certain backgrounds."

"Yes," Yoko said. "Japanese Americans as well as Italians and Germans were put in camps." Where was Pansy going with this? Had Hardy been involved in military looting? He was too young to be in WWII. Pansy's next words set Yoko straight.

"Thomas followed his dad into the Marines," Pansy said. "His dad was a major and had a pal in the battalion who was a financial wizard. That pal found a way to siphon off funds from the frozen assets of the people who were locked up during the war. After his father died, Thomas inherited his dad's share."

"Which group?" Hans asked. "Japanese Americans?"

"Right. Italians too," Pansy said.

Yoko was speechless. She'd read that the amount "lost" by Japanese Americans had been over $27 million. She'd never discovered figures for financial losses for Italians who were locked up. The US government had made reparations to Japanese American survivors of the incarceration in the camps but Yoko hadn't seen any information about reparations to Italians.

"Yes," Pansy admitted. "Before I discovered the online file, one night when we were out drinking with Anna and Bert, Thomas made a stupid joke about people—he actually said, 'Your people,' to Bert—never knowing what happened to their funds when the government put them in camps during World War II. 'Someone knows,' he said, all mysterious."

"What did Bert say?"

"He was livid, accused Thomas of stealing money or knowing who did."

"Thomas flat out denied that, said he'd read it online."

"Do you think Bert believed your husband?"

"Bert was suspicious. So was I, something didn't feel right. Days later I discovered the e-file by pure accident. I had to find out more so I kept looking for info. I feel betrayed after all these years." Pansy put her head in her hands and wept.

"I'm so sorry." Yoko thought back to the tense body language and irate talk she'd seen between Hardy and Balducci at Ben's wake. Even if he didn't know Hardy's secret, the possibility would have rankled with Bert.

Pansy sighed and mopped her tears. "That's it, the whole gory story. What a sham of a marriage. I know damn all about my husband. But I still love him. Am I a fool?"

Yoko looked at Hans. How did one answer that?

"The heart wants what it wants," Hans said.

A ghost of a smile crossed Pansy's face and she turned to Yoko. "I won't be a victim. Do you think he'll change?"

Yoko leaned over and hugged Pansy. "Change is possible but your husband would have to want it." Why add that change took hard work.

Pansy was quiet. Had she told all she knew? Yoko had to ask. "Your husband was able to hide the drugs from you?"

"He must have kept them on his truck," Pansy admitted, anger flaring. "He kept the truck locked, claimed he didn't want valuable tools and equipment disappearing. The truck is off the streets when he's not driving it." Pansy's comments were peppered with sniffs and gulps. "He has a deal with the owner of some ritzy house in the Village where the private garage isn't used. When I asked, he said the family hired limos, didn't have cars." Pansy subsided into a gloomy silence.

Yoko waited. It was obvious no more revelations were coming. "Did you find out the type of drugs your husband was buying?" She held her breath. This was important.

"I checked the names, they were for anxiety. He would never go to a doctor, insisted he was fine. All these years, taking drugs behind my back."

A nurse came in. "Time to check Mrs. Hardy's vital signs."

"Do you want us to wait outside?"

"If you would."

Yoko and Hans were standing in the hall outside Pansy's room when the nurse came out. "A quick word," the nurse said. "Mrs. Hardy's blood pressure is up more than we like. The doctor has stressed she is to have as little stimulation as possible. The police who came this morning were only here for a short time and her vitals were okay afterwards. Do you think you'll be much longer?"

"No, just a few minutes," Yoko said. The nurse hurried off and Yoko said to Hans, "I was planning to ask Pansy what she knew about Hardy tapping phones though she said she'd told us everything. What do you think?"

"Right now, Pansy is a bundle of raw nerve endings," Hans said. "It doesn't sound as if she knew about the phones. Learning about one more of Hardy's deceptions might send her over the edge."

"True." Yoko thought for a moment. "This calls for diplomacy."

Pansy was intent on her cellphone when Yoko and Hans went back into the room. She looked up, her reluctance obvious. "I thought we were done."

"We are," Yoko said. "Before we say goodbye, I wondered if there's anything more you wanted to share with us?"

"My God. I told you everything." Pansy's laughter bordered on hysterics and Yoko was glad she'd kept the question low key. Pansy had laid her soul bare. It was unlikely she knew about Hardy tapping phones. The poor woman had been through enough. Time for a graceful exit.

"Thank you, Pansy, you've been very helpful," Yoko said. "Rest up."

Hans murmured his goodbyes and before he and Yoko were out of the room, Pansy was immersed in wordless communication with her cellphone. She looked as if she was about to throw it across the room.

14 Denouement?

"Dr. Kamimura, Detective Zeissing is waiting for you in the chief's office," the desk sergeant at the one-three said. He assessed Hans in a rapid glance and looked at Yoko in query.

"Mr. Reiniger is expected," Yoko said and the desk sergeant waved them on.

Yoko was surprised to find Dan as well as Zoran in the chief's office.

"I wouldn't miss this for the world," Dan said, picking up on her astonishment. "The chief is off for a few days, family trip with his wife. I'm free of CT work. Another bonus, his office is available for us to meet."

"Detective Riley is correct," Zoran said, seating himself behind the chief's desk. "Chief Sanders is on leave and has given us permission to use his office. He was aware we would have Mr. Reiniger joining us." Zoran was silent until everyone was settled. He and Dan exchanged looks. Zoran gave the subtlest of nods and Dan picked up the conversation.

"For someone who'd been tranquilized and taken into custody after an epic rant, Hardy surfaced long enough to break out of the hospital. He must have the constitution of an ox. At least he wasn't armed."

Was Dan playing one of his jokes? One look at the chagrin on Zoran's face told Yoko this was not funny.

"We believe he hid behind the bathroom door after the psychiatrist's visit. A hospital orderly came in to check Hardy's vitals and thought the room was empty. She and the policeman on duty outside Hardy's room rushed down to the nurses' station. The coast was clear! Hardy walked out, bold as brass."

The silence in the chief's office stretched across weighty seconds as Yoko and Hans absorbed the shocking news.

"Is Hardy still free?" Yoko asked.

"Did you catch him yet?" Hans said a second later.

Again there was a subtle nod to Dan from Zoran. Yoko had never seen the brilliant detective looking so morose.

"We think we've got a handle on his whereabouts," Dan said. He tried to sound confident. "It won't be long before we pick him up."

"Dr. Kamimura, until we have the news that Mr. Hardy is back at the hospital, would you tell us what you learned from Mrs. Hardy?" Zoran asked.

Yoko, with occasional additions from Hans, shared what they'd heard.

"What?" Dan said. He looked astounded.

"Thank you. You will be interested to hear what we learned," Zoran said. "Our IT department discovered material on the two computers taken from the Hardy loft at LaGuardia Place that presents a different analysis." Zoran launched into an explanation that left Yoko and Hans dumbfounded.

"Mrs. Hardy was keeping more than one set of books of financial matters. It is common enough among people who wish to defraud the government and others. It is obvious that one set was for the IRS. It would seem that the computer had files her husband could access but the laptop was for her exclusive use and had yet a third set of books. The laptop also had a file showing a bank account in her name, not her husband's, and the funds in that account were substantial."

"*So?*" The word exploded from Hans. Everyone looked at him in surprise. Hans apologized. "I was shocked, I spoke in my Romani language," Hans said. "*So* means What?"

"Pansy Hardy told us it was her husband who'd been keeping a secret account." Yoko struggled to keep disbelief out of her voice.

"She told us a pack of lies." Hans was disgusted.

"Devious woman," Yoko murmured. "To think I felt sorry for her."

The look Zoran fixed on Yoko was thoughtful. "The computer files have the true story," he said. "We have been in touch with the bank and Mrs. Hardy was in fact the owner of the account that is in her name. The laptop is a MacBook Pro and the software is different from that of the large computer, which uses Windows. It was a clever way to discourage Mr. Hardy from using the laptop."

Zoran's phone rang and the others twitched in nervous reaction. What fresh news was surfacing? Zoran ended the short call with a brief, "Thank you." He stood and the change in his body language was dramatic. He was back leading the quest for justice. Yoko had seen this in Zoran before, his response to the challenge of police work.

"Mrs. Hardy is under arrest. On returning to her home and discovering the computers had been removed, she started to rant about the intrusion of privacy, demanding that her property be returned." Bemusement flitted across Zoran's face. "She lost control of her senses." It was clear that Zoran was surprised someone would allow themselves to behave in such a way. "Mrs. Hardy tried to wrestle the gun from the police officer who had accompanied her from the hospital. We have ascertained that Mrs. Hardy was an active member of the Westside Rifle and Pistol Range." Zoran paused, then added, deadpan, "Despite frequent visits, Mrs. Hardy was not considered an accurate shot."

Zoran allowed a moment for his stunned audience to absorb the news. "Mr. Hardy also has been captured and returned to the hospital. It is time for us to interview him and ascertain the truth." As he spoke, Zoran was heading out of the chief's office, making his way to the street.

"You want us to come with you?" Dan asked, hurrying to keep up with his partner. Dan never presumed to understand what went through Zoran's mind. He'd learned it was best to check each time, every time. Zoran always had a plan and it never ever was what anyone else would have considered. Dan had given up any effort to anticipate what might happen, preferring to ask direct questions, knowing he'd get direct answers.

"Yes. Detective Riley, on your way out, will you please pick up a tape recorder? Choose the strongest. I will use my small tape recorder but I want appropriate back up. Will you bring Mr. Reiniger with you to the hospital? I will take Dr. Kamimura. I propose that you and I interview Mr. Hardy. I want Dr. Kamimura and Mr. Reiniger stationed outside the room, listening in and monitoring the tape recorder."

To Yoko's frustration, Zoran observed the speed limit on the drive to the hospital. Why didn't Zoran use the damn siren? The OCD detective didn't speak until they reached the hospital and he had parked with meticulous care. "Now that we have heard the scenario Mrs. Hardy concocted, we will be able to compare it to whatever her husband reveals."

"What did Dr. Roz say about her interview with Thomas Hardy?" Yoko asked.

"That it was a difficult session but TBI was confirmed by the psychiatrist. Further, Dr. Roz explained that in his military schooling, Mr. Hardy learned a sense of detachment from his emotions and thus did not feel any connection with those he threatened."

"Do you think Hardy realized he had TBI if he was buying anti-anxiety drugs?" Yoko asked.

"Perhaps not in his conscious mind," Zoran replied. "Remember, Mrs. Hardy was also buying illegal drugs and somehow ensuring her husband had them, perhaps mixing them in his food."

"To think I felt pity for her," Yoko grumbled.

"Frustrating indeed," Zoran agreed. "Mrs. Hardy was clever enough to slant the facts so that she was viewed as the victim."

"She's a convincing actor," Yoko said. "Whatever set Hardy off on the rampage, it wasn't what Pansy told us."

Yoko shuddered, recalling the terrifying standoff that had been created from a fabric of lies. Incredible no one had been shot or seriously injured. TBI triggered damage, emotional and physical. When the dust settled and the case was put to rest, Yoko would let Thomas Hardy know he could go to one of the SUNY clinics or visit a practitioner of optometric vision therapy for help.

Zoran and Yoko waited in the hospital lobby for Dan and Hans to catch up with them.

"Hard to believe the power in this tiny piece. It's astonishing." Hans showed them the recording unit he was carrying. "Dan has the receiver in his pocket. We'll be able to record everything even though we'll be outside Hardy's room."

The group walked down the hall to Hardy's room, Zoran and Dan in the lead, Yoko narrowly avoided bumping into Zoran when he stopped abruptly. She caught sight of the empty chair outside Hardy's room. What the hell now? Where was the policeman who was supposed to be on duty and guarding the door?

Dan reached a warning hand behind him. "Yoko, Hans, stay back." He pulled out his revolver. Zoran slowly withdrew his. He rapped on the door and flung it open. The only sound was the noise the door made as it crashed back against the wall. Yoko's breathing rasped in her ears like a buzz saw. The two detectives moved cautiously across the threshold, stopping inside the room. Yoko craned to see around Dan and spotted a figure sprawled near the open window. Other than the man on the floor—an officer from the one-three, was he dead?—the room looked empty.

Zoran and Dan fanned out with swift steps, Dan moved toward the bathroom, Zoran to the open window. Zoran looked out of the window then, satisfied Hardy was not to be seen outside, he turned back and bent over the officer. He felt the man's jugular and called in a quiet voice, "Officer down, no sign of a wound. Breathing regular. Dr. Kamimura, will you alert hospital staff?"

Zoran bent over the prone figure again. This time, he felt for the officer's gun but came up empty-handed. Yoko's heart sank. Hardy hadn't shot the officer but had stolen the gun. She was reluctant to budge from her place at the door, her attention riveted on the situation in the room.

"Want me to take the message to the nurses' station?" Hans whispered when Yoko didn't move.

"Would you?" Yoko said, grateful for his offer. She watched as Zoran joined Dan outside the bathroom door. Dan jerked open the door and he and Zoran stepped back on either side of it. "Police, come out with your hands up." No sound was heard. Dan stepped into the bathroom cautiously. "Man down," he called. Zoran followed Dan and disappeared from Yoko's sight. Seconds later Zoran walked out of the bathroom.

"Hardy is unconscious. He is bleeding from a head wound. Dan is staunching the blood with a towel. Will you alert the hospital staff to this additional need for expert care?" Zoran shook his head and felt in his pocket for one of the sanitary wipes he always carried. He might not have touched Hardy or the blood but Zoran was a germophobe and his overriding obsession was with cleanliness. Zoran called hospitals germ factories and loathed them more than most everything else on his list of what to avoid. Only the urgent call to duty propelled him inside Beth Israel, despite his inclination to avoid the place.

Hospital staff arrived. The policeman on the floor, still out cold, was moved to a different room. Zoran requested a report on the man's condition and a nurse returned to explain, "The officer has recovered consciousness. He has a massive bruise on the back of his head and is not sure what happened."

Two orderlies carried Hardy to his bed so that the doctor could evaluate the wound. Zoran directed Yoko and Hans to be prepared to sit outside the room and activate the recording device. "If we are able to conduct an interview, you will be ready to make a backup recording of the conversation," he said. "I am calling for more officers. We do not need a repeat of an escape."

"It's not serious," the doctor explained, as he tended to Hardy's head. "Mr. Hardy may have been trying to kill himself. If so, the bullet was wide of the mark."

"Strange," Dan said. "He was in the Marines, must know how to operate a gun."

"Not all suicide attempts are serious," the doctor said. "Many are pleas for help."

Hardy regained consciousness as the doctor was finishing his ministrations. The nurse at the doctor's side had an injection ready to help calm the patient. Alarm flared in Hardy's eyes at the sight of Zoran and Dan. His eyes widened more when he saw Yoko and Hans standing near the door.

Zoran knew what to do. "Let us move outside." Zoran led the way to the hall, where the four waited to learn what would be next. The group swelled to seven when they were joined by three officers from the one-three. Nods were exchanged and the group stood ready for whatever action Zoran ordered.

The doctor came out of the room. "Doctor, when do you think Detective Riley and I can talk to Mr. Hardy?" Zoran asked.

"I can't think of any reason for you to wait," the doctor said. "I'm not sure how cooperative he'll be but he is calm at the moment."

Before Zoran could speak, a cell phone rang. Hans was surprised to find it was his.

"Excuse me," he said and walked a few paces down the hall to take the call. The group heard him say, "I'll come right away." He hurried back to where the others stood. "That was Bert Balducci. He and Anna just came back from Long Island. Anna's ill. They went straight to Mount Sinai Hospital."

"That's the closest hospital to Grand Central," Dan said and turned to Yoko. "It might be helpful if you went with Hans."

"You're right," Yoko agreed. "What do you think, Hans?"

Hans hesitated. "What about the back-up recording?"

Zoran smiled. "We have people here now who can help. Please, both of you go. You can listen to the recordings later and we will confer." He turned to one of the officers. "Will you drive Dr. Kamimura and Mr. Reiniger to Mount Sinai Hospital then return here?"

"Has Anna Balducci been admitted?" Yoko asked at Mount Sinai's ER reception desk. Minutes later, she and Hans were shown to the cubicle where Anna lay, tethered to the bed by IVs. Bert, looking anxious, was fidgeting by her side.

"You came," Bert said. "Thank you. Anna's on meds but the doctor doesn't know what the problem is."

"Hi," Anna said, her voice faint. "I'm puzzling the doc."

One look at Anna and Yoko had such a strong sense of déjà vu that she bit her cheek to stop herself blurting, "Oh, God, no."

Anna's extreme pallor and irregular breathing was exactly what Yoko had witnessed when she'd rushed to see Ben at Beth Israel. The shocking clincher was that the pupils of Anna's eyes were shrunk to pinpoints. This was a serious indicator of trouble but what was the cause? Was this another situation where it was impossible to diagnose and therefore treat the illness?

"What is it, Yoko?" Hans asked. "Do you feel sick? You're almost as pale as Anna."

The question dragged Yoko back to the present with a start. She shook her head, unable to answer.

"What does the doctor say?" Hans asked Bert.

"He isn't sure but it may be intestinal or chemical poisoning. They're waiting for lab reports."

Anna groaned and clutched her abdomen. She was sweating heavily.

A nurse arrived and the doctor, who was holding a sheet of paper, was behind her. The nurse prepared to add something to one of Anna's IVs.

"Doctor, what can you do to help my wife?" Bert asked.

Yoko was certain she could predict the answer and the doctor's reply confirmed this.

"Your wife is receiving intravenous fluids to restore the loss of body fluids. The lab report rules out intestinal disease. This leaves us with poisoning, which is why we've started injections of atropine intramuscularly. This will help counteract any neuromuscular symptoms, which have the potential to be dangerous."

Bert shook his head, bewildered. "We just came back from a day visit to family in Long Island. We often go out there. I ate . . . we all ate . . . the same lunch, I made it myself, pasta primavera with broccoli, snow peas and zucchini, all fresh from the farmers' market. No one else is sick."

"Did you have shellfish?"

"No, no fish. Just pasta and veggies," Bert said.

"What did you drink?" Hans asked.

"Wine from the family vineyard," Bert said. "We all had the same wine."

Yoko was sure she knew why Hans asked his question. Had Anna drunk a lot? Could she have alcohol poisoning? Wouldn't the doctor have picked up on that?

Bert hesitated then said, "Would she be sick because she drank too much?" An annoyed "Bert!" came from Anna and Bert backpedaled. "She's a slip of a woman, a little goes a long way."

It was the doctor's turn to look puzzled. "It's not alcohol poisoning," he said. "The patient doesn't have any symptoms like blue-tinged skin, low body temperature to the point of hypothermia, vomiting or signs of confusion."

"I guess that's a relief," Bert said.

"I'll get back to you when I have the rest of the lab reports." The doctor left.

Hans touched Yoko's arm. "Let's talk outside," he said. Yoko followed him out.

"What is it?" Hans asked, his voice low. "You know something?"

"Anna has the same symptoms Ben had," Yoko whispered.

Hans was shocked. "Are you sure?"

"Dante Nicosian, the city's top coroner, did the autopsy. He ran a number of tests and so far has failed to be certain about the cause of Ben's death."

Once Yoko had said aloud what she'd been thinking, she felt she'd cleared a hurdle. She started searching for answers. "I don't think Ben ever went out to Long Island but there must be some connection between his illness and Anna's."

"You're right, somewhere there has to be a link," Hans said.

"Hans, something else. It's strange neither you nor Ben knew Bert had family in the camps, that's if what Hardy said is true. If you find the right moment, can you ask Bert about that?" Hans nodded and he and Yoko walked back to where Bert sat beside Anna's bed.

"Bert, can we talk outside for a moment?" Yoko led the way out and Bert followed. When they were a distance from Anna's cubicle, Yoko stopped and asked, "Bert, did Ben ever go with you to Long Island?"

"Never."

"I wish I didn't have to tell you this but Anna's symptoms are the same as Ben's when I saw him in the hospital."

A troubled understanding filled Bert's eyes. He said, "Ben felt better and went home and died the next day?"

"Yes."

"Did they ever find out what killed him?"

"No. The autopsy was done by the city's top coroner, who has run a number of tests but so far hasn't been able to come up with a conclusive diagnosis."

"Dear God, what can we do?" Bert said.

"I think there's a connection between Ben and Anna that links their illnesses," Yoko said. "We have to work out what it is."

Bert's face was blank. "I can't think of anything," he said. "Let me get back to Anna, I don't want to leave her." He walked back down the hall but stopped. His back was to Yoko but she heard him mutter, "White wine. Is that the link?"

"What?"

"White wine. If she has her druthers, Anna goes for white wine." Bert stopped outside Anna's cubicle. "Does that make any sense? Could it be the wine?"

Yoko shook her head. "I don't know. What would be different about *that* white wine? Wouldn't more people be sick if it is the wine?"

"I don't know but I'll call my uncle."

"Rather than waiting to hear from your uncle, we ought to tell the doctor that something might have been wrong with the wine Anna drank today," Yoko said. Bert nodded in agreement. Yoko hurried down to the nurses' station. The doctor was there, talking to one of the staff. He listened when Yoko explained about the similarity between Ben's illness and Anna's. "We don't know if the link is white wine. Is there any treatment that might help?"

The doctor thought for a moment. "The wine came from a Long Island vineyard?"

"Yes."

"I haven't heard of any outbreaks on Long Island but I can test for organic phosphate poisoning. It's one of the toxic chemicals used in agriculture. Perhaps the vineyard is near an area that was sprayed."

"Is that why the parasympathetic nerves were overstimulated?" Yoko asked, remembering what Ben's doctor had said.

"Yes," the doctor said. "Atropine helps with overstimulation. It relieves the threatening symptoms. The trouble is, we don't get at the source. Atropine doesn't eliminate the poison. There's a drug for that but I'd have to test the patient's blood to measure the levels in the plasma and the red cells of the enzyme cholinesterase to be able to identify the poison with any certainty."

Ben had responded to the atropine injections, had felt better and left the hospital but the poison was still in his system. Yoko recalled seeing the mug half filled with what smelled like wine on the kitchen table when she and Zoran searched Ben's apartment. Had Ben drunk more of the wine? If the wine was the cause of his illness, had Ben intensified the poison already in his body?

The doctor gave a nurse instructions to draw blood from Anna. "If the test comes back positive, we'll give the patient pralidoxime chloride." Yoko went back to where Anna now lay sleeping. Hans and Bert, heads close, were talking in hushed voices.

"The doctor is testing Anna's blood for phosphate insecticide, it's highly toxic," Yoko said, keeping her voice low. "If the result is positive, there's a drug they can use to treat her."

Relief filled Bert's eyes. Yoko's phone rang. It was Dan. Yoko stepped out into the hallway to take the call.

"How's Anna?"

"Right now, she's sleeping. It looks as if we have a handle on the cause of her illness. The strange thing is it may link to Ben's death." Yoko explained what she'd learned.

Dan let out a low whistle. "That's a major breakthrough. Zoran will want to know, Dante too. I'm calling because we've finished our interview with Hardy and Zoran hopes you can meet us at the one-three to review what we've learned."

"I don't see why I can't leave the hospital now. Hans may want to stay with Bert." Yoko stuck her head round the curtain of the cubicle and waved at Hans, who came out to join her.

"Zoran is anxious for me to meet at the one-three. D'you think Bert will mind if I leave? He'll have you to keep him company."

"I'll be glad to stay," Hans said. "Bert and I go back a long way."

"Thanks. I've something important to ask you. After Bert hears from his uncle about the wine, will you ask Bert if he had family in the camps? I think it would be better if you ask him rather than me. Mind you, it's possible Hardy was lying."

"It was strange how Hardy sprang that on us," Hans said. "Now that the doctor knows what to do for Anna, Bert will feel less stressed and I can find a time to ask him."

Yoko found Dan and Zoran in the chief's office.

"How was the interview with Hardy?" she asked.

"Bizarre." Dan said. "When he started, Hardy was full of bluster. He denied tapping the phones, swore up and down he wasn't guilty," Dan said. "Zoran confronted Hardy with proof from our IT department—something about his digital fingerprints being all over the installation of the equipment. Hardy caved and admitted he'd tapped the phones."

"Why?"

"Hard to believe but he was adamant he needed to test his equipment." Dan grinned and shook his head.

"The report from the psychiatrist clarified much about the behavior of Mr. Hardy," Zoran took up the explanation. "Dr. Roz pointed out that it is rare for criminal behavior to have rhyme or reason."

"Dr. Roz said Hardy's TBI was aggravated by his self-medicating," Dan added. "The anti-anxiety drugs he used weren't the right combo. Hardy had delusions of persecution as well as unwarranted jealously and he developed full-blown paranoia. Dr. Roz doesn't think he's schizophrenic. It's more that the drug abuse has triggered an exaggerated self-importance and he knows he's always correct in his thinking." Dan raised a single eyebrow, one of his favorite party tricks. "You know how easy it is to think you are correct." He smiled, innocence itself, and continued, "Hardy swore to us that the people he spent time with, guys like Ben and Hans and Bert who he thought were his friends, were talking about him behind his back, denigrating him. He was obsessed, ergo he had to listen to their phone conversations for proof."

Yoko felt pity for Hardy, a man with a damaged soul.

"As you know, it is my belief that unless we have an understandable and acceptable motive, we have nothing," Zoran said. "It is obvious that delusions and paranoia led Mr. Hardy to illegal phone tapping. Ultimately, the man had a mental breakdown and caused a dangerous hostage situation. He threatened his wife and members of the force when armed. That cannot be gainsayed. However, a file on the MacBook Pro revealed Mrs. Hardy had an account with an illegal pharmacy and was ordering drugs and giving them to her husband without his knowledge. It was systematic and deliberate. Legal counsel will be able to make a compelling case of mitigating circumstances for the situation caused by Mr. Hardy. We have played our part and Mr. Hardy and his wife are now the responsibility of the criminal justice system."

"We just catch the villains," Dan said.

"We still have the issue of who fired at Hans when we were in Central Park," Yoko said. "Was it random?"

Zoran acknowledged the query. "I believe we will find that it was Mrs. Hardy."

The insight startled Yoko but it made sense and she nodded in agreement.

Without missing a beat, Zoran continued. "The challenge facing us now is to find out more about a link between the illness and death of Mr. Sasaki and the illness of Mrs. Balducci," Zoran said. "I understand there is a question about wine being a causal factor."

"How can it be wine?" Dan asked. "A lot more people than two would have been ill if it was wine."

"Hans told me the family vineyard had problems and a batch of wine had to be destroyed," Yoko explained. "Bert didn't tell Hans what was wrong with the wine. Now that Anna's illness mirrors Ben's, Bert is going to talk to his uncle about the wine. What if all the wine wasn't destroyed and a few bottles were left behind by mistake?"

"That is a possibility," Zoran said.

"Something else," Yoko said. "When I left the hospital, I asked Hans to see if he could persuade to Bert Balducci to talk about something Hardy let drop, that Bert had family interned in the WII camps."

Dan and Zoran stared at Yoko in surprise.

"Is that true?" Dan asked.

"It may be a lie, something Hardy made up for shock value."

Yoko's phone rang. It was Hans.

"I'm about to leave the hospital. Good news all round. The results of

Anna's blood test showed she did have organic phosphate poisoning so the doctor gave her the drug to counteract it. She's sleeping. Bert's going to try and grab forty winks so I'm on my way out. Are you still at the precinct?"

"Yes," Yoko said. "What a relief to hear Anna's going to be all right. Do you have any other news?"

"I do. You'll find it quite interesting. I'll join you as soon as possible."

While they waited for Hans, Dan made a food run to the deli. Hans arrived just as Dan returned with sandwiches and containers of hot coffee and iced tea, catering to all tastes. The food disappeared in no time and while Hans sipped on tea, Zoran filled him in on what they'd learned about Hardy. When he finished, Zoran sat back and looked expectantly at the Romani.

"I believe you have information for us, Mr. Reiniger," Zoran said.

"I do." Hans had a strange look on his face. "It's a mixed bag but I'll start from when the results of Anna's blood work came in and Bert knew Anna was going to be okay. That's when he called his uncle at the winery on Long Island."

Yoko held her breath. At last a breakthrough?

"The wine had been contaminated all right," Hans said. "A batch of wine was going through the bottling process a few weeks ago and Bert's uncle spotted an empty container of organic phosphate lying near the open fermentation tank. He knew it was poison. It's never used on the property but crops on farms close by are sprayed with it. He had the wine checked, it was contaminated. It must have been deliberate, a worker had been fired the day before. They thought all the bottles had been destroyed but one of the workers said he'd noticed two bottles at the back of a shelf. The grandfather—Bert says he's a real tyrant—insisted he'd handle it. No one thought to check the bottles really had been discarded. When Bert called, the uncle confronted the grandfather, who admitted that when he went to finish the job, the bottles were gone and he thought someone had disposed of them."

The silence in the chief's office was heavy as they considered the tragic consequences of a stranger's anger. Yoko ignored the tears rolling down her face, grappling with the question of how *did* Ben have any of the wine if he'd never been to the vineyard. She took a deep breath, she had one more query.

"Hans, did you ask Bert whether he had family in the WWII camps?"

"I did." Hans sighed. "Bert started trembling when I brought this up. It was obvious the answer was yes. He calmed down and the story came out. 'Umberto, my grandfather's brother, was interned,' he said. 'I was named after him. Umberto lived in Florida. He died a few weeks ago. He was in the Manzanar camp for a while. The government put him there, said he was a troublemaker. He taught history in a Florida high school but was very political and outspoken about people's rights and lost that job. He was sent to Manzanar and ran into trouble with informants there ratting on him about his rants. Not long after Umberto arrived in Manzanar, Ben and his family moved to another camp. Almost right away, word circulated in Manzanar that Ben had been one of the informants.'"

Yoko bit her lip. Emiko had told her about the accusations.

"I knew there was something more," Hans said wearily. "It took a while, but Bert told me that when they visited Long Island, Anna often told his family about the potlucks we enjoyed with friends. Bert said, 'My grandfather picked up on Anna's description of Ben. He came to me and badgered me until I gave him Ben's address.'"

"I didn't understand what Bert meant and I asked why his grandfather wanted the address," Hans said. "Bert began to weep and said, so quiet it was hard to hear, 'If I hadn't given him Ben's address, Umberto wouldn't have been able to send Ben those threatening notes.'"

"Ah, an explanation about the threats." Zoran sounded satisfied.

Yoko nodded in distracted agreement, still wondering how Ben ever came to drink any contaminated wine. What was the common denominator? Bert and Anna were the only two people in the circle of friends who visited the vineyard on Long Island. Yoko turned to Hans and said, words coming out in a rush.

"Will you ask Bert if Anna ever brought wine back from Long Island?"

"I'll do it right now," Hans said. The group listened to the conversation, which Hans put on speakerphone. Loud and clear they heard Anna's reply to Bert.

"Yes," Anna said. "Last time we were out on Long Island, it was two or three weeks, I went down to the wine cellar and saw two bottles of white on the shelf. I took one to Ben."

Bert groaned. "What about today?"

They could hear Anna crying as she realized what had happened. "When we had lunch today, it's almost always red wine on the table. No one remembers I like white. I went down to the cellar and ferreted around until I found the last bottle of white like the one I took to Ben. He told me he liked it." Anna sobbed. "I almost didn't find the bottle, it was tucked away on a back shelf."

15 The Scene Changes

Yoko wasn't in New York when the Hardy case came to trial. She wasn't even in the U.S. Scant days after the bulging file of the Hardy case was passed to the District Attorney's office, Yoko was summoned to the dean's office. To her surprise, Bob Williams was there. She'd only had time for a brief chat with him before she'd led the NORA attendees on what had been a successful Central Park tour. She hadn't known he was still in town.

Dean Kate Green waved Yoko to a chair and after the usual pleasantries said, "Yoko, Bob has an intriguing proposition for you." She sat back, gaze steady on Yoko, perhaps to gauge the effect of her comment.

Bob Williams was equally direct. "How would you like a trip to the UK?" he asked, a smile on his face. "If I recall correctly, you were at the OEP conference in Bournemouth a few years back."

"I was at that conference," Yoko answered. "Ah, I'd never say no to a UK trip."

"If you've kept up with Hannu Laukkanen's travel, you know he's the inveterate voyager."

"Yes." Yoko was mystified.

"On one of his trips to China, Hannu stopped off in the UK. He was asked if he could recommend an experienced researcher to work with a group of UK practitioners on a large optometric vision therapy project they've undertaken."

"Oh," Yoko said. Was *she* was the experienced researcher?

"Your name topped the list," Bob Williams said. "You're the first person we're approaching. All of the UK optometrists involved have busy practices and they need someone whose attention is devoted to the project. It might take three to four months, perhaps longer. Free room and board is offered and Kate has agreed that SUNY will continue your salary while you are away."

187

Yoko was tempted to pinch herself to be sure this wasn't a dream.

The dean laughed. "You have a lot to think over. Do you want to take a day or two before you answer?"

"No, I'm in," Yoko said without hesitating. Hours later, after she'd had time to think about the effect such an absence would have on her personal life, she called Dan. She'd kept her excitement in check but her spirits soared at his response when she shared the news.

"Congratulations, kiddo, that's an offer you can't refuse. I guess I'll be spending my vacation time on long weekends in the UK. It's a six-hour flight, right?" Without missing a beat, Dan added, "What about the cats? I'd offer to look after them but there are those long weekends when I'll be travelling."

Yoko laughed. "Not to worry. Chris, the super's wife, always has offered to come in daily and feed them and scoop out the litter box. I asked her already and she's even willing to sit in the living room and read her newspaper in the mornings so they don't feel abandoned."

In the busy weeks before she left for England, Yoko settled her SUNY work. She could handle some of it long distance, other projects that needed to be based in New York were passed on to others. The night before she was due to leave, she and Dan had a farewell meal at Good Eats.

"Congratulations. Enjoy the beer in England," Pete said when she told him the news. "Don't forget where you have the best good eats. We'll see you when you return." He brought over their bowls of borscht then left them to their conversation.

"What did I miss about the wrap-up of the Hardy case," Yoko asked Dan.

"Dr. Roz had a field day with Pansy Hardy," Dan shook his head at the memory. "Quite the scheming wife. Vengeance with a capital V."

"But why?"

"About a year ago, Thomas Hardy confessed he'd had an affair. It was over but Pansy wasn't able to forgive and forget. The woman had moved to California and Pansy told Anna Balducci she was convinced that's the only reason the affair ended. Anna knew Pansy was squirreling away money because she wanted a divorce."

"So that made it okay for Pansy to lie to us about what *he* was doing?"

"At least she didn't copy Othello and commit murder," Dan said. "Hell hath . . ." Yoko didn't let him complete the worn adage.

"I dare you to add 'A woman scorned' to that!" Yoko warned. "Pansy was poisoning her husband with a dangerous mix of drugs. What I remember of my psych classes, that sort of deep jealousy is often mixed with violence and confrontation." Yoko thought back to Pansy's insistence on having a drink after Ben's wake and the persistent way she'd questioned Hans. "Did they check to see if Pansy was taking any illegal drugs?"

"She was."

"So they both had addled thinking. Add that to feelings of jealousy and it's a combustible mix."

Dan reached across the table and took Yoko's hand. "If you promise not to give me illegal drugs, I promise never to play around."

"I know you won't, Dan. You already have another woman in your life."

"What?"

"Your work. You're wedded to it."

Dan's grin was sheepish. He made a valiant recovery. "You're the icing on the cake, Yoko. You know that."

"And you're the icing on my cake, Dan."

On the flight to Heathrow, Yoko wondered how long she'd be involved in the optometric project in the UK. She didn't know what the future held. No one did. It had taken decades but she had learned about her family's past, fact by painful fact. Mystery no longer surrounded Ben's death. Revenge had been the cause of the accident that took his life, revenge based on hatred. Yoko's parents had chosen to focus on the positive and move past wrongs, filling their lives with love and hope.

"Are you happy?" Yoko once asked her Auntie Ai as they sat together in Ai's Brooklyn apartment after a meal.

"Yes, I am, Yoko. I have my freedom."

Postscript to the Reader

Elements of Truth

Fact and fiction mingle in *Eyes on the Past*. Dr. Yoko Kamimura, the protagonist, is fictional. Optometric vision therapy—the field in which she works—is fact. This therapy, often called behavioral or developmental optometry, is an optometric specialty that is available in more than forty countries. It is a valuable health care that has helped countless individuals whose eyesight was excellent but whose vision needed help. The roll call of professional and amateur sports teams includes the New York Yankees, Seattle Mariners, Chicago Black Hawks, San Francisco 49ers and U.S Olympic medalists.

Eyes on the Past has real people, from Ansel Adams, the renowned photographer and environmentalist to flesh-and-blood practitioners of optometry. These include Doctors H. Laukkanen, Clinical Professor of Optometry at Pacific University, C. Forkiotis (deceased), a nationally recognized Expert Witness who lectured on vision at the Connecticut State Police Academy for decades, and E. Robert Bertolli, also a decades-long lecturer at the Connecticut State Police Academy.

The College of Optometry of the State University of New York (SUNY) is one of twenty colleges in the U.S. offering postdoctoral degrees in optometric vision therapy. Robert A. Williams, former Executive Director of the OEP Foundation (retired) and former Executive Director of NORA is real and ever tireless on behalf of this valuable optometric therapy. Readers are encouraged to contact www.noravisionrehab.com and www.oepf.org for more information. Organizations like the Neuro-Optometric Rehabilitation Association International (NORA), the Optometric Extension Program Foundation (OEPF), the College of Optometrists in Vision Development (COVD), and international counterparts, the Australasian College of Behavioural Optometrists

(ACBO), the British Association of Behavioural Optometrists (BABO), the Consejo Mexicano De Optometria Funcional (COMOF) and the Behavioral Optometric Academy Foundation (BOAF) support and advance the profession of optometric vision therapy in meaningful ways.

As you can see from the Bibliography, a number of books were consulted for the writing of *Eyes on the Past* in an effort to portray the events of that time as accurately as possible. Certainly there are more books than those listed, which are the ones I bought or borrowed. Two books stand out in particular: *In Defense of Our Neighbors, The Walt and Milly Woodward Story* by Mary Woodward, and *Born Free and Equal, The Story of Loyal Japanese-Americans* by Ansel Adams. Both books have superb illustrations and their texts clarify the reality of one of the darkest chapters in the history of the U.S., the shameful treatment of Japanese American during World War II.

When Loren Kramer loaned me *Born Free and Equal, the Story of Loyal Japanese-Americans*, the book by Ansel Adams, I discovered the photos are in the public domain. A bevy of generous, clever friends scanned and cropped some of the photos so they could be included in the paperback and the e-book. Adams was invited by Ralph Palmer Merritt, the camp director of Manzanar, to visit (Manzanar was one of the ten camps where Japanese Americans were incarcerated). Adams stayed for some three months.

Although well reviewed, the Ansel Adams book had limited circulation, perhaps due to the political climate of wartime America. Adams noted, "It was met with some distressing resistance and was rejected by many as disloyal." Offering the collection to the Library of Congress, Adams wrote, "All in all, I think this Manzanar Collection is an important historical document, and I trust it can be put to good use . . . . The purpose of my work was to show how these people, suffering under a great injustice, and loss of property, businesses and professions, had overcome the sense of defeat and despair by building for themselves a vital community in an arid (but magnificent) environment."

In 2013, the Book Club of New Jersey's Ocean City Free Public Library invited me to visit to talk about the first Dr. Yoko mysteries, *Eye Sleuth* and *Eye Witness*. Some of the club members said they were disappointed not to read more about what had happened to Japanese Americans during WWII. This was all I needed to prompt me to re-search then weave the history of the tragic WWII incarceration of Japanese Americans throughout *Eyes on the Past*. What I learned from the research is that the similarity between those WW II years and life in the 21st century is alarming. In the 21st century, we struggle still with the racism and xenophobia that was evident in the 1940s. The history of the WWII incarceration of Japanese Americans is a stark reminder of how precious our civil liberties are, and how easily they can be lost.

Gallery of Photographs of Manzanar Camp
by Ansel Adams from his book,

Born Free and Equal,
The Story of Loyal Japanese-Americans

The arid Mohave Desert surrounded Manzanar. The massive wall of the Sierra Nevada rose to the west, the high, barren range of the Inoy to the east.

This cadet nurse shows her pride at being in her country's military. Uniforms had to be remade to fit the women of Japanese heritage.

A young couple at the door to their hut smile despite the camp's harsh conditions.

Youngsters chose to eat with friends, eroding family traditions. Lines out-side mess halls were inevitable.

Farmers and engineers labored to transform the desert into an oasis of beauty with ponds, bridges and trees.

Eventually, Manzanar had power but still mountains loomed, dust was ever present and the land was bleak where hard work hadn't transformed it.

Yoko stared hard at the photo, it could have been Ben and his parents. Ansel Adams had written, "A young lawyer and his family."

Homegrown veggies from Manzanar's north farm, the fruit of expertise and backbreaking work.

Manzanar had its own newspaper, *The Free Press*.

Nobutero Harry Sumida, a veteran of the Spanish-American war and one of the oldest people in Manzanar.

Spinach-tofu Quiche

1 package frozen, chopped spinach or a bag of fresh
    spinach
2 small onions (or one large one), chopped fine
1 unbaked 9" pie crust
1/2 cup grated cheese of choice (Yoko sometimes uses soy
    mozzarella)
1 lb soft tofu
3 eggs
1 tsp salt
1/2 tsp nutmeg
dash of pepper

Preheat oven to 350 degrees.

Blend eggs and seasonings. While blender is running, drop in tofu,
1/4lb at a time. Blend until smooth.

Cook spinach—do not overcook. Drain well.

Combine egg-tofu mixture and spinach and onions in a bowl & mix.

Pour into unbaked pie shell and cover with grated cheese.

Bake for 30 minutes.

You can use any other veggies, it's your choice.

Bean-nut Loaf

1 small onion, chopped fine & sauteed in small amount of
  oil of choice.
2 cups cooked, drained beans (Yoko uses akudi, any beans
  are fine)
1/2 cup bread crumbs (Yoko prefers gluten-free)
1/2 cup sunflower seeds or walnut pieces
1/2 tsp sage or thyme
2 TBS flour (Yoko often uses rice flour)
2 eggs, beaten
1/2 cup vegetable stock or water (Yoko likes a dash of
  Braggs liquid aminos)
1 TBS vinegar (apple cider)
sesame seeds (to sprinkle on top)

Preheat oven to 350. Mix all ingredients & put in greased loaf pan.
Bake for 30 minutes covered with parchment wrap or a cookie sheet,
then for 10 minutes uncovered.

Tapenade

1 can of tuna (olive oil preferable, water OK, you can add
    o. oil)
2 tsp anchovy paste or a tin of anchovies (if you use a tin
    of anchovies, cut the anchovies into small pieces before
    blending unless you have a mighty strong blender)
Garlic (1 clove minced or chopped)
3 TBS lemon juice (Yoko used the organic bottled kind)
3 TBS good olive oil
1/4 cup pitted and chopped olives
1 TBS drained capers
Optional: 1 tsp salt, 1 tsp freshly ground black pepper

Drain all but a tablespoon of olive oil from the tuna and blend.

Add anchovy paste or cut up anchovies and garlic and pulse a few times. Add the lemon juice, 3 TBS of olive oil, and process until almost smooth. Add the olives, capers, salt, and pepper and pulse to incorporate.

Refrigerate for at least 1 hour.

This freezes well & also doubles nicely.

Fruit Cobbler

This is an easy cobbler.

Lightly cook any fruit—berries, apples, peaches.

Sweeten to your taste with maple syrup or honey.

Yoko always adds a dash of vanilla

Butter a glass dish and pour in the cooked fruit.

Yoko takes the easy way out—she crumbles gluten-free shortbread cookies over the top of the fruit. Mix in to the fruit lightly.

Bake at 300 degrees for 20 minutes.

Marinated Greens

This will make about 8 cups of greens (you can make less & adjust the marinade accordingly).

  1/3 cup olive oil
  1/4 tsp salt
  1 clove garlic (Yoko minced it)
  1 TBS fresh ginger, grated
  1 TBS Braggs
  1/2 cup water
  pinch cayenne (optional)
  Large bunch of greens—kale, collards, etc.

Cut/tear greens into bite-sized pieces.

Blend marinade ingredients in blender (or blend by hand, one less item to clean).

Pour marinade over greens & mix well. Cover & let sit for at least a few hours, preferably overnight. This is even better the next day. Use any variety of greens for this, kale, collards, Swiss chard, spinach, etc. Strangely, this doesn't work well with dinosaur (aka lacinata) kale.

Bibliography

Born Free and Equal, The Story of Loyal Japanese-Americans at Manzanar Relocation Center, Inyo County, California. Text and photographs by Ansel Adams. New York, 1944, U.S. Camera.

Dandelion through the crack, The Sato family quest for the American Dream by Kiyo Sato. 2007. Willow Valley Press.

Farewell to Manzanar by Jeanne Wakatsuki Houston and James D. Houston. 1973. Houghton Mifflin.

Go for Broke: The Nisei Warriors Who Conquered Germany, Japan, and American Bigotry, copyright 2015, C. Douglas Sterner. American Legacy Historical Press, 1544 W 1620 N. Ste 2-A, Clearfield, Utah, 84015-8423.

Going for Broke: Japanese American Soldiers in the War against Nazi Germany (Campaigns and Commanders Series), by Dr. James M. McCaffrey (Author) University of Oklahoma Press, April 30, 2013.

Honor by Fire: Japanese Americans at War in Europe and the Pacific Hardcover January 15, 1997 by Lyn Crost (Author). The story of the Nisei (first-generation Japanese Americans) Purple-Heart Battalion.

In Defense of Our Neighbors, The Walt and Milly Woodward Story by Mary Woodward. Foreword by David Guterson. 2008 by Bainbridge Island Japanese American Community. Manuscript copyright 2008 by Mary Woodward. Fenwick Publishing Group, Inc., 3147 Point White Drive, Ste. 100, Bainbridge Island, WA 98110.

Nisei Daughter by Monica Sone, 1953. Originally published as an Atlantic Monthly Press Book by Little, Brown and Company. University of Washington Press paperback edition published in 1979. Sixth printing in 1991.

Serving Our Country, Japanese American Women in the Military during World War II, by Brenda L. Moore. 2003. Rutgers University Press.

Snow Falling on Cedars by David Guterson. 1994. Harcourt Brace.

Strawberry Days by David A. Neiwert, 2005. "How Internment destroyed a Japanese American community." Palgrave MacMillan, the global academic imprint of the Palgrave Macmillan division of St. Martin's Press.

The Legend of Fire Horse Woman by Jeanne Wakatsuki Houson. 2003. Kensington Publishing Corp.

The Living Fire (E Zhivindi Yag) (2009) by Ron Lee (the republication of *Goddam Gypsy* under the author's originally intended title). Magoria Books in 2009.

The Politics of Fieldwork, Research in an American Concentration Camp by Lane Ryo Hirabayashi. 1999. The University of Arizona Press, Tucson.

Unlikely Liberators The Men of the 100th and 442nd, by Masayo Umezawa Duus (Author), Peter Duus (Translator), copyright 1983. Stanford, CT. Interviews with veterans provide a look at the horrors of war overseas and the social and political rejection at home.

Citations for TBI (Traumatic Brain Injury)

Neurovision Rehabilitation Guide, by Drs. Amy Chang, S. E. Ritter and Xiao Xi Yu (available from oepf.org) is a valuable resource for the health care professional working with patients with visual dysfunction as a consequence of traumatic brain injury and neurological disorders. It covers the concepts of visual dysfunction as well as assessment and step-by-step treatment plans. The neurology of visual processing before and after a brain injury is covered. The concepts behind neurovision rehabilitation are explained as are the ways to examine and treat patients' visual deficits. It also covers the evaluation of visual perceptual deficits and treatment of the traumatic brain injury patient.

The guide contains more than 80 vision therapy procedures, with step-by-step instructions as well as sequencing guides for each category of therapy (oculomotor, accommodation, binocular, perceptual).

The Ghost in My Brain: How a Concussion Stole My Life and How the New Science of Brain Plasticity Helped Me Get It Back, by Clark Elliott, Ph.D. In 1999, Clark Elliott suffered a concussion when his car was rear-ended. Overnight, his life changed from that of a rising professor with a research career in artificial intelligence to a humbled man struggling to get through a single day. At times he couldn't walk across a room or even name his five children. Doctors told him he would never fully recover.

After eight years, the cognitive demands of his job and of being a single parent finally became more than he could manage. As a result of one last effort to recover, he crossed paths with two brilliant research-clinicians in the Chicago area—one a specialized optometrist [behavioral optometrist Deborah Zelinsky, O.D., F.N.O.R.A., F.C.O.V.D.], the other a cognitive psychologist, Donalee Marcus, Ph.D. These practitioners were working on the leading edge of brain plasticity. Within weeks, the ghost of who Elliott had been started to re-emerge. He kept detailed notes throughout his experience, from the moment of impact to the final stages of his recovery. This astounding documentation is the basis of the fascinating book, *The Ghost in My Brain.* It offers hope to the millions who suffer from head injuries each year and provides a unique and informative window into the world's most complex computational device: the human brain. (Dr. Elliott spoke at the NORA annual conference in 2015.)

Jillian's Story: How Vision Therapy Changed My Daughter's Life, by Robin and Jilian Benoit, was published in 2010. Soon, teenager Jillian Benoit began to receive countless e-mails from individuals around the world who shared their amazing stories of optometric vision therapy success. A second book, *Dear Jillian,* shares the amazing and inspirational true stories of twenty-two individuals, children and adults, who have had their lives changed by optometric vision therapy. It is a personal, deeply moving, and thought-provoking look into the lives of these people. Optometric vision therapy helped those struggling with traumatic brain injury, autism, Down syndrome, stroke, sports-related concussion, polyneuritis, anxiety, learning problems and other vision problems such as amblyopia, strabismus, and convergence insufficiency. They all credit their success to optometric vision therapy.

Dr. Theodore S. Kadet, "Visual Rehabilitation in Traumatic Brain Injury," is a charter Fellow of the College of Optometrists in Vision Development (FCOVD), the certification body for Developmental Optometry and Neuro-Optometry. He is a member of the Neuro-Optometric Rehabilitation Association (NORA); a Clinical Associate of the Optometric Extension Program Foundation (OEPF); the Washington Association of Optometric Physicians and the American Optometric Association. Dr. Kadet is also an Adjunct Professor, College of Optometry at Pacific Grove University, Forest Grove, Oregon.

Stephen Leslie, B. O.D. "Optometric rehabilitative assessment of people with acquired brain injuries in long term residential care." *Behavioral Optometry,* Vol. 8, No. 1.

Harris, Monica, O.D. "Optometric Care and Vision Rehabilitation for Acquired Brain Injury Patients."

Hazel Dawkins lives in western Massachusetts in a particularly bucolic part of New England. Her years of work in communications were in London, Paris and New York.

Dawkins has also written factual books on behavioral optometry, a specialty in optometry that is available in forty countries. These titles, including *The Suddenly Successful Student and Friends,* are published by—and available from—the OEP Foundation, the professional organization for optometrists (www.oepf.org).

Eyes on the Past is the fourth Dr. Yoko mystery. The first, *Eye Sleuth,* was followed by *Eye Witness* (the latter was created in amiable collaboration with writer Dennis Berry of Oregon). The third, *Eye Sleuth's Ghostly Vacations,* is only available as an e-book but a paperback may well emerge at some point. Each Dr. Yoko mystery has photos in the back of locations and activities described in the book. You can find all the titles on Amazon.

www.ingramcontent.com/pod-product-compliance
Lightning Source LLC
Chambersburg PA
CBHW060042150626
46556CB00018BA/2425